I0614367

The Sound of Creation

by

Gabriella Zielke

3

The Sound of Creation

Cover Art by *Debbie Taylor*

The Wild Rose Press, Inc.
PO Box 708
Adams Basin, NY 14410-0708
Visit us at www.thewildrosepress.com

Publishing History
First Edition, 2022
Trade Paperback ISBN 978-1-5092-3913-9
Digital ISBN 978-1-5092-3914-6

Published in the United States of America

"It is believed there are multiple locations on Earth where one may access the great knowledge, though we don't know exactly how many." He drew a poor representation of the continents in the dirt and arranged smaller sticks to show the various divides. "This little patch of land…" He gestured with the drawing stick in the direction of where they were on the map, "is the North American point."

"What is the great knowledge?" Ava asked, her ankle forgotten. "And how do you know this is the place?"

"Patience," he answered with a finger to his mouth. "For each point there is a guide, or a translator of the knowledge. We do not know if any have been located yet. They will be born and find their place when the time is right."

Zek cut in. "A human is supposed to be the translator."

"Hold on, Zek," Tony said calmly. "Why don't you tell her what you know of this place?"

"Millions of years ago, while the continents were still forming according to the governing rules of this universe and dimension, it was decided that those rules, those truths, should be revealed when the inhabitants were sentient enough to transcend them. The code was hidden among the areas of separation to wait for the translators to be born." Zek's eyes shone with an intensity directed toward a place and time far away.

Praise for Gabriella Zielke

"I have never met someone in my life who does not like music. But what if music is used as a tool to make you tell the truth? What if music opens your eyes to the reality around you? Then you suddenly realise that what you believed to be true is not. How can you live life after such a revelation?

What if music becomes a weapon to control humanity, would you listen to it again?

The Sound of Creation is a mind-bending book filled with big questions about our existence. It takes you on a journey disrupted by action scenes and strange characters. You will find yourself floating on dimensions you did not know even existed. This book is a mind game. You have been warned."

~George Papa, author of The Manual and The Architect's typist for The Code

Dedication

To my son, Philip, who inspires me to be a better person and gives me great writing feedback. You are my best creation.

Acknowledgments

If I had known the amount of work I would put into this book before writing it, you would be reading something different. The first time doing anything is done on faith. That faith was built by many people who helped me along the way.

I decided when I started my company that I would write a novel once I sold it and my son was in college. That was in 2009. My first attempts at short stories and scenes were with the help of wonderful authors who taught at The Writer's Path at Southern Methodist University.

When I didn't know what I wanted to write, Chris Feola handed me a copy of The Diamond Age and given my background in technology, I had to facepalm at the obviousness of science fiction. It's the genre of ideas and philosophy. It has shaped our present and our future. It makes people wonder "what if…"

Thanks to my partners, investors, mentors, and founders at Tech Wildcatters for so many great years. And thanks to Ricky Tejapaibul for leading it into its second phase.

Michael Gorton deserves a lot of credit for going through my first draft and providing feedback. I appreciate the help of quite a few others who went through early versions of the manuscript; Kiki Mason, who also taught me to dance with fire, Jim Hudson, Cory Rohde, Kim Bunting, Anna Enns, my forever sister Lisa Coachbuilder, and my son Philip. My husband Peter deserves plenty of credit for trying to make sense of my ideas before he's had his morning coffee.

This book wouldn't be in the shape it's in without the help of Sally Kemp, Craig Gabrysch, and Ally Robertson.

And thank you to all of you readers who make writing worth it!

Chapter 1

Los Angeles – present day

It was the scratching that woke her.

The noise reached Ava Lawson's ears not too long after she laid down on her office futon to catch a few hours of sleep. She had two weeks to prove to her investors that her trading system produced alpha or she and her team were finished.

Alpha, known as the truth to some investment managers, career life or death to others, in reality measures an investment return against a market return like the Dow Jones. It was as elusive to Ava as it is to most return wranglers.

Until the music began to play.

The other sounds: a conch shell, leaves rustling, a wolf maybe, entered and exited her subconscious without ringing any alerts.

The scratching though. She would know it anywhere. A sound from her childhood when her father came to visit.

She sat up. There was more to the sounds than what she could hear. The only way to describe it was a presence, some life force, was in the room with her. Across the long office, past the small conference table, all the way to the wall behind her white desk; she was alone. Yet, the room was full with an air of confidence and knowing, like a football player putting on his third

Superbowl ring or an actress setting her fourth Oscar next to the others on a shelf.

Ava saw only blinking LEDs on the other side of the long glass wall separating her space from the company war room where most of the developers worked, but the feeling wasn't coming from there. The scratching intensified.

All the men from her father's village were given a *popoyo* as teenagers. The fist-sized dried fruit receptacle held burnt seashells that they crushed into lime and mixed with coca leaves. It had a long stick to extract the powdery lime from the tall neck. Her father had worn his around his neck.

The scratch, turn, wipe, scratch used to put her at ease. When she heard it as a child, she knew he was there, safe, protected, and protecting her and her mother in the Colombian mountains where she spent her first fourteen years. She hadn't heard the sound since. It was no longer comforting. The tiny hairs on her arms stood on guard.

The scratching fused with the other noises to create a melody. It was coming from her laptop. Strange, she thought. She had left the new algorithm running against the Chinese currency market while she napped.

Ava crossed the room and sat in front of her wide, curved monitor. Something was wrong. The entire screen showed green figures against the black background. There's no way a trading system would show all gains and none of the red blood of losses. She hit refresh. Still green.

When she increased the time stamp to two hours the red finally showed. It was the last ten minutes of trading that resulted in all gains.

The music intensified. It began to take on the drumming she remembered from her mother's work. She closed her eyes and listened for a singing bowl. That exact moment, it came to life with an eerie vibrating whine.

She opened her eyes. It's just a coincidence, the logical voice in her head said. Another voice steamrolled over it and reverberated through her body.

You have done it, the deep voice bellowed between her ears.

Without thinking, she slammed the laptop shut and yelled, "What?" The room went silent, and she shivered.

There was only one word she could think of to describe the feeling, the sounds, the words: *otherworldly*.

Chapter 2

Renzo – Creators' World in Seventh Dimension

Zek took a deep breath and crouched through the hatchway of the capsule that took up a third of his living and work quarters. Once inside, he pressed a glowing red button. The door hissed to a close. His feet lifted off the ground slowly and he crossed his legs under him.

His rig, like all of those used in the seventh dimension Creation Guild, offered enough room for his lithe body to turn around and nothing more. However, once he spoke the command "activate" into its dark corners, the physical confines disappeared and gave way to infinite space. Only then could he enter the multiverse network in creation mode.

All senses, save the thought sense, deactivated to preserve a creators' mind in the rig. Zek could reactivate any of his eight senses as he needed them.

When it came to creating planets, he needed his senses in varying intervals.

He mentally reviewed the plans his Master drew up for the latest planet he expected Zek to spawn. He sighed then commanded, "Activate magnetism."

He directed his magnetic sense to draw in the elements needed from his rig's portal to the Laer Guild's creation platform. Zek had refused to use the platform for his final project as an apprentice, much to the consternation of the Creation Guild elders. He wanted to build planets that would grow the multiverse network rather than only improve what currently existed.

Laer allowed planet creation above the fourth dimension only, after souls gained awareness of the network and their place in it. At the time Zek began his project planet for three dimensional souls, the rate of ascensions from the third to the fourth dimension had slowed to almost zero. Since then, his planet, Earth, had already produced more soul ascensions than anyone currently in the Creation Guild could remember.

He was anxious to complete his Master's request so that he could switch views and check in on the humans. It was nearing time for his third and last intervention on his project planet. Once his finishing touches were in place, he would present his project for final approval and gain membership in the Creation Guild.

Zek focused on his Master's current task of using the Laer system to assemble the protons, neutrons, electrons, quarks, and other particles into gases, which all compressed into a tiny ball of energy. When the process was complete, Zek closed his eyes.

All went still.

Energy pulsed around and through him. He waited until the compression intensified to the edge of his control, then opened his eyes wide. Blue light burst forth. Energy and matter spewed, spun, and stuck together. Master Vezon's newest planet would allow fifth dimension souls the opportunity to expand their newly unlocked senses and ascend to the sixth dimension, where they would master their new powers and unlock the next.

Zek called out, "Complete." Each of his senses slowly reactivated at the same rate the rig interior glowed brighter, as if a single sun rose over a horizon. The darkness that remained was his pure black flesh, the color that absorbs all colors.

"View Earth," he commanded. His planet came into focus. He tuned into the consciousness level of the dominant species and narrowed his eyes. The reading was not as he expected.

He sensed a presence nearby. Someone was in his apprentice quarters. He grasped the exit bar to steady himself and pressed the glowing button at its end. Gravity pulled gently on his limbs until it was fully restored, and he could walk steadily. He folded through the entrance of the tiny capsule.

"Zek, you are expected in the Great Hall."

The apprentice's ice blue eyes flashed on his Guildmaster, Vezon, who stood pristine in white formal robes. They shared the same smooth, space-black skin and long limbs, but the similarities ended there. Zek searched for his robes; found them crumpled in a dark lump on the stone floor. He shuffled sideways between the rig and his narrow bed before bending down to retrieve them.

His master sighed. "They wait for your final progress report."

"It is not time, Master Vezon. I was only now observing the planet to complete my plan for the third intervention."

"A change was observed. It is time." Vezon swept his arm toward the direction of the Great Hall. "They are assembled."

Zek grabbed the robes and threw them around his shoulders before following the brisk, light steps of his Master. They exited the low walled Apprentice Hall and rushed across the main lawn in the center of the complex. The Great Hall loomed at the opposite end. If one combined Zek's building and its adjoining classrooms, five of them would fit easily inside the great stone walls, stacked one on top of the other.

"Master, please tell me, what change?" Zek shouted to Vezon's back, who pulled even farther ahead. He jogged to catch up.

The stark quiet in the large, open gallery at the center of the Great Hall made it sound as if there were no audience for the meeting, but Zek sensed the consciousness of every single guild master, craftsman, and journeyman. The slap of his hurried steps on the white stone floor echoed loudly as he rushed to stand beside his master. He peeked up at the galleries to the left and right where the other apprentices stood in aisles beside guild members who were packed onto the long stone benches, just as they had been for his first two progress meetings.

Grandmaster Zalor's voice boomed through the audience. "We are assembled to examine an anomaly in apprentice Zek's creation."

Zek slowed his labored breathing, straightened his shoulders and fastened the wrinkled robes. It was unusual for the Grandmaster to preside.

The anomaly was either very good or very, very bad.

"Thank you for the opportunity to share Zek's progress so that he may continue on the path to creator," Master Vezon said.

Zek lifted his eyes to the elder's gallery where the Grandmaster sat. Fear of breaking protocol kept him from gaping at the public galleries flanking him and Vezon on both sides of the long stone hall.

The Grandmaster continued. "Earth, built for three dimensional beings to expand and ascend, is experiencing the anticipated rise into fourth dimension consciousness. The apprentice's thesis around mass ascension of a species could soon come to pass." Gasps and whispers whirled through the galleries.

Zek beamed. Would they now recognize the genius behind his creation?

The Grandmaster lifted his arms and the Great Hall fell silent. "We are convened in order for the guild leadership to convey our deep concern over the direction Zek's world is advancing."

Zek's face fell. He fought the urge to yell out. What would he have observed if he hadn't been interrupted in his rig?

"It was an ambitious plan, and we applaud the apprentice's effort. Now, let us examine the failures so he may further understand the ways of the seventh dimension creator."

"Failures?" Zek muttered to himself. What happened? On the verge of breaking silence, an infraction that could permanently end his quest for guild membership, Zek glanced sideways.

Vezon put his finger to his lips and shook his head slightly.

"You were gracious to allow an apprentice to embark on such an ambitious creation, the largest ever for an apprentice in fact. We are grateful for your trust and belief in Apprentice Zek's skills." Vezon bowed his head and paused.

Zek waited, eyes steady on the gallery above, for his master's rebuttal to the accusation of failure. It never came.

"Yes," the Grandmaster said. "It was a foolish effort on the part of the apprentice to attempt creation without the safeguards of the Laer platform. It put him in danger of losing his soul to the network void, as creators did before Laer was built. However," he paused and focused an intense glare on Zek. "We observed a property that is of high concern. Because of it, the upper dimensions are at risk of lower beings gaining access to the network without awareness of it. I do not believe the apprentice understands the threat his failed creation now presents for the multiverse as we know it."

Zek's icy blue eyes burned as he continued to face the elders. They knew the safety of Laer created dangers of its own. A creator could choose elemental combinations, run a simulation, then build a world without any idea of how it actually worked. The Grandmaster himself told Zek that he feared the Laer Guild had designed the platform to slow down ascensions.

"Raw ambition without awareness is foolish, I agree. However, he has not used his third and final intervention. Will we not grant him the same opportunity to learn from and correct his mistakes, as we have every apprentice before him, before declaring his creation a failure?" His master risked sanction for openly defending a non-guild member.

"Apprentice Zek. Will you please enlighten the guild as to your expectations regarding your disregard for our long-held practices?" the Grandmaster asked.

Zek's mouth fell open. Titters from the spectator galleries interrupted his thoughts.

Grandmaster Zalor shifted his eyes around the hall. The noise stopped once again.

"W-with apologies, Grandmaster," Zek said. "What is meant by disregard?"

Master Vezon sucked in his breath almost imperceptibly beside him.

Zek dared another glance sideways and saw his master's pursed lips. *What had he done wrong now?*

"Apprentice Zek." The Grandmaster stood.

Zek snapped his head back up. *This was not going in the right direction.*

"Deciding to eschew the creator's platform and build a planet without it left us all..." He gestured widely to the room and continued, "in danger. Your disregard was for everyone but yourself. I have examined the recent anomaly on Earth in great detail. The consciousness spikes are of a nature we have never encountered. The humans' conscious activation is, for some unknown reason, decoupled from their awareness. That lack of awareness could have disastrous consequences if they are able to access the network. You are hereby ordered to destroy the species so that their souls may inhabit a proper planet and ascend according to our known laws."

"What? You can't do that!" He covered his mouth with his hand.

The Grandmaster glared down at him. "Apprentice Zek." He paused. "We have all watched with much hope as you ascended through your guild training. Your quick mind and decisive actions inspired a great many to continue in the tradition of creator, which was in decline. The great balance was threatened. As news of your brilliant ability swept the membership, we sat in anticipation of welcoming you as a craftsman and possibly naming you our Grandmaster one day. Such is the nature of your immense talent."

The proclamation was far from gratuitous. Zek was the prodigy who restored much of the reputation and power of the guild. It was why they had allowed him to create Earth, from scratch. Or so he thought.

Zek raised his chin, straightened his shoulders, the muscles in his face tightened. His peers, who finished their apprenticeships far ahead of him, had laughed at the amount of work he had put into building a world from the most basic particles. It mattered not. He was not like them.

"However," the Grandmaster said. "Your defiance of the great system and what we now recognize as recklessness and obsession to prove a point, are a threat to our entire society. Impetuousness is the death of creation, pride the antithesis. Now you must complete the circle and restore balance. Do you understand why we command this, Apprentice Zek?"

"With respect sir, no, I do not. I chose not to incorporate Laer because I believe true creation is only possible from chaos, not from the ordered rules of another guild. Their methods are outdated and too restrictive for growth of the network. Without the ability to determine the base particles in my lower dimension creation, Earth never would have progressed this far. The humans will usher in a new way, a better way of ascending the dimensions and building the collective informational stream of the network. Earth already accounts for more soul ascensions than any other planet in its dimension. You'll see. We must allow them to continue!"

Murmurs from around the hall grew in volume. Zek lowered his voice. "The project is not complete, Grandmaster. How can it be ended before completion? How can you deny me a third intervention? That is against the fifth bylaw in the Guild constitution. Please understand that all I wish is to complete my work to either success or failure. It is unlawful to force an unnatural end."

All eyes were on the leader of the guild as he contemplated the outspoken apprentice. "It is true we may not force you to destroy your creation." His tone was slow and measured, as if he were speaking to a being from a lower dimension. "It must be of your free will. But you see, young apprentice, free will is a complicated thing. One you do not seem to completely understand. You are at all times free to do as you wish. What you missed in your calculations, which manifested in your attempted creation, is risk. Defiance of the wishes of guild membership comes with the risk of expulsion. Of this I assume you are well aware, but for some reason do not consider a variable in this discussion."

Zek considered the reply and all its repercussions. He had pushed too far.

"Grandmaster, I see the wisdom of your argument." He bowed his smooth dark head. "With your blessing, I request I be allowed to present a plan for destruction of Earth after I learn the true nature of that which you deem a destined failure." This should buy him some cycles. Restoring his former place would take more work. One step at a time, he reminded himself.

"I must take into consideration the wisdom of the guild elders for a decision of this importance. We will confer in absentia," the Grandmaster said. He closed his eyes. All the elders, including Zek's master Vezon, followed the Grandmaster's lead and closed their eyes. Each of their thoughts converged on a higher plane to determine what should be done with the apprentice and his rogue creation. One by one, a cylinder of light surrounded each elder before it dissipated, and their thoughts were added to the collective discussion taking place in a higher realm.

Chapter 3

Several hours after the music played, Ava lifted her head at the light rap on her office door. Michael, frequently referred to as Ava's Ass because of his military title -- Special Assistant to the President -- must have seen the massive surge in their overnight returns.

The coffee mug next to her on the desk was full and cold. She had fallen asleep before figuring out what was responsible for the change, and for the strange sounds.

Michael watched her from the open war room outside her office as she wiped drool from her cheek. Glass walls had their drawbacks.

She mouthed, "Get Rys."

Michael stepped left to unblock the view of her lead software architect who furiously typed with one hand while the other held his laptop. His long, frizzy brown curls bounced in rhythm to his keystrokes.

She nodded them in and pulled her waist length, thick red hair into its usual knot at the base of her neck. She thought back to the memories conjured earlier that morning. Maybe the weird music would have a more tangible purpose than the random noises her music healing, free spirited mom would make with bowls and drums. If it led to investment returns, she would listen to anything.

"Well boys, what the hell was that?" They all got

alerts when the system did something unexpected.

Rys would have immediately checked the office security cameras to see what was happening. He probably saw her bolt out of her chair and scream to herself. No wonder they had waited until a reasonable hour to show up. She checked her phone. Six qualified as reasonable.

She glanced at the two men in her office. Rys had dropped into one of two leather chairs that flanked her desk. He was still typing but wouldn't miss a word of their conversation. Michael was taking her uneaten frozen dinner out of the microwave. He lifted it to show her and shook his head. She shrugged.

"It's that house on Venice Beach for me if we can reproduce it," Rys said. "If we had been trading real dollars, we would've made about $50 million in those ten minutes. Why did it shut down?"

"That's what we need to figure out," Ava said. "The thing was playing weird noises, some kind of creepy music. I don't know."

"Like Marilyn Manson creepy or Death Grips creepy?" Rys asked. Ava rolled her eyes at him.

She turned to Michael. "Get everyone together at seven. We've only got a couple of weeks to get this sorted and close our next round of funding."

Michael nodded and took out his phone. Sense Labs wasn't one of the snowflake factories people worshipped in the tech world. They took their mission seriously, their coffee black, and everyone showed up early and could be depended on. Those who couldn't handle the team's high expectations self-selected and quickly left.

"Rys, I'm guessing you were panting at the door

because you're trying to get Seneca to turn on again. Have you figured out how?" Ava kicked around under her desk for her black flats, put them on, and stood up.

"I've been trying to isolate any changes you made overnight," Rys said, "but I don't have access to some of the files." He stood and gestured to her laptop. "Can I drive?"

"Be my guest." Ava logged in to her machine then stepped aside.

Rys pulled up her activity monitor and pointed. "It looks like a stream you had open interfered with the system. Don't tell me you looked at your home security system or car data on your work computer again." He shook his head. "Dude. Have I taught you nothing?"

Ava frowned. She and Rys spent enough time studying and recreating old hacks that she knew better. "I know, I know, but it may be what changed. I could kick myself for not starting there."

She leaned over Rys and pointed to an icon. He clicked it and the feed from her late uncle's cabin in Montana sprang to life displaying views from a dozen different cameras.

"I had these installed last month after a drifter got a little too curious. The live video feeds must have been playing in the background when I ran the program. Do you think it interfered with the database?"

Rys looked around her. "Turn it up. How sensitive are the microphones? Put it on your office speakers."

Her screen showed twelve views around the property that were split between the cabin, cooperage, front gate, and the Little Blackfoot River. First pecking, then a squeak, broken by rustling leaves and wind. As she separated the different noises, babbling from the river at the north end became apparent. A gray wolf stalked prey hidden in the trees. The deafening solitude of nature filled the office.

Rys pointed. "I swear I can hear that bird walking in the brush. There, on camera nine. Isolate it".

"I don't want to state the obvious," Michael said, "but can we skip the wildlife lesson for now and try running the program again?"

Ava laughed. "That's probably a better place to start, huh?" She hit a few keys and waited. She felt it first, the sensation of another presence in the room. Then a series of long, languid, humming sounds flowed from her laptop.

"Seneca, connect to office speakers," Ava whispered.

Seneca, a Stoic philosopher who also happened to be one of the richest men in Rome in his day, was a fitting name for her trading platform.

Heads cocked then stopped moving outside her glass window in the now half full war room. A few employees sank into chairs with dreamlike smiles on their faces.

Ava looked first at Rys, then at Michael. These men and the team outside her office had become her entire life. This office her home. But what for? She had no family left. Her parents had died together in a small plane crash that had left her a teenaged orphan in her uncle's care. Her uncle, a former music producer, had left his beloved Montana cabin and moved her to his other home in L.A. where she had attended a prestigious arts and science magnet school. She was at Cal Tech four years later when he died of a massive heart attack. Would he be proud of what she had created? Would her parents? Of course not, she thought, they were artists. What she did was logical, rational, productive. What she did was safe.

Ava shook her head. Why was she thinking of them, again? She blinked away the water in her eyes.

Yelling from beyond her glass office wall grabbed her attention in time to see a junior developer punch one of the project managers.

"What the…" She moved around her desk and ran out of her office. Michael and Rys, who had ceased typing, followed.

Before reaching the desk where Paul, the unfortunate project manager, held his bleeding nose, they were interrupted by a loud crash from the left. Ava watched in horror as another developer repeatedly smashed his laptop on the glass desk in front of him. Avoiding the flying shards, she ran over to him and grabbed the mangled machine from his hands.

"Danny, stop! What has gotten into you guys?" She whirled around and cut her hand across her neck.

Rys nodded and hit a few keys on the laptop held open in the crook of his elbow. The music stopped and everyone froze.

"What the hell is going on out here?" Ava sat the laptop on the desk that had miraculously survived the beating.

"You two." She pointed and walked over to John, the junior developer who threw the punch, and Paul who was shoving Kleenex up his nose. "This is completely unacceptable."

John spoke up first. "Paul grabbed Melanie's ass. I told him it was uncool, and he told me to go fuck myself. I didn't realize my arm was moving until my knuckles made contact with his jaw. I don't know what to say. I've never done anything like that before."

Melanie's startled eyes and vigorous nod told Ava that what John said was true. Paul stared hard at the shining concrete.

She pointed back across the room at Danny, the laptop smasher. "And you?"

"That's my fault," said a barely audible voice from behind him. Mei, another developer stepped out with her head down. Her long, black hair curtained her eyes. She quickly tucked it behind her ears. "Danny asked me what I thought about his ongoing project, and I told him his code sucks. I didn't mean to. The words just sort of fell out of my mouth."

Danny shook his head. "It wasn't Mei I was mad at. She's right. The code I've been working on the past six months needs to be scrapped, but it's too late to start over. I know the company doesn't have money to waste on a lousy job. I guess I couldn't handle hearing the truth from someone else."

"So, you decided destroying company property was the best solution?" Ava's eyes bore into him.

She turned to address the entire room. "Okay, everyone, we need a breather. I want you all to take the day off."

A few hesitant protests stopped at Ava's glare. "Hit the beach, hit the bottle, hit the gym. Just don't hit each other or do any more work today. Be back at 7 a.m. tomorrow for an all hands so we can get back to work. Clear?"

Employees slowly gathered their things and one by one headed for the front door. No one spoke a word.

Michael touched Ava's elbow and raised an

eyebrow when she turned.

She gave a quick nod toward her office. She didn't need to watch if everyone left. They were a good crew. She followed Rys and Michael back into her office and closed the door.

They stood for a few moments staring at one another. Finally, Ava broke the silence. "What just happened? Any ideas?"

Rys stuck out his hand.

"Not now, dammit." She shook her head and grabbed a dollar off her desk. Rys' payment for catching her using a weak word. Just, sorry, I think – as a leader she couldn't afford to litter her messages with them, and so she paid up as a reminder that they were costly.

Rys pocketed the money, but neither man answered her.

Ava dropped into her desk chair. Her hair had come loose from its knot when she grabbed Danny's computer, so she swept it back on top of her head before continuing. "I want system access limited to the three of us until we understand what those noises are doing and why."

She motioned for the men to sit down. "Also, we need to bring in the new data scientist to help out. What's her name again?" she asked Michael. "She's a neurology and music major, right? We need to run some tests."

"Her name is Sarah. And yes. Strange combination." He texted while he talked. "The fewer of us with access to the database and code, and especially those cameras feeds, the better. I recommend we keep access limited to you and Rys for now."

Rys smirked. "Don't worry, dude. I know you won't mess up the code."

Ava nodded. "Michael has a point. We can program some listening devices for him and Sarah but keep the codebase access to you and me." She closed her eyes and pinched the bridge of her nose. It wasn't just her crew that needed a break.

"Whatever." Rys turned his laptop to face her. "You and I are the only ones with full access to the system now." He closed it and templed his fingers under his chin. "Now what in the hell was that *Lord of the Flies* crap in there?"

Michael pointed at the glass wall where only a few employees remained. "I'm not worried about me or messing up the code. I'm worried about it getting into the wrong hands. Look what happened out there when you turned on Seneca. People went nutso."

"He's right," Ava said. "There's obviously a strangeness to the sounds, or at least what they do to people. I felt it too. We'll keep the code between the two of us until we figure out what all the weird behavior is and what Seneca has to do with it."

She faced Michael. "And find Drew. He needs to be here." Her Chief Operating Officer should have been handling the employees and strategizing with them. He should have been the one to break up the fight. He was usually the first employee at work every morning.

"You know Drew was in the building when the noises started last night. This morning, I mean," Rys said. "I watched the office cameras from the time it came on. You should check out his office."

"Why would I care about Drew's office?" Ava shook her head. He was new to the team, a requirement from her institutional investors. In six months, he had implemented needed order and policies so that Ava could focus on building her system.

"It was pretty weird." Rys swept his eyes around the room then continued. "He was throwing stuff. A lot like what happened out there." He nodded outside her office.

"Throwing stuff?" Ava grimaced. She knew Drew liked his Scotch more than the average executive, but she had never seen him lose his temper. "Let's hope it was that awful print hanging in his office that sent him over the edge. You know, the one of the dogs playing poker." She laughed.

Rys and Michael exchanged raised eyebrows.

So much for lightening the mood. "I'll go check it out now and then take a quick shower."

"Sarah will be here when you're done." Michael slipped his phone in his pocket. "She's getting coffee around the corner. I'll go brief her while you do your thing."

"Check out what?" a voice behind Ava asked.

She jumped and whirled around. How long had Drew been listening to them?

"Where is everyone? It's after seven." Drew's eyes went from Ava to Michael, then to Rys.

Ava took a deep breath to slow her heart rate. Drew looked as if he had gotten a solid night's sleep, not like he had been tossing things around his office a few hours before. Every tiny strand in his black crew cut was in perfect order. His heavily starched dress shirt was tucked neatly into starched and creased jeans. She still puzzled that dry cleaners would do that to jeans.

"I sent them home," Ava said. "Rys told me you

were here when the music turned on. If what he says is true about your office, a few of the employees had similar reactions to yours. What happened?"

Drew narrowed his eyes.

Ava took an involuntary step back.

"You sent them home? Are you kidding me? Ava, we have less than a month to get this funding round closed. If we don't raise more money, they'll have all the time off they want."

Michael crept out of the office. Rys did a fake march behind Drew's back before leaving. Ava was too stunned to giggle.

"Are *you* kidding me? Did you hear what happened? Team members were throwing punches, for God's sake." She shook her head.

Frustrated, she sat down at her desk and rebooted her laptop. "We made huge gains last night when the noise first started. As long as we can reproduce the results, we'll get the funding from the investors on the Board at the quarterly meeting in a couple of weeks. Hell, we may not even need them by then."

When he didn't respond, she continued. "Did you listen to it? It's not Mozart, but there's something about it. I can't put my finger on it. Maybe we're onto something more, you know?"

"I wish I hadn't," he sneered. "It'll make my job harder having to sell something that sounds so awful."

Her smile dropped. She stared. Kept her face passive. Of course he could insult Seneca. He hadn't done a single thing to help build it. The investors' request, written into their legal docs so that it was more of a demand, was for Ava to hire a COO they approved of. Drew, an old classmate of hers from college, happened to contact her and wanted to catch up the week she signed the papers. She figured it was serendipity as he was the only MBA she knew, and he was looking for a job in L.A. Turned out he already knew one of the investors who lobbied hard for him after she brought up his name for consideration. She still wondered about the coincidence.

"I actually wanted to run my plan by you to get us through the cash crunch." He sat down in front of her desk. "You know my buddy who looked at the last round, but just couldn't get there on valuation for the company? Said it wasn't worth what you thought it was without any real results to show. He wants to meet again this week, and with Seneca working I can probably get them to your number."

She sat opposite him. "You mean the one who asked where the adult supervision was? Were you planning to tell me you were meeting with him? I thought I was clear on my position."

"Come on now. You know that's just something they say. It isn't personal."

Ava rolled her eyes.

Drew sat forward. "Do you want to let me do my job or keep shooting down every solution I bring you?"

She rubbed her eyes and gazed at the futon across the room. "You win. Tell me about the deal." When was the last time she slept in her bed at home?

"Never mind. I can't talk to you when you're like this. I don't know why you get so emotional. It's just money."

"Drew." She sighed. "You know this is about more than money to me. To us." She gestured to the empty desks outside her office. "We need investors who believe in our vision and our ability to execute on it. I talked to some of the founders your friends backed. Most of them were replaced with new CEOs within six months and the companies were broken into pieces and sold off." She leaned back and closed her eyes. "Not. Interested."

"Fine, Ava. I've talked to everyone in town. No one else wants to work with you."

She sat up and glared at him.

"Don't shoot the messenger! All I'm saying is you shouldn't be so difficult. I still don't understand why you don't put the money in yourself. It's not like you can't afford to with your inheritance."

"That money is locked up for three more years. I want to do this on my own anyway. And for the record, no, I don't want to bring in an investor who thinks it's perfectly normal to hold most of his meetings at a strip club. Who asks what kind of birth control I use? I mean what the actual fuck, Drew? I know you've worked with some of the Valley's best investors. Let's bring them to the table now."

"This is why no one wants to fund Seneca. You can't deal with basic facts about how things work. You take it all personally." He paused and softened his tone. "Why don't you let me handle the meetings and I'll keep them in check? Haven't I done a good job with our other investors?"

It was true. She had been worried about the two venture funds who invested in the first round. So far, they were easy to work with and Drew managed all their requests so that she could focus on building Seneca.

"Fine." Her eyes were so dry. She rubbed them

again. "It's been a long night. I'm excited, but I'm also exhausted and worried about how we're going to make payroll this month."

"Wait, you're not a machine?" He laughed.

"Very funny." She tossed a pen at him.

He fell out of his chair. "Employee abuse! I'm telling HR." He stood up and straightened his shirt. "Look Ava. I know we'll get this figured out. You got the tech working. Now it's my job to close the funding."

Her laugh didn't reach her eyes. How was it that someone who made her feel small and weak could, in the same conversation, make her feel like she could accomplish anything? It was complicated.

Chapter 4

An hour later, Ava stepped out of the cavernous locker room shower. The number of showerheads exceeded the five female employees at Sense Labs. She rarely crossed paths with any of them during her quick morning routine.

She wrapped a huge bath sheet around her petite frame. It hung to her ankles.

Her favorite part about this office was its history. It had been a gym before they took it over and converted it to office space. She had kept the men's and women's locker rooms and one of the fitness rooms intact to use as their company gym. She also negotiated to keep a stair climber, treadmill, cable machine, and free weight set with a couple of benches. The gym equipment made her habit of sleeping at the office far more bearable. When she was stuck on a problem, breaking a sweat helped her break out of a rut.

Her laptop sat on the purple velvet loveseat in the lounge area, another leftover from the quirky gym. Seeing it made her heart pound audibly. She didn't want to admit to the others what had happened to her when Seneca started playing the first time.

She had hit "end" on the program involuntarily. When she listened to the recording after, there were only sounds, no voices.

If her employees had experiences even remotely like hers, Ava thought, then she could never release Seneca to the public. Her latest encounter with it had evoked an emotional response that wasn't sadness, loneliness, or confusion. It was irrational, seething, limitless anger. Anger over something she didn't want to face.

She never wanted to create something that would have made her parents proud, but thinking of them while Seneca played had stirred up deeply hidden beliefs Ava was not consciously aware of until then. It had nothing to do with pride.

Ava believed her mother was responsible for getting herself and Ava's father killed. She knew her mom was trying to help one of the most notorious drug lords of the time. Her father was nervous about it, but Ava's mom had said she couldn't turn away those who desired to be healed. The details around their crash were sparse and the authorities deemed it an accident. Ava was terrified it was something else. So, she had taken the safe, busy path of chasing money.

No one wants to confront that kind of truth.

She knew she had to listen to the music again. Her new headphones were in her locker, just five short steps away from the shower where she stood. Another four steps to the loveseat and her laptop. An ocean of avoidance in between.

She went to the mirror instead. Brushed out her hair and coiled it at the nape of her neck. She studied her hazel eyes and rubbed eye cream into the dark circles under them. Why was she allowing the past to interfere with her work?

"Ava, you're being ridiculous." She stuck out her tongue at her reflection. "It was just some emotions, you weirdo." She smiled and shook her head.

The headphones were from a crowdfunding site.

They supposedly read brainwaves and gave readouts with suggestions for sleep, meditation, or deep work. So far, she had only worn them during sweat sessions on the stair climber. She laid her head on the soft velvet arm of the loveseat and propped her feet up on the other side. Her laptop rested on her stomach.

"Okay, Seneca, what do you have for me this time," she muttered and hit "Start."

Ava closed her eyes. Immediately, the feeling of not being alone overwhelmed her. She fought the urge to take off the headphones. She sensed the same presence as before but refused to open her eyes. No one would be there.

The tempo of different noises working together picked up. The intensity grew until it sounded like a freight train bearing down on her. She raised her arms over her head, shielded it.

The voice in her head again, loud, commanding. *"Don't trust him."*

A thundering crescendo of drums, then silence. The soft *bum bum bum* of a tuba as the sounds settled into a melody.

The tiny strawberry hairs on Ava's arms stood on end. Her uncle had told her the same thing once. A year before he died, when she was working on a group project for a history class. Drew had introduced himself to her uncle, all smiles and compliments. Uncle Jack had said he knew the type but hadn't elaborated.

"I have to trust him," she said into the empty room. "He knows his job better than I do."

"When you do not trust yourself, you give that trust away and become the source of your own betrayal. You trust blindly because you truly trust no one at all. Blind

trust is naïve. You will allow people to be hurt."

"This is bullshit!" She slammed the laptop shut for the second time that day. She ripped off the headphones and reared back to throw them at the wall.

Then, her own little voice in the back of her head spoke up. *It speaks truth.*

Ava froze. "Oh shit," she whispered. She could deal with the blind trust revelation later. What her intuition had said changed everything.

She tore off the towel and found a fresh pair of tights and tunic in her locker. She texted Michael before pulling them on. Then she ran through the gym that connected her office's back door to the locker room.

If Seneca did what she thought, the world would never be the same.

Chapter 5

"Fellow creationists and those still learning the way." Grandmaster Zalor commanded the attention of all in the hall and those listening in.

None listened so closely as the apprentice standing before the elders.

"We find ourselves in an unusual situation. While convening in the other realm, the elders and I determined we do not understand the true nature of what Zek created in his project world. Our insistence on Earth's destruction was made in haste and fear. We recognize our lower order logic for what it was."

A shout from the crowd broke the silence. "It is chaos!" Other voices rose. "It is destruction!"

"Yes!" the Grandmaster replied. "The chaos that has infiltrated the Network is already infecting minds, but we cannot allow it to affect the order, the rules, we have held in place for so long."

He lifted his arms high, hushing the excited cries. "Apprentice Zek, you are ordered to embark on your final intervention to seek understanding of the consciousness anomaly in the humans. You will bring this knowledge back to share with the guild. The only action you are permitted is to destroy the planet when the time comes. Do you have any questions for the elders in order to meet the desire of the guild?"

Zek felt the collective energy projected on him. What kind of an intervention consists of no action, he wanted to yell.

Vezon nudged Zek with his elbow.

Right. This was not the time. Zek hadn't saved Earth, but at least he had a chance to. Surely the Grandmaster would forgive any action he took to fix the problem.

He replied with a simple nod and deadpan eyes. "As you wish, Grandmaster."

****

Zek's quarters were simple. His rig sat in the far right corner like a recently laid upright egg. His narrow bed was beside it, a flat stone table at its foot.

Each of the senior level apprentices were given a semi-private space like his once they began their final projects. The interior walls went to the tops of their heads and there were no doors. Nowhere to be alone unless they were in the rig, but that was limited to creating or observing times only. They would be granted private creation rooms once they became full members of the guild.

He rested his elbows on the table and watched a miniature holographic version of himself reenact the progress meeting on its surface. He paused then replayed the Grandmaster's words.

"The humans' conscious activation is, for some unknown reason, decoupled from their awareness."

How could consciousness exist without awareness?

The tiny figures moved on the table once again. The alternative to joining the guild made him shudder. He would descend back to the sixth dimension and have to start all over again with only his dreams to remind him of life in the guild. Few souls who descended ever make it back.

If Earth were destroyed, his time in the seventh dimension would immediately come to an end. If he defied Zalor's orders, he would likely be expelled as an apprentice and suffer the same fate. He dropped his head in his hands.

Mez, the apprentice who worked next to him, entered his space without asking and pointed to the projected memory. "We have all experienced the need to learn from our failures, Zek, but this is spectacular! I have never seen a meeting like that."

Zek tapped the table and the hologram disappeared. "Do you not have work of your own to bother with?"

"None of us will remain if your humans ascend and ruin everything." He kicked Zek's robes aside and sat on his bed. "What will you do?"

"I will do as Grandmaster Zalor commands." Zek picked up his robes and hung them on the hook beside the entrance to his creation rig. "I have work to complete."

"That means certain descension!" Mez leaned back on the bed and crossed his lithe arms behind his head. "You may as well give up now. How will you do it? Will they see it coming?"

Zek shook his head. "I believe the humans will work it out themselves. My second intervention set things in motion to handle situations such as this."

"Oh yes, your secret society on Earth." He sat back up. "I never understood that one. Your first intervention was far simpler with much broader repercussions. To think one could add a little chromosome that made half the planet's creatures present their feminine side while the other half presents male. Then use the union to make them unconscious creators. That part is odd though it was an elegant solution. Will you not do something like that again?"

Zek stood by the door with his arms crossed. "Sometimes the best solution is to trust others. The human species evolved to embrace order. They simply needed a little nudge from the network's wisdom. The secret society, as you call it, will restore the proper balance."

"The part that disturbs me is how your species evolved to look and sound so much like us. Except why are they different colors? And the hair." He touched his smooth black head. "Laer would never have allowed it."

Zek responded by closing his eyes and directing his thoughts to his world. He hoped the other apprentice would get the message. He soon felt Mez's presence move away.

The Grandmaster was right. Zek didn't understand the complete nature of his creation or its dominant species. He understood what he had programmed it for, the starting conditions he had set, and the adjustments he had built in during his interventions. It was time to observe the anomaly himself.

Another presence pulled him from his questions. Zek opened his eyes to find his teacher standing before him. Vezon's formal robes were changed in favor of the loose, simple smock most creators wore while working.

"I was afraid you might have already gone," his Master said. "I believe I may be able to help you on your quest."

"You have done so much for me already." Zek stood and bowed his head. "Thank you for speaking for me in the meeting."

"Zek, your creation, whether the others recognize it or not, is a masterpiece. They seek to understand so that they may not fear it. You have not helped them to do this. You are responsible for eliminating their fear of your project."

"Yet I now fear it," Zek said. "I do not understand why the humans behave as they do. The balance they maintain lies at the extremes, but their progress rapidly gains speed. What if they succeed in bringing their chaos into the network? I cannot allow that to happen. There is no need to return to handle the problem. I can study it here, review the evolution of Earth to understand what went wrong. What may be done differently next time. The planet may be able to continue without the humans. Might I convince the elders to allow a new species on Earth to host souls that are near the point of ascension?"

"So, you would destroy them before doing everything possible to save them?"

"You heard Grandmaster Zalor. I was ordered not to intervene, and so what would be the purpose of returning?"

"You will defy the other half of the orders then? You will not return to Earth?" Vezon folded his hands and stared down at the apprentice.

Zek shook his head. "I see no need. I will report my findings to the guild once I have studied the world and its creatures in detail, after they are eliminated."

"I urge you to heed the full orders of the elders and return." Vezon gestured to Zek's creation rig. "There may be larger forces at play. Forces that wish to see you fail. Forces that should not be interfering. A new species would not solve a problem such as this. Please let me know how I can be of assistance." He turned to leave.

Zek grabbed his arm. "What do you mean forces? What do you know that I am unaware of?"

Vezon stopped and spoke over his shoulder. "Do you consider it odd that your planet experiences so much trouble? Do you not understand there are those who wish to see you fail?" He shook his head. "It is up to you, apprentice. I have said everything I came to say."

Zek's mouth hung open. It was declared forbidden to interfere with a creator's world millions of cycles before, when the Laer Guild first delivered its platform to the Creation Guild. Surely Laer had not broken the long-held practice.

Zek stepped into his creation rig and deactivated all senses save consciousness. He focused on Earth.

He waited for the consciousness spikes. The normal moves into higher and lower dimensions. Humans called it death. Some souls collapsed back to a lower realm while others expanded into the next dimension. The rest remained in the unpredictable third dimension. Correction, the fourth dimension populated by three dimensional beings unaware of their expansion potential.

Zek's thesis went beyond creating a planet in a dimension not supported by Laer. It went further than restoring the rate of ascensions into the network. He wanted to prove that three dimensional souls could gain conscious awareness of the network and open new network pathways.

He moved past the anticipated spikes. Zalor had been right. There was an ever so slight elevation in the planet's consciousness. He concentrated on it.

It was expected to originate from a human in one of the special power sites he set up in the previous intervention. It did not.

Zek leapt out of his creation rig the moment gravity was restored and made swiftly for the Grandmaster's chamber. Only he would understand the reading.

To become Grandmasters, creators must reach and sustain eighth dimension consciousness without passing fully through to the next dimension. It could not be explained or taught, only experienced. It was the basis on which Zek established his hypothesis for Earth. Conscious elevation without passing through to the next dimension. Grandmasters essentially formed a bridge between the two dimensions.

The chamber doors at the back of the great hall were open and the voice inside boomed as he approached. "You may enter, Zek."

He tore in. "Something is happening, Grandmaster!"

"Then it appears to be a good time to fulfill the wishes of the guild. Are you prepared to return?"

Zek stopped short and took a ragged breath. "We can figure this out from here."

"Can you explain to me the change you observed?" Zalor's smooth, dark face revealed nothing.

Zek stared. "I…well…there is a consciousness elevation."

"I believe we have established that." The Grandmaster moved directly in front of the apprentice. "Zek, you will one day be an extremely powerful creator. In many ways, you already are. However, by failing to understand your creation, you put us all in danger of it. You criticize Laer for allowing creation without the need to understand the underlying elements of building planets. You know how to manipulate elements to create a planet, yet you do not understand the results of your creation. Do you believe what you observed in the human consciousness level is the outcome you anticipated?"

"It is not. It should be coming from one of the designated humans. That is what I wanted to discuss with you. Master Vezon believes there may be interference with Earth. If that is the case, it changes everything."

"It does not change the threat from the humans, I am afraid." The Grandmaster moved past Zek and closed his chamber doors.

He turned around. "There are those who believe ascension is to be achieved only in balancing souls, not in the expansion of them. For every ascension, there must be a descension."

Zek frowned. "Yes, the Statics. It is unfortunate for those who wish to ascend."

"Regardless, many of them do ascend, and thus seek to rebalance by encouraging descensions."

The apprentice shifted his weight from one foot to the other in rapid succession. "Yes Grandmaster. Earth is an attempt to prove that the Expansionists are right. The multiverse can only continue if it expands."

"Who might prefer to prove otherwise?"

"If I prove it, the Statics will believe as you and I and all of the other Expansionists do." Zek smiled.

The Grandmaster sighed. "I sometimes wonder how it is that you made your way to this dimension. You are so talented yet still so very…"

Zek's eyes widened. "Hopeful?"

A small smile formed on the Grandmaster's lips, then dropped. "It is not allowable to interfere with the creation made by an apprentice, but you and Master Vezon believe it has happened."

Zek did not smile.

"You will return to Earth and learn the truth. Only then will you be welcome back at the guild. You will learn the nature of this consciousness elevation and any interference with Earth. Then you will destroy it before any further chaos is brought to the upper dimensions." The Grandmaster turned his back to the apprentice.

Heat rose in Zek's cheeks. "Will I be welcomed into the guild if I do your bidding Grandmaster? If there is interference and I end the project, as you ask. Will I become a creator?"

"You are a creator, Zek. Titles do not bestow the distinction of who you are. To become a member of the Creation Guild, you must present a fully functioning and balanced creation. I cannot change this."

The Grandmaster stood directly in front of Zek and held his shoulders. "However, if you are not able to determine the nature of what is occurring on Earth," he said and paused, "there may not be a guild to return to."

Zek stepped back. "I don't understand."

"You must learn to." The Grandmaster lowered his head. "There is no more that I may explain. Please do not fail us." He closed his eyes and light emanated from the top of his head. He was no longer present in the room with Zek.

****

Zek had more questions than answers as he prepared to return to Earth. From proclaimed failure to possible success to bewilderment at the Grandmaster's request; what did it all mean?

Stepping back into his rig, he set aside his concern and viewed the data from Earth's conscious field. The anomaly remained, and had increased.

The humans are so close. How could they be unaware of what was happening within them?

He pinpointed the location of the plateau and tuned in at the individual level. What the granularity revealed surprised him.

It was a woman. And something else.

Chapter 6

Ava sat up on the futon and stretched her arms over her head. She glanced down at her watch. Four hours of uninterrupted sleep were better than she had managed all week. She rubbed her dry eyes.

Three more days until the board meeting that would decide the fate of the company and the future of Seneca.

She wasn't sure if it was the late nights or her indecision on what to present to the investors that left her with a permanent headache. It wouldn't be so concerning if she could clear out the accompanying fog clouding her thoughts and dulling her senses. She dropped a pod in the coffee machine and headed to the locker room.

Steam billowed from the shower room. "Heads up," Ava yelled. The warm air clung to her skin.

The running water trickled to a stop. "Morning, boss!" rang out from haze.

"Oh, Sarah. I wondered if that was you." The couch, with its upended throw pillows and crumpled blanket, was surrounded by a castle moat of printouts. Ava wasn't the only one not sleeping.

"So far these test results are impossible to understand." Sarah walked out with a pink and blue striped beach towel wrapped around her athletic frame. Her shoulder length brown hair was already drying into tight spirals. "Any luck deciding which direction to go on commercialization?"

"The test results are the problem," Ava said. "The trading system is getting returns, but nothing like the first time Seneca played those sounds. Drew is handling the market tests. It's anyone's guess how long the numbers will hold."

She hoped they would hold long enough for their backup plan to work. Drew said if she took out a home equity loan that he would invest it using Seneca and all their problems would be solved. Without investors. It had only been a few days though.

Sarah pulled clothes out of her locker. "I don't envy you. Rys and I aren't doing much better with the music and its neurological effects,"

Ava turned around and spoke over her shoulder. "Are we calling it music now?"

"You can turn around." Sarah pulled a long, flowy dress over the towel. The towel dropped to the floor. "Yes, Seneca is definitely playing music. Creating it, more like."

"Huh," Ava said. "Interesting."

"We're going back to the university today to see if Rys' sister will help us run more brain scans. We noticed something else yesterday."

"What's that?" Ava wasn't sure *her* brain could handle much more. She yawned.

"When we left the music running after the tests, subjects were easier to talk to and, well, you can never be too sure, but it seemed like they were telling the truth. Like, the actual truth, not just what they thought we wanted to hear. We want to home in on that some more. Rys said he wanted to try it at a bar tonight." Sarah laughed and pulled her hair back with a headband.

Ava's mind raced. "Some kind of truth serum?" She went to her locker and fished out a large bottle of ibuprofen.

"That would be pretty cool, huh?" Sarah slipped a leather cord over her head. She adjusted the heavily lacquered pinecone pendant to hang just below her collarbone "Remember when we met and I told you why I studied music alongside neurology?"

Ava thought back to the Sunday afternoon on Maui when she had decided to check out a nude beach. She hadn't expected so many people. She hadn't expected most of them to have carried drums up and over the rocks. Sarah had set up next to Ava's towel and asked her what was going on.

"You thought music was the key to unlocking secrets to the primitive parts of our brain. It's why I hired you actually. Abstract connection. Not the easiest trait to find."

"Don't you think it's strange that your neural network started playing nature sounds, then created music as opposed to speaking or some other task first?"

Ava narrowed her eyes. "You think it's starting at the beginning? Like humans did? With music." She sucked in air. "I've been trying to understand how Seneca uses the stream from the video cameras. The answer is right there, but my mind has been so fuzzy the past couple of weeks, I can't seem to touch it."

"Then start at the beginning." Sarah folded the blanket then gathered up the printouts. "I'm meeting Rys at that diner on Culver. We should have more for you tonight."

Ava nodded and went to use the bathroom. Sarah

was gone when she came back out.

****

A quick run on the treadmill and shower later, Ava decided to do something she had been putting off. She pulled out her phone and searched for Tony Makoi, her late uncle's neighbor in Montana and his closest friend. She had memorized the number over a decade ago, but now let technology do its job. He picked up on the fifth ring.

"Yello," he answered slowly. She never could place his slight accent.

"Hi Tony, it's Ava. Jack's niece. I'm glad I caught you."

"Ava. Well, it's been damn near a spell since we heard from you. Are you comin' to visit?"

He asked her the same thing every time they spoke. It wasn't often. She hadn't been to the cabin since her uncle's funeral eight years before, and hadn't spent a night there since she was fourteen.

"The company has me busy these days. How are you?" No getting to the point with Tony. Niceties went a long way in that part of the country. She could hear his wife, Renata's, thick Brazilian accent in the background asking who was on the phone.

"Oh, about the same. Getting ready for the big pow wow in Iowa next month. Got a couple of projects to finish. How's the fast life?"

Small talk. She bristled at the thought of wasting time on unproductive banter about the weather or other mundane subjects. Seriously, what did his question even mean?

"It's great. We've made a major breakthrough. Actually, it's why I'm calling."

"A major breakthrough huh? Does this have anything to do with those cameras you had me install around your cabin last month?"

Ava caught the coffee mug before it slipped out of her grasp. Half of its contents sloshed on the floor and her tights. She hardly felt the burning liquid. Tony mumbled in the background, and she heard Renata let out a sharp gasp.

"H--How did you guess?" She had tested every kind of livestream she could think of, from musical performances to other security cameras, but none made Seneca play music or noise of any kind.

Focus, Ava.

"I'm curious if there's something special about the cameras," she said. "Or maybe where you placed them."

When he spoke next, the joviality had dropped from his voice. "It's time you take a trip up here."

Her watch buzzed. Ten minutes until her next meeting. "I...what...can you just tell me over the phone? There's no time for a trip. I have to get this figured out so we can close our next round." She cringed at the desperation in her voice.

"There are some things we should discuss in person," Tony said. "Here. I can arrange a jet that would have you in and out in no time. If it's money, you know the estate can fund whatever you need."

This was not the fun-loving hick she knew from the ranch with his thin, gray ponytail, Wrangler jeans, and elk hide vest dotted with intricate native beadwork. This Tony was the executor of her parents' and uncle's estates. The Tony who found her at the *payé's* hut when her parents didn't return from Bogotá. The Tony who guided her through the jungle to Ecuador and flew her out of South America and to her new life in the United States.

Ava fiddled with a pen. "Let me take care of things with the company, then I'll come up next month. Does that work?"

"Ava, if what you discovered has anything to do with those cameras, you need to be careful. There are forces at play you aren't aware of."

Not this again. Tony meant well, but he was superstitious about everything. Always quick with a fantastic story to explain the mundane.

"I'll visit soon," she said. "I promise. Until then, what can you tell me that might help?"

"There's nothing special about the cameras or their specific placement." He sighed and added, "but there is someone here you need to meet. He can help answer some questions about your mother."

Ava stood up. "My mom?" She paced the shiny concrete floor. "Who is this person? Did they know her?"

"This can't be done over the telephone. You must be here."

She wondered if she could get there and back to LA in a day but couldn't get the timing to work in her head. Probably not. The urgency in his voice told her she should still try.

"You know I would give anything to find out if the crash really was an accident, but this is the most critical month ever in the company. How about after the board meeting? It's in a few days. Will the person be around that long? Can you get them to stay? Will you be back from your pow wow by then?"

"I don't know, but I'll try to keep him here," he said softly. "Please be careful."

Ava shook her head. Her uncle had had the strangest friends.

"Okay. Thanks, Tony. Have a great time at the pow wow."

"I'll see you soon, Little Star." The line went dead.

She hadn't heard that name in a while. She held the now silent phone and smiled at the memory of her parents calling her by the nickname that her uncle and Tony also used.

Maybe it wouldn't be so bad if she couldn't raise more funding. She could always sell her house and move into the cabin. That kind of cash might keep Sense Labs going long enough to perfect Seneca. Or at least figure it out.

And who was this stranger talking to Tony about her parents? Calling Tony was supposed to make her feel better. The knot in her stomach tightened.

Chapter 7

Ava confirmed the agenda and checked to see that the board packages were ready to go one last time. The board meeting would determine the future of not only Seneca, but also her life's work and all her team's livelihoods. She had to be *on*.

Michael interrupted her obsessive double-checking with a tap on her shoulder. "You'll only work yourself up, Ava. Why don't you take a quick break? I have this handled."

The board packages had been emailed the day before, and so he was right. No last-minute adjustments would help or even be possible.

One of the graduate interns, commonly underestimated and whispered about due to her model perfect 5'9" frame and long blond hair, finished setting out the catering.

They had about forty minutes until everyone showed up. Just enough time for one more Seneca session, Ava thought. On her way out of the conference room, she noticed the intern about to set up the telepresence system.

"We won't be needing that. All the board members will be in the office," Ava told her.

The girl's blue eyes widened like a reprimanded child. "Drew s-said he needed it for his presentation."

She wasn't behaving at all like the self-assured woman Ava remembered from the interview a few months before. She made a mental note to handle the exit interview herself when the intern headed back to school.

"That's odd," Ava replied. "Michael said we didn't put anything from Drew on the agenda other than basic financials." She realized this had nothing to do with the girl and changed tracks. "Carry on then. You're doing a great job." She hoped the praise would calm the girl so that she wouldn't spread more nervous energy.

Ava walked back to her office and thought through her notes on the presentation. Her intuition said she was missing a key point. If their theories about Seneca were correct, it would help her locate it.

She pulled out her phone and opened the new app she had created for listening to the music. Then she reached for her noise cancelling headphones and lay down on the futon.

As she listened to Seneca's music, she marveled again at its remarkable power. She recognized flaws in her logic quicker than usual when it played. She slowed down at the same time. The engineer in her called it finding signal through the noise. It had helped her decision making for the commercialization plan she was about to present. Yet she could only listen to it a few minutes at a time before getting a headache. Her sessions with Seneca always ended with the feeling of confrontation.

What was nagging her about the impending board meeting? Was it the friction between the two institutional investors, each of whom had a seat on the board with her, Drew, and the billionaire angel investor? Ideally, investors would vote together, company executives would vote together, and an independent would break any ties. However, they had no independent member, only Nathan, the super angel investor. He usually sided with Ava. Drew had voted against her decision on more than one occasion, and she could never be certain what the two institutional investors would do. They both represented large funds but didn't always see things the same way.

Given the level of additional investment needed to commercialize Seneca, it was uncertain who would vote to support and ultimately fund her plan. She internalized the question, but her instincts, or was it Seneca, said this wasn't what bothered her. She asked herself what did.

Her skin tingled. The presence was there in the office with her again, yet she was alone. She shuddered. It spoke in her head.

It is too late to change what has been done.

She frowned. There was no time left to contemplate. A notification from Michael alerted her that two of the three outside board members had arrived.

Showtime.

****

"Rhonda, Tim, how are you?" Pleasantries were one of the less comfortable parts of Ava's job.

Rhonda Chambers was a founding partner of one of the most successful venture firms in the valley, though it had been around less than a decade. A few big, quick hits put it on the path to icon status and Rhonda was widely considered to be the secret behind their Midas touch.

Tim Lafferty was a former tech CEO who had founded and sold a company before Ava was born. He took a languid approach to the investment world and became a venture partner at one of the valley's oldest firms about the time they invested in Ava's company. Like all the best funds that weren't named after their partners, it was named after a tree. She knew him from a guest lecture she had attended at her university years before, and suspected he got his new cushy role when the firm was angling to lead her investment round.

"We're ready for you in the conference room," Michael said behind them.

Rhonda wasted no time. "Let's do it. I want to see what our star CEO has come up with." She grabbed Ava's shoulder and gave it a friendly squeeze. At six foot one, she towered over Ava and most other people, but her gregarious attitude made even the most awkward engineers feel comfortable.

"Couldn't do it without this great team," Ava said. "We're all about to change the world. But we need to wait for Nathan to get started."

Nathan Klepacz, their independent board member was a fairly reclusive billionaire, known for his eccentricities and hyper genius mind. The hedge fund he started in his twenties boasted some of the most significant returns in the industry before he shut it down to pursue other interests, like investing in Ava's sproutling of a company.

Tim broke in. "I saw him over there with your other Pollack. What those two find to talk about is a mystery. Such a weird language."

"Rys is joining the meeting for the technical portion, and so maybe you'll find out." Ava worked to keep her voice steady. Had Tim always been this blatantly disrespectful? Heat flared up the back of her neck.

She turned to the two, deep in conversation in their native tongue, and motioned to Rys that it was time to get started. He responded with a nod. The other man nodded. His gray eyes caught Ava's and lingered.

Everyone converged on the conference room at one time, loudly catching up, getting in coffee orders, and grabbing sandwiches from the credenza at the end of the room. Once they settled in, Ava stood.

"Is everyone ready to go?" she asked.

The room grew quiet. Heads nodded and yeses were mumbled between bites. Michael waited for Ava's cue.

"Great. As mentioned in the agenda emailed earlier this week, we're varying the flow a bit because we have a big announcement, which will require a major change in strategy. Mostly because I can't get through all the business of the past quarter without exploding and telling you everything first, we're starting with the big news.

"You're killing us, Ava!" Rhonda teased. "Out with it."

Ava nodded to Michael who tapped twice on the screen in front of him. The conference room lights dimmed, and the projector screen lit up with her first slide.

"Since the first days of man, we have struggled with the meaning of this thing called life. Beginning with Aristotle claiming that every life has a purpose to Thoreau prophesizing that government would not be needed in the face of each person living their unique value, to ancient and modern-day religions putting the answers in the hands of deities, even technology companies determined to change the world; we are all searching in our own way. But something stops us from questioning further, from fulfilling who we know deep down that we are."

Pictures of history's great philosophers, inventors, explorers, scientists, and revolutionaries appeared one by one on the screen. Cheesy, but effective.

Ava continued. "That something, our brakes so to speak, is none other than our nurture. We can blame circumstances, other people, God even, but as we learn from the greats and those who reinvent themselves, we hold both the key and the lock to uncover our greatest selves. We let fear, and external forces hide that key."

"But what if, with the help of artificial intelligence, which doesn't suffer from the human condition, we could seize that key and unlock our highest potential?"

Tim snickered across the table to Drew who kept a poker face. Ava ignored him.

"We would like to present Seneca, the world's first ever autonomous music creation brain." She paused. "With a side effect."

The music began its ethereal dance into their ears. Ava noted the quizzical faces around the room. Perfect.

Rhonda smiled at Tim. "I don't think we can sell it for the sound,"

Ava turned to her. "What do you want to do that no one knows about, Rhonda?"

"To fulfill the mission I was sent here for," she said with no hesitation.

Tim couldn't handle it any longer and roared with laughter.

Rhonda's crystal blue eyes flashed, then she joined him laughing. "I mean, aren't we all here to help you fulfill the mission of Sense Labs?" She spread her hands, palms up.

"Uh, okay," Ava said. "What about you, Tim? What do you want to do more than anything but don't think you can?"

"To get a divorce and marry my lover, Randall."

The room went dead silent. Ava's eyes darted to his. His hand flew to his mouth.

Red faced, he shouted, "Turn that off!"

"Tim, I…we didn't know." Ava motioned to Michael to turn off the music. "Before we continue, I would like to remind everyone in the room of the non-disclosure agreements we all signed. Not a word from this meeting can be shared with anyone outside these doors."

Heads nodded around the room. Sweat dripped down Tim's temples.

Nathan spoke up. "Any of us could be lying, regardless of whatever thing we say out of character. How do we know it's the truth?"

"What you've just experienced is real," Ava replied. "While we can't anticipate what people will say, we have learned a lot about what happens in the brain when this music is played."

Sarah pointed to her graphics on the slide while Ava spoke.

"After considering multiple possibilities for commercialization, we have determined that it should only be administered in controlled environments for now. I believe you can see why." Ava nodded toward Tim. "Facing one's deepest self is not the simplest matter."

She paused then flipped to the next slide which

held only two words. *The Future*. "Therefore, we propose to start with a technology-enabled life coaching practice, whereby the music is administered in a controlled setting by trained professionals."

"This is step one and will be used to train the system for the ultimate goal." Another slide, this time with a picture of an infant. "What if we train the system so well, collect enough data points, everything from DNA to in utero experience, to predict a person's purpose and gifts before they can even speak? As Thoreau claimed, governance and rules wouldn't be necessary if everyone did the right thing, in line with their purpose. If we could align nurturing with our individual natures, what could humanity accomplish? This could very well usher in a new age of man. An age of transcendentalism."

Nathan, usually silent during board meetings, surprised Ava by speaking up again. "That doesn't even scratch the surface of what is possible. You aren't kidding when you say we're going to change the world. To think that everyone could be brought up to play their best game, instead of the one that is forced on them by society. How does the music do it?"

"Rys and Sarah prepared a technical preparation that will explain what we know so far, but it was a lucky accident that made it play the first time," Ava began.

Drew stood up. "Everyone, myself included, has been on this day and night since the discovery. I would like to present a few things before we get into the technical details. Ava, may I?"

Rys, Sarah, and Michael raised their eyebrows at one another. Blood rushed to Ava's head.

Chapter 8

Ava cleared her throat and gestured that the floor was his. "Of course."

"I was planning another demonstration of the technology, which we can get to, but I have another matter to discuss before we get too far down the rabbit hole." He held up an envelope and a multi-page typewritten letter that had been folded to fit inside.

Ava sat up in her chair. She thought she had been crystal clear about the day's agenda.

"This," he said and held out the letter, "came in today, addressed to the board of directors. It was sent from a FedEx store in New York, but I haven't been able to identify the sender yet. I would like to tear it up and never bother any of you with it. However, as an officer of the company, I feel it is my fiduciary duty to deliver it to the board so that we can all decide how to handle it."

"What does it say?" Rhonda asked. "Give us the gist."

"It's mostly about Ava. I don't know what to say, other than you should read it for yourselves."

Ava, tight lipped, kept still. She remembered the words she heard when Seneca played earlier that morning.

"Just read the first few paragraphs then," Rhonda said.

Drew hesitated then began. "Dear Sense Labs

Board of Directors. You have been had. Four of you anyway. You are probably sitting there listening to Ava's latest magical, mystical, Pollyanna plan to change the world. That is not what she really has planned. Did you actually think she was all that good and innocent? Allow me to introduce you to the real Ava Lawson." He paused, looked around without making eye contact. "I can't do this."

"Ava, do you want him to continue?" Rhonda asked, her serious green eyes steady on the CEO.

Ava kept her voice steady. "Could everyone on the board stay in the room and everyone else step out please?" As the intern, Michael, Rys, and Sarah scurried out leaving everything behind, she mouthed *I'll fill you in.*

She shifted her eyes to glare at Drew once the door closed. "Please continue."

"I can't," he said softly.

"Give me that." She shot her hand out and yanked the papers from him. Glancing over the first page, her eyebrows raised then quickly returned to her practiced expressionless state.

She began reading where he left off. "The real Ava Lawson. Or should we say Ava Andrews-- whose parents were killed in a plane crash in the jungle while she escaped, untouched? Whose uncle took her in and met with calamity upon calamity, and ultimately death. But not before Ava got her piece of his estate locked up in a trust. Then she turned her sights on the real money, raising over $20 million for an artificial intelligence scheme. Has she presented a plan to you? Let me guess. It displays absolutely no regard for your capital, or for the people who will be affected by it. Does she want even more money, so that she can keep funneling it into her 'special projects' budget? When will she account for all the money that she has spent? It is time you do your fiduciary duty and ask the tough questions. She is still going behind your backs, sleeping with investors she plans to use to dilute you out. Did you not get your piece of tail while you could? Maybe it's not too late! Just don't let it be too late to save your investment and reputation. One final question…who has access to the codebase? Don't know? Ask her. Sincerely, Archangel."

She sat the letter down in front of her. "There are some additional pages from what appear to be screenshots of our accounting system and database trees. I don't know what to say."

Nathan jumped up. "This is ridiculous!"

He was the last person she expected to come to her defense. He was well known for being a justice vigilante. "Ava, you don't have to answer to any of this. I did my due diligence and know everything I need to about your family and past. Somebody obviously wants to divide the board at the most critical time in the company."

"My dear, it seems you're being initiated," Rhonda said. "Congratulations. Only the best get trolls of this nature." She leaned back in her chair and crossed her arms.

Tim, still red-faced, broke in. "I didn't know this about your past. It seems you've hidden it well, changing your name and all." He sat forward, elbows on the conference room table.

"My uncle adopted me after the accident, and I took his name a couple of years later," Ava said.

Lighten up on the defensive tone, she told herself.

"Yeah, but you have to admit, you lied about it in college when we met," Drew said. "I'm just saying, if this gets out in the press, you and the company won't get the benefit of the doubt. It could hurt everything you've built." He pointed to the glass wall. "Everything they've built."

"Oh, dear Lord. Why can't we just do our jobs and leave personal lives out of it? My parents have no relevance on the work we do." Ava's voice rose with each sentence.

"I'm more concerned with what may happen if word of this gets out," Drew said. "The one thing the author is right about is our fiduciary duty." He always played the consummate professional in groups of three or more.

"Exactly," agreed Tim. "I don't have any choice but to take this to my partnership and get their thoughts. In the meantime, I recommend that we investigate these allegations and consider moving Ava to a less visible role."

"You're taking this cowardly anonymous crap seriously because it has a few half-truths in it? Accusations from my childhood? You can't be serious!"

Ava looked to Nathan for support. He had sat down and was staring at his hands.

This is how it happens, she thought. *This is how I get pushed out of the company I started. This is how they steal my work.* She closed her eyes and shook her head.

"Everyone calm down," Drew said. "As luck would have it, we may be able to resolve this right here." He stood and walked to the telepresence system that was wheeled in by the unsuspecting intern before the meeting.

"While Ava and the team were working on their little coaching idea, I talked to a few of my buddies in Washington about ways we can use the music as it is now, without additional investment. They've prepared a demonstration, if you'll allow me." The screen flicked on and a man in uniform in front of a blank white wall greeted them.

"Good morning, Sense Labs! Can you hear me okay?" The man waited for their answer before moving his camera to get a broad view of the room he was in. Nothing but white walls, one with a large mirror next to a steel door, and a table in the middle with a man in an orange jumpsuit chained to it.

The prisoner's dark complexion stood in high contrast to the speaker's pasty skin and close-cropped white hair. The chained man's dark features couldn't hide the purple bruising and his nearly closed, bloodshot right eye. There was no sign of pain on his face, only pure exhaustion.

"What's going on, Drew? I don't like the look of this." Ava's voice edged up a notch.

"Ava, this should get you excited. Your creation will be the biggest advance in counterterrorism methods in centuries, possibly ever. Watch." He clapped his hands together like a child at his first circus.

The military man put on a headset and motioned with his right hand toward the mirror. Familiar music began to play.

"Prisoner 11. Are you prepared to answer our questions?" The other man sat stone-faced at the table and stared straight ahead, seemingly lost in his internal world.

"Prisoner 11. Can you hear me?"

"Yes," he said. He immediately put his hand to his mouth; his eyes raced.

"That's better. Now why don't you tell us who you work for?" the officer asked.

"Because they will kill my family."

"I meant…" The white-haired man paused and held his index fingers on the headphone ear pieces. "Who do you work for?"

"I only know him by the name Khalid. Please don't make me say more. My children, my wife, they will all die," the prisoner cried.

"Would you recognize this man if you saw a photo?"

"Yes," he said through a sob.

"Now we're finally getting somewhere. Isn't this easier than the other way, Prisoner 11?"

"No. I have failed my family."

"Well, maybe you shouldn't have put American lives in danger."

"But I am only a cook. I did nothing," the prisoner said. His eyes pleaded with the camera.

"Let's not waste these people's time any longer. I want you to tell me when you see Khalid's photo."

Drew broke in. "That won't work. You must ask him specifically about each picture. I think we've made our point to the board though. Thank you for your time, General Shaw." The General nodded at the camera and Drew turned it off.

"Is that what I think it is?" Nathan stated rather than asked.

"How did you get the music?" Ava whispered.

"As Ava said, the music invokes truth," Drew said. "While it's nice to believe the world can be a better place eventually, inducing wrongdoers to tell the truth is a far more effective tool for achieving that now. I used the audio from our security cameras and we've tested it on a few dozen subjects so far, with amazing results. The U.S. government is ready to write a blank check." He smiled with self-satisfaction.

Ava still fumed over the letter, but this betrayal was a whole new level of terrifying. No way he would get her approval. "Have these prisoners given consent?"

"I'm pretty sure they didn't ask their victims for consent," he spat.

"Don't all prisoners get basic Constitutional rights? What about the fifth amendment? The right to stay silent." Ava could hear her volume increasing. "It didn't appear as if he had any control over what he said."

"You're getting shrill, Ava." Drew moved around the table, closer to her. "Are you seriously saying that just because we played some music to get him to talk but didn't ask his permission, that it doesn't matter if he is complicit in the deaths of thousands of Americans? This is a completely humane way of getting information that requires absolutely no physical contact and could save many thousands more lives." By the time he finished, he stood over her, glaring. Beads of sweat dotted his upper lip.

"I'm with Drew on this one," Tim said. "It sounds like a far better plan than getting a bunch of hipsters to realize they should quit eating animals or whatever. This is tangible, and productive. If everyone ran around doing exactly what they wanted, or we start glad-handing obvious criminals, nothing would ever get accomplished, and society would cease to exist as we know it. With an application like this, we would all be national heroes."

"Whoa!" Rhonda said. "We all need to take a minute. This may be too much to deal with at once. I'm still trying to understand what it is you all have discovered, but it's clear there is a lot at stake here. The timing and nature of the letter proves it." She pointed to the sheets of paper in front of Ava.

"That's what I was saying about the tech." Drew shifted his eyes to Rhonda. "If Ava will grant us access, we can turn on the music and ask her about what the letter says. Problem solved."

Nathan didn't look up from the phone he was typing on under the table as he spoke. "By that statement, one might assume you wrote the letter, Drew."

"Drew is right though," Tim said. "If Ava agrees to answer questions about what the letter says, I would be fine not pursuing other action. I also think we need to give his plan serious consideration."

Rhonda turned to Ava. "What do you want to do?"

"Are you actually suggesting that I be subjected to interrogation based on that misogynistic, hateful letter? What about all of you? Can we also go around the room and ask who knew about the letter?"

Employees outside the glass wall of the conference room pretended not to hear her shouting.

Tim put his hand on his chest. "Well, I never."

"We can only deal with what we have," Rhonda said. "Given the unusual circumstances, and what's at stake, I think it would be a good idea for Ava to consult her personal attorney."

She rose and turned to Ava. "If this is libel, you need to sort it out. In the meantime, we must make sure the source code is in good shape and check out the financial models for both of your commercialization ideas. Does that sound like a plan that works for everyone?" She moved back to her seat. "We can reconvene in a week to make some decisions. For now, we need more information."

Tim stood. "I think it's more obvious now that Ava has something to hide, or else she would let us ask questions with the music on. If we give her a week, she might take off with all of the company's intellectual property."

Nathan handed Ava his phone so that she could read his open texts. He moved toward the door. "She's not saying another word. I've seen how these things play out. Let's go, Ava. My attorney will meet us in thirty minutes." He turned accusing eyes on the other board members. "This isn't how it's going to work this time."

Ava collected her things and they left the room, then the building, without another word.

Chapter 9

"Dammit!" Nathan yelled after both doors closed on the new Napier green McLaren.

Of all Ava's investors and advisors, Nathan remained a mystery. He wasn't the outgoing type and, just when she thought he was a complete hermit cheap ass, he would show up with an ostentatious neon green, half million-dollar car. It was an amazing piece of machinery. She couldn't blame him for the splurge. Nothing was out of character for him, she had learned since their first meeting. She wasn't surprised at his reaction in the board meeting either. Curiosity more than fear drove her to follow him out.

"So that didn't go the way I planned," she said with a laugh. Why did she always laugh when she was uncomfortable? Her unusual, but customary reaction during those times confused people and sent all the wrong signals.

Nathan's eyes didn't leave the road as they pulled out of the parking garage and into the chaos of daytime traffic. Tourists mixed with bright-eyed dreamers and old school hustlers to create general chaos during work hours and gridlock before and after. He and Ava were catching the end of the lunch hour rush. The engine purred like a mama tiger beneath them.

"I don't know how I missed it," Ava said. "It's obviously Drew. I wouldn't be surprised if Tim were in on it, too. Do you think they're working together?"

"Do you have any concept of what you've created?" Nathan's inability to answer anything directly frustrated her in meetings. She would be ready to wrap things in a neat little bow and he would throw out some random question that would destroy her carefully built argument. She hated to admit it, but after his complete obliteration of whatever plan she presented, his questioning always forced a far better strategy in the end. Didn't change her urge to choke him when he did it though.

Now, she suppressed that urge because he was right. This was serious, and it had more to do with her creation than herself, regardless of what the letter alleged.

"I understand what Seneca is capable of, sure. I didn't realize Drew was going behind my back. He kept telling us to build and he would handle all the boring stuff." Ava's face dropped into her hands. "Why didn't I let him go a few weeks ago? I knew then he was going to be a problem."

"Cut it out!" Nathan stopped for a red light and turned to her. "Useless thoughts like that take you out and we don't have the luxury of it now."

"Take me out?" It felt like a reprimand. That was not what she needed right then. She needed answers and a plan; hopefully one that included slapping the shit out of Drew's smug face.

Nathan stepped on the gas and roared away from the light. "When you're stuck on blaming yourself or feeling guilty, you can't focus on solutions. Your mind is clouded with useless thoughts that lead to bad decisions. Waste of energy. Takes you out of the game. Weakens you. You're not weak Ava, so stop it."

Not exactly a reprimand. Nathan's words reminded her of some of the less comfortable personal insights that came to her while listening to Seneca.

The phone in her hand buzzed. She read the thirteenth text from Michael asking what was going on. Sent him a quick reply not to worry. She would explain later. Read his response that the other three board members were sequestered in her office and had just pulled Rys in. Michael and Sarah had been told not to leave under any circumstances.

Nathan broke through her digital distraction. "Someone wants control of the tech, and they made it pretty obvious who or what that someone is. Drew, Tim, whoever, are just messengers. You're falling into a trap they set. Do you see it?"

"The government?" She considered him with fresh eyes. "You've been through this before," she guessed.

"With my first two hedge funds. People in that world would do anything for Alpha. They all want to know how you do it and will stop at nothing to find out."

He paused and lowered his voice. "My grandparents went through the worst manifestation of truth suppression in Poland. Their truth was education. It landed them on the *Intelligenzaktion* list. They weren't lucky enough for the gas chamber at Auschwitz. That was reserved for the innocent. Political prisoners were worked, beaten, and starved to death for the crime of knowledge. Then my parents, who immigrated to the U.S. during the Cold War, were accused of being spies. Yes, I am too familiar with the power plays against those who know truth."

"I had no idea."

"The circumstances are not important. Only the outcome. We can't let the source code get into any government's hands. Do you have it on lockdown?" He flicked on the left blinker and turned toward the water, away from the office buildings on their right.

"Rys, Michael, and I were the only ones with full access. I thought it was weird at the time, but Michael asked that I remove his full permissions when all this started, and so Rys is the only other one with access now. Do you suppose Michael knew this would happen?" A lot of strange behavior was starting to make sense.

"Good. He is perceptive and wanted to protect you. I don't know if he knew. That is for him to tell. Ryszard will need instruction. I can handle that. Do you trust him?"

Nathan was a much thicker onion to peel than she realized. "Of course," she said. "Do you know Rys outside the company?" How had she missed that?

"I can reach him securely. That leaves you."

"I have a backup stashed away in a secret spot. Running around South America as a kid made me a privacy freak." She mentally crossed her fingers that the package she snail mailed the week before had made it safely to Montana.

"Good," Nathan said. "It will come in handy. Destroy everything except one copy. That one will stay with you no matter what."

"Okay, hold on. This is getting a little bit ridiculous. It's not like we have a basket of three-letter agencies secretly following us." This time she laughed for real.

"Not yet," he said. He reversed in one fluid motion

into a parallel parking spot. "We're changing cars. Get your bag but leave your phone and laptop. If you have anything else with a signal in there, it's best to leave it, too."

"Are we meeting your lawyer here?" She pointed to the beach, well populated with testosterone-fueled bodies and fleshy, sunburned tourists playing on their phones. What was usually a common sight suddenly felt foreign, disconnected. As if she no longer belonged.

"We will call her. For now, we're having lunch and then getting you somewhere safe. You choose what to do from there. Okay?" He pushed his door up and turned back to her.

Genuine concern filled his broad, ruddy features giving him a beauty she had never noticed. His flecked gray eyes fixed on her. He suddenly became a person, not just an investor, advisor, billionaire, or whatever other label was attached to him in her mind. He was Nathan and he was worried about her.

She fired off a final text to Michael, took the sim card out of her phone and used the tiny toolkit in her bag to dislodge the hard drive from the laptop. She slipped the sim and hard drive back in her bag before handing the devices to Nathan. She didn't know him that well.

"I need to change shirts," she said. "This one is full of sensors. Nothing long range but anyone from the team could pick it up if they were close."

It was her first time off the grid for more than a few minutes since she started the company two years before. Her stomach clenched. Instinct made her reach for the phone that was no longer there to check that the sensor alert from her shirt functioned properly. How would she keep track of her vitals? Her team? She tasted bile in the back of her throat.

Nathan climbed out under the raised door. Tourists were already snapping selfies in front of the audacious vehicle, gawking to see if he was famous. For all his reclusiveness, he was once photographed with an up-and-coming starlet on the red carpet. Whenever a story came out, those pictures resurfaced and reinforced the public's view of him as a typical rich playboy.

Ten years later and minus a tux and bright lights, he was nearly unrecognizable. He ducked his head back in. "Don't worry about that here."

She nodded and shoved her workout gear back in the bag. Pulling herself up and out of the tiny hatch was less than graceful. "Lead the way." She followed him down the boardwalk into an alley where an old Jeep sat, ready for its beach bum owner to return.

"Go ahead and change shirts. I'll keep an eye out." He turned around.

"I'm not that modest." She stripped off the sleeveless turtleneck and replaced it with a generic cotton tank top. "Just didn't want that photo on tonight's news." He took the wire-filled shirt from her and tossed it in a dumpster before jumping in the driver's seat of the Jeep.

The hotel turned out to be a small cottage on the beach north of the city. Less chance of being recognized. Over lunch on the expansive redwood deck, Nathan shared stories from the two management coups in his first companies, as well as his grandparents' early demise at the hands of the Nazis. Nervous energy clung to the salt air.

"Your grandfather was one of the professors from

Jagiellonian University?" The news shocked her, as it was a detail she had not uncovered when she had done her usual exhaustive diligence on Nathan. "I spent a semester there during undergrad and was fascinated with its long history, especially the story of the professors sent to the prison camps. I never imagined I would meet anyone who had family from that group. I'm so sorry."

"My mother's father. My grandmother was captured shortly after as well and was sent to the same camp in Berlin at first. They were both on the list. They were not so different from you and me, just living in different times. Different political climate."

"How did your mother survive?" Ava's fascination in learning Nathan's life story was all consuming, though she caught herself feeling for her phone more than a few times. Dread sunk into her bones with each passing unplugged minute. When Nathan offered wine, she gladly accepted, hoping it would take the edge off.

"They suspected what would happen. She was just a baby. They sent her with a letter and all the money they had to live with relatives who were leaving for America."

"What did it say?"

"The usual stuff about how much they loved her and would miss her. They also said that they couldn't run from what they were, and she never should either. It took her a long time to understand what they meant. She and my father were very tough."

"It seems to have worked. I bet they're very proud of your success."

"Enough about me," he said. "It's too bad you didn't get to finish your presentation. I was hoping to experience more of Seneca."

"Most people have a breakthrough of sorts when listening to it. Did anything happen for you?" Would he tell her if it had? That's what she really wanted to know.

"Not to ruin your excitement, but it didn't reveal some hidden truth. I made peace with myself years ago. It was more of a reminder. My gift is that I see people, and I saw you in more depth. With more clarity."

Her heart skipped. "And?"

"I'm not here to tell you that anything you've done is wrong, or how you should be. I exist to protect what you are. Your gifts of creation are otherworldly. Knowing people as I do, I can see what you represent to them. You aren't safe here, just as my grandparents weren't safe in Krakow."

She drew in a deep breath. The shock of another person revealing what she knew deep down but was too terrified to admit filled her with both hope and dread. Like listening to Seneca. "Can you come be CEO and I'll just work for you?" Her nervous laugh kicked in again and she covered her mouth.

"Ava, the only way you will get through this is to accept who you are. I can't help you with that, but I can advise you to seek refuge while you do. Staying here to fight is not the way."

She nodded halfheartedly. He wanted to protect her, but she needed to protect her team and their discovery.

Chapter 10

The sun filled the patio with its softer end of day rays. Nathan seemed to come out of a trance when his phone buzzed. "Ride's here," he said.

"Thank you." She brushed her fingers against his arm. "I mean it. For everything. But I'm going home. I can't run away from my team and my company." She knew he wanted to keep her safe, but his experiences were different from hers. She wasn't in any danger other than losing the company and running away wouldn't solve anything. She had to face it head on.

"Please, don't decide now." He covered the hand that still rested on his arm with his larger, rougher one. "Not tonight. Stay here. Don't go home. Just for one night."

She shook her head while he talked. "I'll be fine Nathan. I've been running from the story of my parents for too long. That letter cut extra deep because the truth is that I've been ashamed of them since they died. It was all over the media. American couple tied to drug trade died in tragic plane crash. Teenage daughter missing. It's time I face that truth."

He trained his eyes on hers. "There's a burner phone and a laptop in the bedroom. Trust me on this one. They'll do something tonight, and you'll see what you're up against. Make your decision in the morning."

He took her hand from his arm, kissed the knuckles and pressed it to his chest. "Thank you for trusting me today, not just with helping you get out of there, but with your story. You're an amazing woman."

"Okay." She was sorry that he took his hand away, wanted to stay on the patio with him longer. "But only tonight. Then I'm going to the office in the morning to sort everything out and see where we stand. Just like your grandparents told your mother, I can't run from this."

"Take the Jeep. There is cash in the bag with the laptop and phone. It's yours if you decide to go." He closed his eyes and put his lips to her forehead.

The gentle touch of his mouth sent a shock through her system. She wondered what it might feel like on hers.

****

Ava took a walk around the perimeter of the house. Cameras covered every conceivable angle of the property, the discovery of which was both comforting and disconcerting. As promised, a black nylon backpack with a laptop, phone and a considerable sum of cash sat on the small desk in the bedroom.

The master closet held an impressive collection of women's clothing, mostly her size, though a bit looser and more colorful than she preferred. All still had tags. A tub the size of a small pool was sunk in the middle of the bathroom. Luxury toiletries lined the sink and fresh, fluffy white towels that probably cost as much as some people earn in a week were rolled, hung or draped in strategic locations so that one never need search around dripping and naked.

It was a home she would have chosen for herself, except for its distance to her office, at least an hour of driving, if she went in the middle of the night in perfect conditions.

She opened the laptop. Sweat immediately trickled down the back of her neck. Rather than start it up, she decided on a quick swim in the ocean. A few more minutes wouldn't change anything, but at least she could get some exercise.

The sea was calm as she waded out in the frigid water, illuminated by a half moon. She pushed through the small break, diving under waves, shuddering until her body temperature regulated enough to recover full use of her limbs. She remembered the shock of her first swim in waters that she expected to be as warm as those of the southern Caribbean. Thoughts of her parents and uncle brought the day's events into full focus. Whoever the author of the letter was possessed a level of cruelty she couldn't accept. Tears washed away as soon as they formed. She had to stop swimming and wade back to shallower waters to catch her breath. It was time for her to deal with whatever was happening.

The computer was easy enough to get into. Email was all she felt comfortable checking on an unfamiliar machine. Passwords could be changed, but it was still a risk.

The first forty or so messages were versions of the same basic thing. They asked if she had seen this in the header, with links to various articles in the body, some adding the question "Where are you?" or "Are you okay?"

Most of the links were similar clickbait headlines, from outrageous to outright disgusting. She scrolled through them all, her stoic resolve holding out until she clicked on one that read "Did LA's Tech Sweetheart Kill Parents and Uncle?"

She picked up the laptop and slammed it on the desk. It cracked the bottom casing but left the keys intact. Fuck. She had broken that habit years ago after the replacement costs got a bit too high. Or so she thought. Then she remembered Nathan's words on guilt and felt guilty for feeling guilty. Damn him.

Whoever wrote the letter apparently released it on the web after the meeting. She searched for the story and watched some live videos of her house and office. Nathan was right that she was better off not going home. She desperately wanted to open another one of his great bottles of wine but needed to think. She let the screen go dark and paced the glossy wood floor with bare feet.

A ping from the cell phone interrupted her planning. She crossed the open living area to the desk. It was from an app another billionaire had funded that deleted messages from the server as soon as they were read. Far more secure than an encrypted messaging system.

Agents at all entrances here. I think I will be arrested. If they use the music, they will find out where you are. Get out ASAP. Take anything you need. Go someplace no one knows.

Yours truly,

Nathan

She flipped on the huge flatscreen TV to a local news station. A shot of Nathan's house filled the screen, animated by flashing lights. Black clad officers with assault weapons stood at the ready. Commotion on the back lawn drew the cameras to where Nathan was being put in handcuffs. It all seemed far too melodramatic for a basic corporate issue.

A woman's voice, rapid and grave. "In an unprecedented move by the FBI, reclusive Polish billionaire Nathan Klepacz is being taken into custody on the charge of aiding and abetting a fugitive. The charges stem from a new initiative by the National Intellectual Property Rights Coordination Center called Operation Sentience, which is investigating the case against Sense Labs CEO, Ava Lawson. Klepacz was the last known person seen with Miss Lawson, who we were just notified is wanted for questioning on multiple counts of intellectual property theft and fraud. More later as the story unfolds."

Shouts from the lawn as Nathan was shoved toward a black windowless van. The back door opened from the inside. Nathan was pushed in.

Ava caught a glimpse of a man with large, black headphones as he closed the door behind them. They would know Ava's location in the next few minutes if the music worked as well as Drew and his unknown accomplices believed.

"Oh, shit!" She slammed the laptop shut and grabbed the backpack with the phone and cash, then ran to the closet to throw in a few things. She would need warm clothes where she was headed.

Back to the kitchen for a few bottled waters and any snacks she could grab. She added a couple bottles of wine to the mix as an afterthought.

Ava flew to the front door, snatched the keys off the hall table and made for the Jeep.

Fewer than five minutes passed from the time she witnessed Nathan's arrest on TV until she slammed the five-speed transmission into gear.

Sirens crescendoed toward the house.

Chapter 11

Ava pulled off the two-lane road and hobbled out of the Jeep to enter the code on the electric gate. Cold dry air shocked her unprepared lungs and stiff body. The blinding sun wasn't nearly as warm as it felt from inside the Jeep.

She turned on the heater before pulling onto the half mile of gravel that stood between her and a bed. The final leg of her sixteen-hour escape from California.

She rounded the last curve and took in the view from the top of the hill leading down to the river. The two-story hand-crafted log cabin was almost exactly as she remembered, except for a blue tarp stretched over the back of the roof. Her realtor in L.A. told her once that landscaping is like the eyebrows of a house. She laughed thinking the cabin's eyebrows had grown a bit Einstein.

She grabbed the warmest item stowed in her backpack and got out of the Jeep to pull it on. The black logo hoodie fell almost to her knees. It enveloped her in a warm hug when she zipped it up to her chin. Her bones cracked in painful gratitude once freed from the confines of the driver's seat. A perfect excuse to wander before resting them.

A metal workshop stood in glaring contrast to the picturesque cabin by the river. The prefab building set on a concrete foundation was still crammed with the tools her uncle used to recreate items from the past. Even through dust and years of neglect, the building maintained the painstaking order imposed upon it by the former owner.

Ava had visited once as a teenager. She devoted an entire summer to learning how to use the dozens of tools she now owned but had no use for.

It had been the summer after her parents died. She had spent her childhood in central and South America, living among the locals. The abrupt change to orphan living with an uncle she hardly knew in Los Angeles was a difficult one. Uncle Jack was a different man here in the wilds of Montana, where she got to know him.

She moved from tool to tool and stopped to chuckle at the century old lathe that used a rusted Ford stick shift to engage gears. Planned obsolescence didn't exist in stores or minds back then. Investors didn't push the "razor blade" model until well after the Great Depression. That old lathe was one of the most trustworthy items she inherited when her uncle passed away just shy of her twenty-first birthday.

Leaving the hybrid cooperage and blacksmith shop, she walked around the cabin's perimeter to get a feel for how it had held up over the years it sat empty. The pier and beam foundation was in decent repair. The tarp that covered the back corner of the roof, closest to the river running north and south through the property, needed attention before the first snowfall sometime in the next month or so.

The new cameras were all in good order around the property. The few months since they were installed hadn't seen much activity, unless one counted Seneca.

A wolf pack had made several return visits and

there was one sighting of a nice-sized black bear. That was nothing compared to the wildlife she encountered when she lived on the property before.

Inside, the cabin was well maintained and stocked in case anyone wandered in to escape the natural elements. It happened often. They usually scribbled a note of thanks, but the most recent visitor caught the attention of local authorities, thus the recent camera installs.

If only life were as simple as this cabin her uncle had loved so much. Ava sighed and walked across the room.

She ran her fingers one by one across the rough logs of the fireplace mantle. What had her grandmother been thinking when she placed them there with her bare hands? Ava wished for words of encouragement from the woman's long forgotten tongue, for inspiration from her mother's lips, or praise from her uncle.

Silence drowned her desire.

There would be news of Sense Labs, of Nathan and her team when she logged on to the laptop. Yet all she wanted to do was curl into a ball and be forgotten. What was the point in any of it?

The backpack she threw hastily together at the beach house lay forgotten on the kitchen table; a small affair pushed against the large picture window with hardly enough room for four chairs.

She pulled out a bottle of wine. Who would care now? One night drowning in her road worn sorrows would change nothing. A few more blissful hours without pings, dings, alerts, problems to be solved. Ava poured the wine without restraint into a chipped Dallas Cowboys coffee mug she found in one of the cabinets.

She crossed to the couch in the middle of the great room and sat down heavily. The same afghan she cuddled up with as a teenager settled over her shoulders in a familiar, soft embrace.

In less than three seconds she was out flat, wine untouched.

Chapter 12

The crunch of gravel prickled Ava's skin. She shot up from the couch, heart pounding in her ears. Golden light from a sun setting on the horizon streamed through the cabin windows. How long had she been out? And who had woken her?

Tony wouldn't return from his event for a few days. No one else knew where she'd fled. She peeked around the edge of the small window over the kitchen sink. She couldn't see inside the pickup truck that pulled up beside the Jeep. It was old, Montana plates. A local checking in, or so she hoped.

Using her thumb to access the safe in the corner, she took out one of the hunting rifles, checked that it was loaded, safety engaged, and set it by the front door before opening it to greet the stranger.

She stood in the doorway with her right hand on the rifle and waited as the man parked the Chevy beater and turned off the ignition. A dark shiny head appeared over the rusty blue door.

Ava stepped back then held firm. He was one of those people you feel before they even walk into a room. The air buzzed with anticipation. A magnate or a mangy beggar, it mattered not. His presence preceded him.

Did he see her surprise with those penetrating ice blue eyes set deep in his flawless midnight black skin? Transfixed, her hand loosened on the muzzle of the rifle.

He walked to the front of the truck with his hands held out low in front of him. His wasn't the unwanted baldness of an old man, but the supple skin of a man closer to thirty. Ava stared at the striking figure before her a few seconds too long.

"Hi, ma'am. Just coming by to drop off your mail and introduce myself. Name's Zek."

The stranger had a peculiar accent. Not like Tony's. Not like any she had ever heard.

"I don't recognize you from around here. Did Jim send you?"

"Only Jim I know is at the lumber yard. Tony said to check in with you while he's out of town. You must be Ava."

He had caught her trap and passed the test. She leaned the gun against the doorjamb and stepped over the threshold. Was this the man Tony told her about?

"Nice to meet you, Zack." She was relieved when he firmly shook her hand, those icy eyes locked on hers. Weak handshakes made her uneasy. His matched the feeling she got when he stepped out of the car. Confident, easy. And again, a presence.

"It's Zek, with an e. Tony said you might start the cooperage back up. I've got some projects if you're interested."

He certainly got right to the point. "No plans other than getting the cabin back in shape and relaxing a bit," she said. "I don't know how long I'll be staying. If you need a shop, we can talk about it, but most of the tools are older than both of us put together."

"I'd be skeptical if they were new. It's a very old art."

There was a familiarity in the easy way he communicated. He leaned back against the front of the truck as if he had all day.

Ava's desire for complete solitude dissolved. She craved this relaxed pace and attitude. She would have to talk to Tony about why this stranger knew her name, but if he trusted the newcomer, she could, too. Still, she would do a little online sleuthing once she got the laptop going. Couldn't be too hard to find someone with a name and appearance like Zek's.

She stepped off the porch and moved closer to him. "It will take me a few days to check out the equipment and see what needs to be done," she said. She motioned toward the front door. "I want to get the cabin fixed up first. If you need work, I could use some help. Any chance you'd be up for a trade?"

Her ability to barter served her well in the early startup days, though things were different now that the company had grown. She slipped back into her comfort zone with ease. Value for value without all the politics and backstabbing.

"Tell you what…I'll see what's working in the shop and get it back up and going. Any hours I help you on the cabin, we can trade for hours on the tools. Sound fair?" At her nod, he extended his hand a second time.

"Deal," she said." They shook again.

She peered around him. "You said something about my mail?"

"Yes ma'am. Got it right here." He pulled a few envelopes from his back pocket and handed them to her.

She couldn't hide her sigh of relief when she clutched the familiar bulky envelope. She knew Tony could be trusted to check her mail every day, like clockwork.

"Call me Ava," she said with a smile.

Zek nodded.

"When can you start?" she asked.

His penetrating gaze lingered longer this time. Debbie Gibson started singing in Ava's head about getting lost in eyes.

"Well, Ava, how about right now?"

"I'd like to check things out on my own today. We can start first thing tomorrow morning. I'm an early riser so first light is good." She was still disoriented from the long drive and wanted to settle in before inviting another person into her space. And, she wanted to get online. There were things to check.

"Sounds good. I'll bring supplies." He walked back around the pickup and climbed in. Tires spit dust and tiny rocks as he turned the truck and headed off the property. The red tape where a taillight should have been reminded her of one of the many vans her mother had driven when she was young, before Ava met her uncle and started life in the states. Since then, it had been all five stars, new cars, and private jets. A far cry from battered buses, broken down vans, and the Colombian jungle.

A local would have spent at least an hour making small talk. Zek was no local. She found it odd that she was smiling. Quiet filled the air around her as his truck drove out of earshot, and the sounds of nature began to return. The soft babbling of the Little Blackfoot River caught her attention. She wanted to clean up before getting to work. She moved back into the cabin, set the mail on the table, and returned the rifle to the safe.

Grabbing a towel and bar of homemade soap from the tiny bathroom downstairs, she mentally braced herself for the cold by stripping down and running the couple hundred feet to the formerly narrow shore where, as a teenager, she had spent hours sunbathing.

The river had widened since her last summer there, and a nice, calm pool had formed by the bank. She dropped the towel and plunged in.

Chapter 13

Zek glided through the trees, illuminated by the waxing gibbous moon. He stopped before the river bank and stepped into a shadow to conceal himself. From there he gazed at the crimson streaks that trailed Ava as she ran toward the water.

The subtle differences in the human species; hair of multiple shades, skin of even more diverse color, and eyes that had not settled into one uniform hue, still struck him with awe. He lifted his black hand to his face, the same as he presented on his home planet, Renzo-- hairless, smooth, unlined.

She let out a shriek when her feet splashed the surface. Zek shifted his gaze back to Ava. Her perky breasts and small, supple muscles informed him of the sensations that accompanied being a human man. In this he had chosen to appear as one of them; in masculine form.

He adjusted his position to accommodate the discomfort in his midsection and replayed the guild meeting in his mind. It was what brought him to this place and time. Soon the pieces would all come together.

Ava was the key to the mystery of the anomaly plaguing Earth and threatening the network and upper dimensions. When he had met her, he sensed no conscious awareness of it in her. She wasn't the Laer operative, if there was one on Earth. Yet she was fearful of something. Learning what it was could bring him closer to the truth.

A deep penetrating growl snapped Zek back to the reality of his created world but didn't distract the woman bathing upriver.

A lone gray wolf's amber glare locked on her. Zek let out a low howl and the wolf returned it, turning its head his way. Then it sauntered back through the white spruce and pine forest out of sight.

Ava continued her chilly bath without interruption. What would she have done if confronted by the curious wolf?

His body overpowered his thought processes once more when she stepped back onto the riverbank and wrapped a towel around herself. She glanced around, her eyes stopping momentarily in his direction, before walking back to the cabin.

He fought the urge to follow. She closed the door behind her. He exhaled long and slowly. He couldn't allow the physical sensations of this world to distract him, no matter how alluring, tempting, distracting.

On his way back through the trees to Tony's house, Zek thought again of Grandmaster Zalor's final words.

Whatever Ava was afraid of may help him understand his creation and what was going wrong with it. He needed more time with her, time to understand her. She was already familiar to him in one way.

She was a true creator. Not simply an unconscious one as he had designed humans, but like him, a soul made to create from the very first dimension.

Tony had shared this with Zek when he first arrived at Tony's door. She made systems that were meant to think as humans did. Zek laughed into the trees. He wondered what her intention was in building such things.

His original intention in creating Earth was to prove he could develop a planet where souls would ascend dimensions with less difficulty. To make the transitions easier on those who passed through after him. Not like his long, tortuous time on harsh planets before he gained awareness. Before he learned he was a creator.

He felt the sudden urge to protect Ava. Was it a Laer interference she was afraid of, too?

Guild creators had used the Laer platform long before he reached the seventh dimension, with great success, if success was to be measured by planets built and not by network expansion.

Zek originally believed the Laer limitation was unintentional. With Vezon and Zalor's final warnings, his belief had changed. He needed to learn why and how Laer was allowed to limit the power of creation. If it was true that they were Statics, why did Expansionists continue using the platform?

Zek reached Tony's driveway and climbed back into his truck. A plan formed in his mind. He needed supplies.

Chapter 14

The slide and click of the deadbolt echoed through the small cabin. Ava took a deep breath and waited for the goosebumps to settle back into her cold, damp skin. It had been so close.

Wolves don't live long enough for it to be the same one that roamed those shores when she was last there. It could very well have been its offspring though. She would have to be more careful. And, what was the drifter, or whatever he was, doing out there hiding in the shadows? He was probably one of those savior types who thought all women need protection, she thought. As long as she didn't give chase, the wolf had no interest in messing with her. The creature was just curious. She was in its territory, even if she did own the land.

But Zek was in their territory, and she didn't know why. People were searching for her. She needed to see Tony. He could tell her more.

In the meantime, she had other work to do. The allure of quiet, stillness, and a wholly different way of life beckoned like sweet honey. She could ignore the whole thing and go on living here forever. This place and its people were so disconnected from her fast-paced world of technology and money at all costs that it wouldn't occur to them to turn her in. Half of them were running from something anyway, kindred spirits.

She closed her internal discussion and opened the

laptop. Nathan was adept enough to give her a Linux machine with Tor already configured so that she wouldn't expose herself pulling updates from the open web. Tor would bounce her traffic to different locations making her machine nearly untraceable, but there was always a risk on exit. Logging in through a VPN connection would complete her anonymity.

The question remained if Rys had already given up their secret domain and crypto key under questioning. He and Ava had built a secure messaging platform after someone at a hacker conference demonstrated how easy it was to infiltrate most of them. They only used the system for particularly sensitive communications. It was encrypted at both ends and messages self-destructed after they were viewed.

She logged into the VPN, opened a Tor browser window, then typed in yunolisten.com. Goosebumps spread over her towel-clad body when she discovered Rys was in the chat room.

She shivered and crossed the room to rummage through the backpack. A pair of fleece tights and the hoodie replaced the towel, which she used to twist up her hair.

She lit a fire before settling on the floor with a mound of pillows and blankets, then perched the laptop on her knees and started typing.

AVA: Did you ever imagine we would use this silly project for something like this? Which con was that?

Her cursor blinked white on the black background of the shared text file. No bells and whistles. It was for messaging and file sharing, not ease of use and entertainment. She would know if it were Rys soon enough.

RYS: Hack in the Box. Believe it's me now? Are you OK? Do you know what's been happening? It's chaos here.

AVA: One question at a time!

AVA: Yes and yes

AVA: Only what I've heard on the radio

AVA: I'm sorry

RYS: Nathan is out of custody, but they used the music on him. They know about the Jeep, computer, phone, cash. He has so many layers of security that he doesn't know enough to give them more info to trace. Still, take precaution.

AVA: I'm somewhere safe. Will figure out new transportation.

RYS: He'll be happy to hear. They separated the team and questioned us individually. I've been put on temporary leave. Sarah and Michael are still at the office. We had to surrender all our electronics, or they threatened arrest. We wiped everything important when Nathan started texting us during the board meeting.

AVA: Really?! Is it all gone?

RYS: He said you had backups. I hope that's true. Turns out, all they want is the source code. They even said you can come back and run the company if you grant them a perpetual license and hand it all over. They'll pay a bundle for it. Nathan and his lawyer are handling negotiations. You need to talk to him.

AVA: Nathan wants us to sell it to them?

RYS: I think it's a stalling tactic, but if that's what gets us back on track, don't you think we should do it? They'll get it anyway. At least this way you get to keep the company and keep working on the system.

AVA: Classic dilemma. I won't ever give up this place, no matter what they try.

RYS: Are you at the cabin?

AVA: Shit. Forget that. I meant this chat room. I want to speak with Nathan though. Find out what he's doing. He said he could reach you. Can you give him access to this app? It feels like the only safe space.

RYS: I don't see why not. They will be in here soon enough. All they have to do is ask the right question and they will get the domain and encryption key from me, so be careful what you reveal.

AVA: Don't worry. I was brought up that way.

AVA: How is everyone?

RYS: I'm scared for you but have to admit I'm having fun. Never dreamed I'd get to use the Degausser wands for real counterintelligence. It wasn't as cool as using microwaves like in the movies, but at least I know they worked. They were pissed when they found all the fried hard drives.

AVA: You're a regular MacGyver. Do you think the team believes what they're saying about me?

RYS: Some of them jumped right in the Drew camp.

AVA: Who?

RYS: Mostly his team, the new ops and biz dev people. That slimy investor, Tim. There are question marks.

AVA: Who are they?

RYS: Rhonda and Michael. I'm not sure what's going on with them. Michael was sequestered with Drew and the feds during the questioning today. He's not responding to any of us. Rhonda is acting as mediator, the good guy go-between. I don't trust that shit.

AVA: She's a brilliant investor. Probably trying to keep the wheels on the bus. Michael is loyal.

RYS: Your golden boy Michael let them in your house. Gave them access to everything.

AVA: They would get it anyway.

RYS: Just be careful, OK?

AVA: This shit is so real it's hard not to find it comical. Truth stranger than fiction and all that.

RYS: They only want you for questioning at this point. Said they won't formally charge you with anything if you come back voluntarily.

AVA: Do you think they're being honest?

RYS: Nathan doesn't. He said to wait until he gets some assurances in writing. They didn't hold him by the way. Let him go after questioning him in the van.

AVA: Get us in touch as soon as you can?

RYS: On it. Jazzing up this app to make it more secure against questioning. A puzzle must be solved in real time to access the platform. You'd enjoy developing it with me, but I'll get it done solo. Should have something in the morning.

AVA: I can't wait. Anything I need to know about before then?

RYS: Check out this video: Tim Lafferty interview.

AVA: Evening entertainment. I can't wait. I'll be back on at 6AM west coast tomorrow. Cool?

RYS: I'll have something ready by then. Night night, fearless leader.

Ava laughed and downloaded the video before shutting down the browser. She didn't feel so fearless. Her laughing stopped when she listened to her investor's answers to the increasingly biased questions from the graying CNN reporter.

Tim's face had the same red coloring she remembered from the boardroom. "As far as I'm concerned, she is guilty of all the charges. No one who is innocent runs. If she's listening to this," Tim said directly into the camera. "I want you to know that I am personally committing as much time and money as it takes to bring you to justice, Ava. We can't let greed and destruction threaten our great country."

"I'm sorry, did you say she is a threat to our country?" The camera stayed on Tim's self-righteous glare while the reporter continued his questions.

"She is wanted by the FBI. That means she poses a threat to the country."

"Isn't that a bit circular? What about being innocent until proven guilty?"

"She hasn't given us the opportunity to question her, and so she doesn't deserve that right as far as I'm concerned. Given her bad decision making and squandering of my limited partners' hard-earned capital, I stand behind my statements."

How much animosity had Tim harbored for her through all those meetings? Without the Sense Labs investment, he never would have been hired by his venture fund. He knew his job was her doing. Some people have a strange way of repaying favors.

Knowing what a bad idea it was, she scrolled through the video's comments section. They didn't disappoint. She was called everything from a liar, cheat, and fraud to a gold digger and slut. She slammed the screen down. Her dream of peace and tranquility shattered. The bottle she uncorked earlier beckoned from the tiny dining table. Perfect time to check its quality.

The first glass went down smoothly and didn't disappoint. Her stomach growled. Wine on an empty stomach wouldn't do. She grabbed a couple of protein bars from her stash, poured a second glass, and sat back in front of the laptop.

"Fuck that guy," she yelled at the rough-hewn logs of the surrounding walls. Logging into the VPN and pulling up a search tab, she typed her name and waited a few seconds for the results. The first two pages were filled with breaking news. The number of shocking headlines was at a fever pitch. New clickbait posted with each auto refresh. She took another long drink of the wine and logged into her blog editor.

Dear Sense Labs Employees, Investors, and All Other Interested Parties,

The past two days are a blur to me. Have you ever been broadsided by an eighteen-wheeler, ejected through a broken window, then run over by elephants? Me neither, but I imagine this is what it feels like. I've been giving myself a lot of grief believing that I should have known. Is one ever prepared for a well-planned *coup*?

Coup you say? Why yes, this entire ordeal is a disgusting attempt to steal breakthrough technology that I and the team at Sense Labs created. I believe it is one of the most important discoveries ever made by humans and I can't wait to bring it to the world. Some people have other ideas about what to do with the technology, and those ideas do not end well for our democracy. This is why I am in hiding. I will return when my safety and that of my company and the technology we created are guaranteed. Under no circumstances will I allow this technology to fall into the wrong hands.

In response to some of the more damning allegations, yes, my name as a child was Ava Andrews. When my parents were killed and I moved to California with my mother's brother, I took the name of my mother's family, Lawson. This was not an attempt to hide. I merely wanted what all fourteen-year-old girls want – to fit in. I still haven't achieved that, but my aim changed along the way.

I now strive to bring truth to the world. Music is one of the oldest forms of communication known to man. Stories were passed down through the generations via songs, relaying the secrets unlocked in individual and group experiences of this thing we call life. By consolidating the largest database of music and sounds in the collective conscience of mankind, we were able to feed what we now call our artificial creativity system, Seneca, all known musical structures as well as sounds from millions of natural phenomena. The result is nothing short of astounding. It is one of the most powerful, profound experiences of my life.

This is the experience I wish to share with the world.

I don't know what the coming weeks and months hold. I am still the CEO of Sense Labs, unless one of two board members have changed their minds. Drew the Usurper and Tim the Ungrateful have made their positions clear.

Now that you are aware of my side of the story, you may make your judgment. I know who I am and what I am responsible for. I will fight for myself, my team, the technology we created, and the company I founded. Most of all, I will fight for truth.

Until I see you again, I remain yours truly,

A

She hit Publish with a flourish and raised her glass. "I see your shade and raise you righteous nerd public opinion." She finished the wine and refilled her glass.

The speed of news and rumors, and the lack of distinction most people made between the two, would work against her if she didn't respond. She hoped her message hit the intended mark and proved she wouldn't stand down in this fight.

Searching her name again, she found the blog post already uploaded to Reddit and all the major news sites. The rash of comments made her smile.

Chapter 15

The September sunrise came fast and bright. Long forgotten noises filled the space within the cabin walls.

The wine bottle sat uncorked on the floor below Ava; drops of liquid barely covering the bottom. She groaned. The last thing she needed right now was an alcohol problem. She would be better off using work to deal with her feelings. And, there was plenty of work to do on the cabin.

Springs squeaked heavily when she hoisted herself off the couch to get coffee going. Thankfully the solar panels were in good repair and so far, the appliances worked fine. She would have to do without milk in her coffee, the least of her concerns.

Designer skinny jeans and a promotional t-shirt from Nathan's second company were the best work clothes she found stuffed in the bag at her feet. Her shopping list kept growing. Maybe she could ask Zek to pick up a few things for her.

"Zek," she said aloud to herself. Such a strange name.

She brewed some of the blue bottle coffee from Nathan's stash and took it to the front porch to enjoy, as much as one could enjoy black coffee anyway. She nearly tripped over a bag in front of the door, plain brown paper with a note taped to the side.

Ava,
I'm in the shop. Thought you might

need a few things this morning. See you soon.

-Zek

She found milk, butter, eggs, bread, white cheese, and two ripe green apples inside. How had he known? Some things are better left unquestioned and just appreciated. At least the day was off to a better start than the one before.

She narrowed her eyes at his old truck parked far down the drive and poured some of the fresh milk into her steaming cup. The porch swing waited patiently for her to sit.

Fifteen minutes into her first morning back, and she was more relaxed than she had been in at least two years. Then she remembered her promise to Rys and everything waiting for her in Los Angeles. It was probably about time to log in and get the latest.

AVA: Did you get the new functions working?

RYS: Obviously. Nice post. You basically own the interwebs right now.

AVA: Dork! What's the addy?

RYS: nutin2c.com

AVA: I'm in. How does it work?

RYS: We shot for elegance, the one thing they won't understand. If philosophers write volumes trying to explain truth, they can never "know" the answer by forcing someone to tell the truth. They must know truth.

AVA: OK? What if one of them does?

RYS: Then we're fucked.

AVA: That's reassuring.

RYS: Which is why we had to go deeper than surface level conversation. We had to assume that all of this can and will be figured out. It's the time element they won't be able to catch up to, so we hope. The riddles cycle every few minutes and build on one another. Messages are encrypted and destroyed after they're viewed. And of course, bioinformatics are required. We're pretty excited about the multi-factor authentication we came up with. Nathan is already coming up with ideas on how we can commercialize it as an online security tool.

AVA: Do I need to know anything else to access the messenger?

RYS: I can't take credit for the real brilliance behind the authentication. Sarah made us all feel like noobs over here.

AVA: Yeah?

RYS: While we were trying to come up with clever puzzles, she pointed out that the elegant solution is found in the problem.

AVA: Easier said than done.

RYS: The system won't unlock if a recording of the music is being played.

AVA: Sweet Jesus. Now I feel like an idiot. Do you need a special microphone?

RYS: We all felt kind of dumb with our cleverness, which is another reason it's so perfect. The laptop Nathan gave you is plenty. It has high-def sound coming in and going out.

AVA: Can't wait to give it a try.

RYS: Try after six tonight. And call 212-555-9462 today at three PST. Lawyer who will take your case. On our side but be careful what you share. Assume people are listening.

AVA: NYC?

RYS: Would appear so. Nathan's person.

AVA: Got it. Later

She shut down the portal and opened her email. A loud groan filled the cabin when she saw over seventeen hundred new messages waiting.

Until she spoke with a lawyer there wasn't much she could, or should, do with them. She poured a fresh cup of coffee.

Chapter 16

"Good morning," Ava said to the dark figure bent over the workbench in the center of the shop. She stood a solid two minutes waiting for a response while his fingertips smoothed oil into metal parts with efficient tenderness. There was no hurry to his work. She opened her mouth to repeat the greeting. The words never left her mouth.

"Brilliant." Zek held up the now gleaming compass plane used to create long sweeping curves in wood. He smiled and handed it to her.

"How long have you been working on that?" She turned the tool around in her hands. "It's probably worth about three hundred bucks more now than it was yesterday." She nodded approvingly.

"It is a start. Everything in here must be given attention before it will perform its job well." He took the plane she handed back to him, held it up for final inspection and wiped a smudge from the larger gear that set the angle.

"Are you ready to begin work on the roof? I brought all the supplies in the truck," he said.

"I was thinking we should check it out before buying a bunch of stuff we may not need." She narrowed her eyes.

"Tony purchased everything last week. He planned to fix it when he returned, but I am happy to help. It's a very nice cabin." He smiled a large, teeth-filled grin.

"I didn't realize." Her voice trailed off. Tony did expect her to visit. She returned Zek's smile. "Thank you for the groceries. It saved my morning."

Maybe he was keeping an eye on her last night. He definitely got an eyeful. She tried to remember the last time a man saw her naked. Work had been her sole lover the past few months.

"It is no problem." He took a small wooden toolbox from one of the shelves and moved around her to the open bay door. "What we have waiting for us on the roof is a problem. The solar panels are getting old and there was a lot of snow last year. You have leaks up there. Tony is looking into new materials, but most of them still aren't available. For now, we patch."

"That guy never ceases to amaze me" She shook her head and stepped to the side. "Lead the way."

The repairs took less time than expected with both of them working together to lift and reinstall the heavy panels after replacing worn shingles. Ava enjoyed the experience of purely physical problem solving. The designer jeans got some not so designer rips in the process.

"Would you like to have a late lunch by the river?" Zek asked after they climbed down from the roof for the last time.

At her nod, he took the two Adirondack chairs stored in the workshop out to water's edge while Ava made some grilled cheese sandwiches to go with the apples from her morning delivery.

She handed him a plate after they settled in. "It's hard to beat a simple grilled cheese on a day like this."

"Is this what you like to eat?" He pulled the two sandwich halves apart and finished the first in two bites.

So far, the extent of their conversation felt like awkward first date Q&A. His answers to the few questions she managed to ask while they fixed the roof were less than revealing.

"I like to eat lots of things, but yes, my favorites are the simple things like this. How about you?"

"I like this, too." He smiled and devoured the rest of his sandwich.

"Tell me more about yourself, Zek." She wasn't answering another question until he started reciprocating. What was it with these farm boys and their attempts at mystery?

"Can you be more specific?"

She paused and turned her head to judge if he were serious or giving her a hard time. He popped a slice of apple in his mouth and flashed a smile of pure innocence.

"Where did you grow up? What are your parents like? Did you go to college? How did you end up in a town with fewer than two hundred people in the middle of Montana? What do you want to be when you grow up? Are you a serial killer or rapist?" She almost added, "Do you wear colored contacts," but stopped herself. He was probably sick of obvious questions like that.

His deep laugh was almost musical. "You ask a lot of questions."

"You answer very few. So spill it. Who is Zek? What kind of a name is that anyway?"

"I grew up far from here. It's very cold there. I never knew my parents. I did not go to college, but I am still a student. I like it here. I will be Guildmaster. And yes, I have it in me to be a serial killer and rapist, as do you. I have committed neither act though and do not intend to. I am Zek, which is the name I was given at the guild."

"You don't go on many second dates, do you?"

This time it was Zek who tilted his head in confusion.

"Never mind," she said. "What guild?"

"It is where I practice my work. I am an apprentice now and my final project is coming to a close soon."

Finally! Learning more about the stranger had become her personal challenge. "What is your final project? What is it that you make?"

"I build worlds. I made a world that turns chaos into order and am waiting for it to do so. It must if I am to earn full guild membership."

"Designing video games is about the last thing I expected you to say. I'm in tech too, but you probably already know that."

She took him in through a fresh lens. "How is it going? Are you almost done?"

"It has been running for quite some time. I must address a few issues, but it will be a success. There is an anomaly I am trying to understand that I believe is the key to success."

His icy eyes held hers with such intensity that she laughed nervously and turned back to stare at the water just in time to see movement in the trees on the other side. Several pairs of amber glints reflected the high sun.

"Don't move," she whispered. "They aren't here to bother us."

He laughed loudly and put his fingers in his mouth. A sharp whistle pierced the air. "Of course they are. They want to join us for lunch."

The leader of the pack emerged from the underbrush into full view. Ava couldn't tell if it was the one from the night before. Even from a distance of at least one hundred yards, she saw the fangs bared in his lowered jaw.

"Zek," she hissed. "Don't provoke them. The river isn't deep here, and they spend a lot of time on the property. We're in their home, not the other way around."

He gestured to the others that were coming into view behind the leader of the pack. "They just want some lunch. Hold on."

He jumped up and jogged toward his truck.

Ava froze. She was dead center in their path if they decided to pursue him. Beads of sweat marched down the sides of her face and into the t-shirt, caking the dust left from their earlier work. Her eyes locked on the leader of the pack's.

The wolf easily outweighed her. It steadily stalked its way toward her followed by a dozen more gray wolves.

Ava didn't turn when she sensed Zek behind her.

"Here." He pressed a paper wrapped package into her hand. "Help me out." The wolves closed in faster as Zek dropped down and started taking his boots off.

"What the fuck are you doing?" she hissed, near the point of hysteria. She fondled the package in her hand but kept close watch on the pack leader. Something dripped from the firm but malleable substance inside the heavy wax paper. She dropped her eyes for a brief second and saw it was blood.

She sensed Zek's eyes on her.

"They're just hungry," he said lightly as he took

the package from her and unwrapped it. "Want to help me?"

He held up a bloody steak from the top of the pile, lifted it behind his head like a baseball pitcher and hurled it to the opposite bank of the river. The leader of the pack finally broke eye contact with her and caught the piece of meat easily in its strong jaws, finishing the large chunk in a few seconds. None of the other animals moved.

"Good boy, Ringo!" Zek yelled. He took the package out of Ava's hands. "Now let the girls eat."

Another steak flew through the air and the same wolf caught it again, but this time dropped it in front of three smaller animals. Zek waded into the water with the remaining steaks, throwing them to the larger wolves in the group.

A smile broke out on Ava's still frozen face when she remembered her uncle forcing her to watch *Dances with Wolves* as a teenager. She giggled. Would Zek go play with the animals now? But he only went a few steps into the water, emptied the package with a few more bloody pitches, and walked backward to settle in his chair.

Ava dropped into the chair beside him. "A game developer who can fix a roof and trains wolves in his spare time." She wiped blood on the thighs of her already ruined two-hundred-dollar jeans and retrieved her half-eaten lunch. "What else have you not told me?"

"Why have you returned here, Ava?"

She nearly dropped her plate. "I…" Had he read the blog? Talked to Tony? "Why do you ask?" She narrowed her eyes and looked directly into his.

"Yes, I read your letter last night."

"Of course. I'm not sure why I would assume you hadn't. Why did you ask if you already knew?"

"What one says publicly and what one experiences are many times different things. It is part of what fascinates me about humans."

"Are you sure you haven't worked in PR?" Ava asked with a snort.

"What is that?"

"Public Relations. The people who talk to outsiders, I guess. It doesn't matter." Quit rambling, Ava.

"What is the truth?"

"Are you asking because of what I wrote in the blog? Or is that a rhetorical question?"

He contemplated the last apple slice on his plate. Ava's had disappeared long before. "What truth do you wish to bring to this world?"

Everything came to a stop in her mind. The one sentence in the blog alluding to what Seneca really was. How did he know the one question to ask? She stared at the flowing river in front of her. He sat quietly by her side.

It was the question she had struggled with since they had learned of the music's side effect. The team discussed it at length yet still no answer emerged. Philosophers hadn't exactly gotten any further in their attempts, and so she didn't feel like a failure. She still couldn't explain in words. It was simply felt. The music helped her feel it.

Telling the stranger all of this would only lead to more confusion. Yet there was something different about Zek. Like Seneca was playing, only he didn't make her uncomfortable. Not the way the music did.

The sun slipped through the pines in the west. Their shadows danced on the water. "I don't know," she said, long after the question was forgotten.

"Maybe that is why you are here," he answered without pause.

Ava collected their plates and stood. "I have to make a call and do some other work. You're welcome to use the shop for the afternoon."

"Thank you for the lunch." He stood up and stretched. "I will rest a bit then catch some dinner. When you're done, we can drive over to the house so that I can cook it for us."

Was he being presumptuous or naïve? Did she care? He was a well-built, helpful distraction. "Where do you live?"

"I thought you knew. I am staying at Tony's."

"Oh. I should have guessed," she said.

As she made her way back to the cabin, she shook her head unconsciously. There was more to Zek, but what was it?

Chapter 17

Ava exchanged the coffee pot for her mug mid drip and watched it slowly fill, steam pouring over its edges. Ten minutes until the call to the lawyer and her mind hopped about in wild circles.

She found herself instinctively reaching for her phantom smartphone every few minutes while she and Zek had worked on the roof, and a few times during lunch. This not being connected stuff was a bigger challenge than some of her toughest programming problems. Those could be solved with her mind. She wanted to check blog comments, the press reaction, email. She also wanted to see what the team had accomplished the past few days. In this, she had to exercise discretion and patience. *Is this what it's like to go mad,* she thought?

Ava took her cup and sat down in front of the laptop. She pulled up a secure calling app. What she needed was a plan to take back the company. Hopefully, the lawyer would have some ideas. She reverse searched the phone number to see who it was but hit a dead end. And, her time was up. She put in earbuds and clicked call from on the laptop screen.

A woman answered with an impatient, "Yes?"

"This is Ava Lawson. I was told you would be expecting my call."

"Yes. Ava. Lisa Statler. I do high profile corporate litigation and intellectual property defense work. I told

Nathan I would take your call, but you need to give me a reason to take your case. So far, you've made about every wrong move possible. Are you getting bad advice or not taking good advice?"

Ava sat back from the screen with a grimace.

"Nice to meet you too, Lisa. Your friend Nathan is the one who advised me to run and hide like a coward, and given what is happening, I don't know that it was bad advice. What would you have suggested?" Were all litigators such assholes? Hopefully, Nathan had a few more suggestions.

"That you follow his advice. I don't believe he recommended that you flash your goodies to the entire internet."

"Do you mean my blog post last night?" The woman clearly understood nothing about how her world worked. "I had to say something. People need to know the truth about what's happening. What they're planning to do with our system. What they've already done."

"If I take your case, I need your assurance that you won't ever do something like that again unless you run it past me first."

Ava couldn't think of a quick answer before the other woman continued.

"At least our cyber team couldn't crack your location, but that will happen in time. Are you planning to knock a few back and do it again tonight?"

"Are we still talking about the blog?" Ava sighed. "Was it that obvious?"

"That you were drinking?" The lawyer's harsh tone grew in force with each sentence. "That you were pissed? That you are way out of your league? Pretty damn obvious."

"What would you have done?" Ava asked. "Not as a lawyer, as a human."

"I would have kicked his teeth in at the board meeting and probably been arrested," she confessed with an unmistakable Texan accent. "Then I would have hired a lawyer and done what she told me to."

Ava laughed. "If Nathan hadn't pulled me out of that room I don't know if I would have cried or started throwing punches."

"You're lucky to have him on your side. You have a long road ahead of you." She paused. The kind of audible pause where you know the other person is searching for words but not done talking. Ava waited.

"Look, I won't lie to you," Lisa said softly. "This will get far worse before it gets better. And, it may not get better. You need to be extremely careful who you trust and what you reveal. If you're not prepared to play at the highest level of the game, I recommend you drop out now. Hand over what they want and stay out of sight. Get a dog or something to keep yourself busy."

"You're not serious?"

"About the preparation or the dog?"

"If you're trying to scare me, it's not working. It's annoying. Tell me what I'm dealing with here and what you think I should do." She would definitely need more lawyers' names.

"The FBI, the military, and God knows who else want what you've built. They will twist words, distort meanings, invent new rules, and outright steal if that's what it takes to get it. This is the government, Ava. They are bigger, older, far more powerful, and ruthless. There is no winning in this scenario. You should be terrified. I'm terrified for you."

Lisa paused for effect. It worked.

"What I suggest you do now is lay low. It's about the tech, not you. Remember that. We will work on getting a deal put together that guarantees your safety. Do not go public in any way until then. No communication other than with me directly. If any of your colleagues want to get in touch, they need to go through me. That means everyone."

"I haven't answered any email or used the phone, other than to call you. This call is routed through the dark web, and so my location can't be traced. I messaged with Rys, my chief architect, also on a dot onion site. It's how I knew to call you. Other than that, I haven't spoken with anyone."

"I need your assurance that you'll cease contact with him until we have a better idea of what we're dealing with here," Lisa said. "What about where you're staying? Are you talking to anyone there?"

"How am I supposed to know what's going on?" Something told Ava not to say anything about Zek until she found out more about him, and what he knew about her. "I'm safe where I am. No need to worry about me."

"You have to trust me, or this won't work. I'm not saying you can't talk to people at all, just that it needs to go through me."

"You owe me a dollar."

"Excuse me?"

"Just is a weak word. I pay everyone a dollar if they catch me using a weak word." Ava laughed nervously and heard silence from the other end. "Why should I choose you to represent me?"

"I have experience with D.C. politics, and this will

end up there, eventually. I'm a friend of Nathan's and believe what he's told me about the power of what you've built. I'm willing to take your case knowing that it could very likely end my career. I'm prepared for that risk, as you should be. Do you have any more questions, or would you like to engage my services?

This kind of problem is why Ava hired Drew in the first place. She didn't want to waste her time and energy second-guessing her administrative decisions. Now she had to decide whether to trust Nathan's recommendation or keep searching for a lawyer on her own. He was as caught up in the situation as she was, but she still didn't know him that well.

"Can I answer that in a couple of hours?"

"I'll email you an engagement letter. If you want me, send it back signed by end of day eastern. Good?"

"Yes. Thank you for your candor, Lisa. I'll be in touch." Ava ended the call and sat contemplating the screen until it went dark.

Chapter 18

Ava's eyes wandered to the unopened envelope at the other end of the table.

She hadn't listened to the music since the morning of the board meeting. A lifetime ago. The truth was that it unsettled her, and she didn't have the time to figure out why. Was it the raw power? Was she afraid of what it revealed?

She pulled out the thumb drive she had mailed after her conversation with Tony the week before. The code would pull data from the Sense Labs servers, but she could cloak her location easily enough.

The board and whoever else was involved in Drew's coup would be monitoring all usage. She would have to mirror the data on new servers with backups tomorrow so that she didn't need to access their servers to play it, but for now there was no harm. They would know someone was listening, but not who or where that person was.

She needed the connection to Seneca. Needed to hear whatever her inner voice had to say.

It started softly, slowly. Filled the cabin with a mournful tune that built to longing then grew in joy. She didn't remember closing her eyes.

The intention. What was her intention in listening this time? Yes, Lisa, the lawyer. Was Lisa a good choice to represent her interests? The message came through loud and clear. She will do well, but you will stand in the way of her success.

Seneca was right. Ava planned to access Rys' new system that evening as planned, regardless of what the lawyer said. She reasoned it was secure and no one else would ever know. Besides, she trusted Rys. What did she know about the lawyer?

The music cut through all her justifications, denials, and attempts to minimize. Anger melted as the truth of what she was dealing with, and how she contributed to it, revealed itself. It wasn't pretty. The sensation was that of observing something important from a vantage point on high, detached from the outcome yet bound to it.

Her thoughts moved to another line of inquiry: Zek.

Had she set this next intention? Or had it just bubbled out from the chaos of her subconscious?

He would change her life in a more drastic way than her current experience. He was important to her future. To the future in general. No clarity was given on why or how. It was simply known.

A crash inside the cabin broke the spell of the music. Or had it come from Seneca? She hit stop and called out, "Is someone there?"

A knock on the front door then a voice. His voice. "May I help, Ava?"

She coughed, not sure whether she was relieved or annoyed at Zek's quick interruption. Interruption of what exactly? Her thoughts of him? She smiled at herself. "I'm fine. Sorry if the music bothered you."

The cabin swallowed all shadows in darkness. How long had she listened? She stood stiffly and felt her way carefully to the door to open it. Still seeing nothing, she flipped on the porch light.

His smile magnified the light on the small deck. Sawdust covered his bare chest like a million stars in the night sky. His eyes blazed. "I love your music."

They stared at one another. Ava couldn't say for how long. She wasn't lost or adrift. She felt every moment consciously as if time stopped and waited for them. She opened the door wider and moved aside.

Zek stepped up from the porch and towered over her. He radiated dormant strength like the boulders flanking the hills across the river. Not an intimidating strength. His presence calmed and uplifted her mood. And, excited her body.

She became acutely aware of the time since she last allowed a man this close to her. Inside her head. Allowed herself to feel the tension and electricity that coursed through her.

He hadn't touched her.

He smiled again. Reading her mind.

Her chin dipped and she returned his smile. They were in the dance, and she wasn't fighting it.

Her eyes adjusted to the dark. A line shimmered where his skin touched the emptiness of the air surrounding them. She followed the line as it curved along his body wishing it continued uninterrupted by the Levi's he wore.

He slid them off easily. How did he know what she was thinking? Just like with the wolves and the shop, he seemed connected in a way she had never encountered. She wanted that connection. That access. Or did she just want him?

The familiar yearning she normally controlled and suppressed refused to do her bidding. She reached out, fingertips brushing the smooth skin of his shoulder and trailing down his torso. They still hadn't broken eye contact.

Thoughts bubbled toward the surface of her consciousness and she allowed them to float by, undisturbed. He held her attention as no thought ever could. She explored his body with her fingertips, learned its contours, discovered the patterns of his pleasure. Rode the pulsing intensity of his gaze and noted the tiny nuances and feedback his body gave her. It made her feel powerful. He allowed her to read all his signs with no interference. She was powerful.

She became aware of his hand on her hair. He gently massaged the back of her neck through the soft tresses. Tension melted down and through her until it was a distant memory.

She took his other hand and guided him to the couch behind her. He sat while she peeled off her t-shirt. A split moment of indecision threatened to take her out of the moment. One decision. To let him see all of her. To expose herself fully in front of this man she hardly knew. The desire to hold back, protective yet stifling, entered with a force as great as his.

His lips touched her breast, and his eyes didn't leave hers. It was safe for her to return to him. A flood washed over. She was more than ready. She was his.

Chapter 19

Drew chuckled and posted another anonymous comment about Ava. He leaned back in his dark leather office chair, Scotch in one hand and cigar in the other.

An alert pinged an end to his laughter. It was the moment he had waited for to set things in motion. He dropped the cigar into a crystal ashtray and picked up the phone.

"Someone is accessing the servers," Drew said. "I know it's her, but I can't get a useful IP. Do you want to get your guys on it?" he asked the FBI Assistant Director of Counterterrorism.

An audible sigh came from the other end of the line. "It's not important. We'll find her. Did you read her blog?"

Who hadn't read Ava's pissy little ranting the night before? Drew spent most of the morning responding to investor calls and emails about it and finally quit answering. What a bunch of idiots. "Only me and the rest of America. Has she responded to your office or engaged a lawyer? We're still waiting over here."

"No. We may have a lead, though. How long has she been accessing the system?"

With a huff, Drew pulled his feet off the desk, threw back the last finger of Scotch, and pulled up the alert. "Eight minutes. If you guys aren't getting on this, I can put my people on it."

"Mr. Hodges, this is in our hands now." The

director spoke in short, clipped sentences. "We will request your assistance when needed. Do you understand?"

"Yes sir. Of course." Drew feigned deference. "I just hope she isn't using the system to discover the truth about your plans." He flashed a grin into his empty glass. "It's too bad you haven't heard the music live."

"Excuse me?"

Drew knew that would get his attention. Best not to show all his cards yet. Cute how they treated him like he was dispensable.

He chuckled with less enthusiasm than before. "Did you assume the live version was the same as the recording?"

The director paused a beat. "Irrelevant. We only care to prevent the music from getting into enemy hands." His tone said otherwise.

"Oh, well, then never mind. Thank you for your time, *assistant* director. I won't bother you again." Drew waited for it.

"Wait. Drew!" Desperation crept at the edge of the reply. "We should follow up on the access. Do you have time to meet with an agent today?"

"With all due respect, sir, this needs attention from the top. I'm not comfortable working with a field agent. I can arrange to meet you in D.C. tomorrow afternoon for lunch if you want to know more."

Something slammed against the desk in the director's office. Drew smiled.

"You don't need to come all the way across the country for something we can discuss over the phone. Why don't you tell me more about the live music so I know who to put on discovery?"

"It's no problem at all," Drew said. "I have access to a private jet. I don't feel comfortable discussing this over the phone. It needs to be in person with someone I trust. I think I can trust you?"

Drew let the question hang in the air briefly. "After all, I brought this to the counterterrorism division because I thought it was my civic duty to address one of our nation's top concerns. You yourself told me you joined for that reason. It's set to be the most visible part of the FBI. We do this right and you're next in line to run the entire department." He stopped himself. He didn't want to lay it on too thick just yet.

"I can meet you at the airport and have lunch brought to the FBO. Reagan?"

Now he had him. The Flight Based Operator would be too private for what Drew had planned, though it might help impress the man. "Why don't I meet you at Monocle at noon and then I'll rely on your good nature to drop me back at Reagan after."

"Fine." He sighed. "I expect to be able to listen to the music live, otherwise this meeting will be considered a waste. We don't appreciate wasting taxpayer dollars."

"Absolutely, sir. You won't be disappointed," Drew said. "See you tomorrow." He hung up, not waiting for a reply. Finally, some action.

He poured himself another drink and called Michael into his office. Ava's lapdog hurried in.

"I need you to get me on a private jet to Reagan immediately. Get a reservation at The Monocle for two at noon tomorrow. I prefer to go as soon as possible and stay overnight at the Jefferson. Think you can handle that?"

Michael stared blankly at Drew who brought a half-smoked cigar to his lips. "I don't make travel arrangements. And, well, we don't have a jet," he stammered.

"You are the Special Assistant to the President, are you not? I am the interim CEO, am I not? That means you do what I tell you," Drew said.

"I have been summoned by the Assistant Director of Counterterrorism at the FBI to brief him on activity concerning Seneca, and the Board agreed to any travel needed to resolve the case with Ava. If you can't make that happen, then I will find someone else who can. Do you understand?" He picked up the crystal snifter, noticed it was empty and set it back down.

"I'll check with the other board members," Michael said. "Maybe we can use one of their planes."

Drew lifted his eyes in time to see the end of the other man's eye roll. "Atta boy. I knew we paid you for something. Get Rhonda on the phone and tell her what I need and why. Patch her through to me so I can explain if she asks many questions." He stopped. "Better yet, tell her I want her guidance on the whole thing. I assume you can arrange that?"

Michael nodded.

"Good. Don't forget the hotel and lunch reservations. You're dismissed." He waved his hand toward the door.

Michael kept the blank stare intact until he was out of the door. He pulled out his personal phone and texted Nathan first. When he made it back to his desk, he lifted the receiver on the landline Drew had them install when he started at the company less than a year before.

Nathan returned the text while Michael waited for

Rhonda to pick up. He had a jet that could be chartered anonymously if Michael needed it in a pinch.

Michael fist pumped the air, then heard a brusque, "Rhonda here," from the phone. He sat up and replied, "Hi, Rhonda. It's Michael from Sense Labs."

"What can I do for you, Michael?" Her voice filled the receiver with as much benevolent authority as it did in person.

"Drew thought you may be able to help with private jet arrangements to D.C. tonight. He has a lunch meeting tomorrow with an FBI agent. He says it can help expedite the case. Would you like to speak with him?" His hand hovered over the dial pad, waiting for the go ahead to transfer her and be done with Drew's demand.

"What do you think about it?" Rhonda asked.

Michael caught himself before saying what he thought about Drew. "Well, we could find him a commercial flight, but he specifically asked for a private jet. That is a decision for the CEO and ultimately the board."

"We have access to private jets. Some people prefer them. They can be very useful for hard to access places and last-minute flights. Do you think his request is excessive?"

What was she getting at? "That's not for me to answer. It isn't how we did things before, but you know, nothing is the same right now. Can I put you through?" His finger touched the transfer button, eager to apply pressure.

"You'll have to choose a side sooner or later, Michael," she said in a motherly tone. "Would you like me to handle the flight request for you?"

He exhaled loudly. "I don't know what's right or wrong anymore. It would be so much better if this came from you. I'll transfer you now." He checked the phone instructions to make sure it was Transfer – Extension – Transfer then hit the buttons and hung up the receiver. Drew's line blinked red for a few seconds, then went steady.

"Who designed this crap?" he muttered to the plastic monstrosity taking up the corner of his desk.

****

Drew waited three rings to pick up. "Rhonda, how are you?"

"Not so good, Drew. What is this I hear about a meeting with the FBI tomorrow and needing a private jet to get there?"

She was speaking down to him. Bitch. "Michael must have misheard what I asked for. I've been summoned to meet with the Assistant Director of Counterterrorism at the FBI to brief him on activity concerning Seneca, and I thought it would be best to present a strong front. We don't want these feds to push us around. Tim mentioned that I should do what it takes to get them, and you know how people react to displays of urgency and importance."

"You believe you need to be the one to handle your guy and show him how powerful you are," Rhonda finished for him. "To what end?"

Drew took a few seconds to process Rhonda's question through the fog of his afternoon indulgences. The perfect counter argument was always there if he waited for it.

"It's for the company," he answered. "I promised to play the live music for him. They've only heard recordings so far."

"How exactly do you expect to play the music live? Did you get access to the code?"

"Well, it would just be a newer recording, unless we find Ava by tomorrow. I may have some leads." He let the words hang. Rhonda was proving to be a pushover. Getting her buy-in and assistance on this small matter should help Drew convince her to vote in favor of replacing Ava for good.

The CEO job would be a great stepping stone if Seneca proved to be a success. If not, it would be a good way to move into D.C. He was the one who uncovered the fraud and would be labeled a hero either way. He smiled and a small laugh slipped through his teeth.

"Is there something funny about all this?" she asked. "How do you expect to find Ava?"

"I'll know more tonight. I may need his help though."

"So, you're setting him up? For what? To give you resources? A contract?"

"These government types are so easy to handle," Drew sneered. "Promise them the job they want and they'll do just about anything. But yes, whatever the company needs. Right now, it's resources. Ultimately it's a fat contract."

"Fine," Rhonda answered. "We have a plane at Santa Monica. Get there by five and they'll get you to Reagan tonight. It needs to be back by six tomorrow, so don't screw around. I'll send an invoice."

"Thank you, Rhonda. I'm glad you understand." Drew sat back. He had known he would have Tim on his side during the board meeting, but Rhonda had played it smoothly…until Ava and Nathan had left. Since then, she remained vague but supportive. He still wasn't sure how far she would go to help him.

"Actually," Rhonda said. "I happen to be in the area. Meet me for drinks when you get in tonight."

He stopped, mid pour on his third drink. "You're in D.C.? Is something wrong?"

"We can discuss it over drinks. You know the Stadium Club?" she asked.

He grinned at the phone. Rhonda suggesting the best strip joint in town was a pleasant surprise. "I never say no to a good time."

The dial tone kicked in before he finished his sentence, but he polished off the drink anyway. Time to go pick out a good, but not too expensive suit for the next day's meeting with the FBI. He was, after all, a servant to the company and his country. His old man would be proud. As for the meeting that night with Rhonda, anything could happen.

Life had gotten a lot more interesting without Ava around.

****

The Challenger landed at Reagan International fourteen minutes past the stroke of midnight. He was pleased to find they sent him in a midsize jet that didn't require refueling.

Although it was from a fractional fleet, his girlfriend Nikki didn't seem to care when she took multiple photos and posted them online. She knew better than to photograph or tag him. For those who might be keeping an eye on him, it was a great reinforcement of his growing influence. An accidental slip on his girlfriend's page would be noticed by the people he wanted to impress.

"You catch a cab and check us into the hotel, baby," he instructed her when they landed. "I've got a meeting to go to."

"What?" she pouted. "I thought we were going out."

"You know I would if I could, but this is a work trip. You go have fun. There's bound to be a bar that's open in the hotel. I'll see you in a few hours."

The plane taxied to the FBO. Drew tore out the second the door opened and jumped in the waiting limo without a glance back.

"Stadium Club," he ordered the driver and poured himself a drink from the small bar.

"The gentlemen's club, sir?"

"Is there any other?" he answered and closed the partition between him and the driver. Ava would never understand that there's no better way to learn a woman's weaknesses, or a man's for that matter, than to meet in a strip club.

"Let's see what she has for me this time," he said to the glass in his hand.

Chapter 20

Zek's truck bounced over the steel cattle grate at the entrance to Tony's property. Ava caught movement through the trees that lined the long driveway where morning sun reflected off a silver Airstream parked by the house.

"Tony's back!" Ava scooted over on the truck's bench to the passenger side. What had possessed her to sit there like a teenager, her leg pressed against Zek's? The night before had been amazing. That morning as well. She covered a small grin with her hand. Time to pull it together and act as if nothing had happened.

Zek stopped the truck beside the camper.

"Tony!" Ava jumped out and jogged toward her late uncle's best friend. Tony stood a full head shorter than Zek, with weathered skin and thinning black hair tied into a long ponytail. Not a thing had changed in his appearance.

"When did you get back?" Ava asked. "Here, let us help you with that." Zek reached for the box in Tony's arms. She went in for a hug before Tony could turn all the way around to face her.

"Little Star." He laughed and hugged her back. "I couldn't be gone while you're here. Besides, those lug heads in Iowa aren't nearly as pretty and interesting."

He let her go and handed Zek another box. "I see you met our new friend. Is everything good at the cabin? How are you doing?" He turned back around and searched her face.

Don't blush, she told herself before turning a shade she hoped Tony would miss. "One question at a time, old man." She bent and avoided his gaze by picking up a box. She handed it to Zek who was stacking them on the porch. "Zek helped me patch the roof and has been working in the shop as a trade. You gave him a project?"

"A few barrels and things for a movie studio. They always want some random props built, but I don't have all the tools here. You good with him using the shop?"

"He keeps the wolves at bay." She winked at Zek. "Supposedly he also cooks. That's why I'm here. We were going to borrow your grill before heading to town for supplies."

"Not to see your old friend, Tony, then?"

Bantering with him made her feel fourteen again. Or was that teenage embarrassment from being caught post coital? She was way too old for that kind of thought. What did it matter if Tony knew?

"Leave the boxes on the porch and come on in the house. I'll finish this in a minute," Tony said.

The house hadn't changed much from what she remembered as a teenager. It was an old lodge, fully outfitted to welcome anyone from a field hand to a king. Her entire cabin could fit inside the spacious living room on the first floor.

"How about something to read while Zek and I finish outside," Tony said. He led her to her favorite room in the back of the house.

What he called a study was a two-level room, lined floor to ceiling with bookshelves on all sides. She ran her hands across the spines of the books to the right of the oversized double pocket doors. Like the living room, it was bigger than her cabin a few miles away. It held thousands of volumes, many of which she had devoured during the tumultuous time in her life after her parents died. She planned to replicate it in her next home once the company was on its feet and she could afford it completely on her own. That dream felt further away now than it ever had.

He handed her a book and pointed to the back deck. "You'll find some tea on the stove out there." Tony looked Ava up and down. "It's good to see you. We have a lot to discuss." He motioned again to the back porch and left her alone.

She found the hot tea, poured herself a cup, and sat down on the outside sofa facing the back of the property. She turned the thin, hard-bound volume over in her lap. *The Ethics* by Benedict de Spinoza. Surprising choice. While Tony had plenty of books on religion and philosophy, he was not a devout man. He drank and swore and could be downright self-righteous. That was on a good day. But he had a reason for every little damn thing he did, and she was curious what his book choice was meant to convey.

Rather than leaf through the book, she took in the unchanged scenery. There were no new houses or neighbors to spy on because he owned the thousands of acres within sight. The row of white oaks they had planted together over a decade before was growing. It was the only change she recognized after so long.

"So much different, eh?" came Tony's voice behind her. "You like the book?" He let out a long sigh, then sat down on the porch swing to her left and popped open a Pepsi.

"It's just like I remember it, same as you. Why this book, old man?"

He leaned forward and turned his head. "Still sassy as ever. Have you ever read it?"

"I'm not that into philosophy or religion these days. Had enough of it as a kid. I remember a little about this work though. It was one of the early writings on reason. Pretty sure the author was killed for his beliefs. And excommunicated."

"Nature is God. The infinite is God. Some of us, not necessarily Spinoza, believe the soul is infinite. Zek is one of those people. I am, too." He leaned back and took a swig of soda.

Had Tony become some kind of religious zealot? Was that what was so mysterious about Zek? Mysterious was the wrong word. The only other word was inhuman. No man had ever come close to doing what he had the night before. It was as if she became closer to herself. Her cheeks burned again. No way Tony would miss it this time.

"You'll need to get me something stronger if we're waxing philosophical today." She pointed to her tea. "Got any coffee?"

"Renata!" He yelled so loud that a flock of birds took flight from the trees. His Brazilian wife popped her head out of the door. "You got any coffee on in there?" he asked.

"Ava!" Renata's bronze face broke into a smile. Her matching golden eyes crinkled at the edges. She glared at her husband and walked out to join them. "You yell at me for coffee but don't tell me Ava is here."

"Jeez, Tony." Ava jumped up to hug Renata and

they both glared at him. Zek climbed the porch steps behind them with the fish in his hands. "Save me from these men," she said.

Renata picked up the book Ava left on the table. "Going here, are you?" Her glare turned into a knowing look at her husband. "I'll get the coffee. Do you still take it with milk?"

Ava nodded.

Renata waved to Zek who was firing up the grill. "Nice to see you again, too." She disappeared back indoors.

Tony continued sipping his Pepsi, occasionally pushing off the deck with his toe to keep the swing on its lazy path. "I was talking about the infinite nature of souls," he told Zek. "What do you think? Finite or infinite? Are souls immortal?"

"There is the issue of decay," Zek said, "but theoretically a soul can live the entire life of the universe it was born into. Then there is the issue of time, which you have not yet mastered, and in which a soul may maneuver forever."

Ava squinted and shifted her gaze from Tony to Zek. It was too early. She had expected a lazy morning cooking breakfast with Zek. The words "playing house" popped into her head and dammit if she didn't blush again. "Is this a physics class or philosophy?" she muttered.

Renata returned with a pot of coffee and some mugs. She poured it quietly and handed Ava one of the streaming clay mugs.

"If we're going straight for the big questions, am I a soul?" Ava asked. "If so, what is my nature?"

Tony and Renata had loved discussing philosophy

and the big questions of life with her uncle. She missed the quiet way he handled her when she had been younger. Guided her. She hadn't wanted to visit the cabin since he passed away. Never wanted to be on this porch talking philosophy again. The memories, sweet at the time, bitter now after his death, threatened to break through her tough exterior. She smiled over the pain of missing her family. Tony and Renata didn't need more to worry about.

Zek answered. "Your philosophers say 'I think therefore I am.' The fact that you can ask the question makes it true, does it not?" he asked. "You say you are a soul, and so you are. The souls that do not continue, those that decay before transcending, they are the ones who do not trust the soul. Those who master time, the fourth dimension power you are here to unlock, eventually become weary of it and transcend. Each dimension has its trappings so that a soul may stay there through eternity. I believe you call this laziness."

"I call it comfortable," Tony said with a low belch. "'Scuse me."

"Are we still on philosophy or are you guys trying to recruit me for a cult?" Ava asked with a nervous laugh. "We were talking souls, and now you're going into different dimensions. Next we'll be sharing energy fields. You guys know I live in California, right?" She smiled at the group and raised her cup. "But I'm happy to be here at the moment. To old friends and new." A hearty "cheers" went around the porch and they each sipped their morning caffeine.

"You won't understand energy fields for at least a few more dimensions," Zek said. "I am curious what you think about it, Ava."

What a weird guy. They had awakened before the sun and had sex again. It was as amazing as the night before. She didn't remember where sleep began and ended, only him.

Now he was the stranger again. The blissful illusion of responsibility-free pleasure dissolved. She turned to face him. "You never finished telling me about yourself. Are you from around here? You know I'm on the run. You could be a spy." She wanted to bring up her current situation so that they could get to more important matters, like a plan to get back to real life. The break was fun and all, but she had far bigger problems than philosophy could fix.

Tony took another gulp. "Don't know I'd necessarily call him a spy."

"He's from a lot of places," Renata said. "Don't worry, we'll get to all of that after breakfast. These are the things that all our daily dramas drown out as we go around too busy to think. There is always time for contemplation of life."

No, time was not on Ava's side. How would she ever get the company back if she stayed out here?

"What was the music you played in the cabin yesterday?" Zek asked.

Ava eyed him for clues to what he was after. "It's why I'm here," she admitted. "The music you heard was created by a machine that my team and I developed. We call it the first true artificial creativity. But it has odd side effects. We've studied it from multiple angles yet still don't understand how or why it works the way it does. I'm hoping to find those answers here before the government succeeds in stealing the tech and the company out from under me.

135

"You're on a mission," Tony blurted out and popped open another Pepsi. "Your new real life." He took a long drink and threw his head back, eyes closed to the world.

She sighed. "Whether I want to be or not. I must save my company and keep the tech out of the wrong hands, but it may be too late. I'm here to figure out the secret behind the music and stay out of sight for a bit. They came to arrest me before I fled here." Why was she discussing all this in front of Zek? Did she trust him that much already?

Renata patted Ava's hand. "Tony kept an eye on what's happening in the news. You might listen to his thoughts on your situation."

"After breakfast," Tony said. "First, I want to know what Ava thinks about Zek's question."

"Fine." She sighed. "You want to know what I think about the big picture. God, purpose, souls, the infinite, the source, the divine. Is that right?" She paused as the others nodded their heads in unison. Ava pondered the question as wind rustled through the surrounding trees. Zek was right; it wasn't something she set time aside to think about as an adult. But she had at one point.

"I had this epiphany when I was a little girl. My parents were very spiritual, as Tony knows. They were healers. My life with them revolved around something of an unreligious spirituality. I read all kinds of books. As many as I could get my hands on."

She laughed remembering what had passed as a library in many of the villages. "Not many books that close to the Amazon before Amazon Books came along."

"The epiphany came as most do. I was minding my business bathing under a little waterfall and thinking back to a man we met the day before. Dad said he had a demon in him. What I saw was a person who could only see the dark and was afraid. He would lash out at himself and others. To me, it seemed as if he were defending himself rather than attacking. Then I had this flash of recognition, like an insight or a knowing. Call it what you will. It told me heaven and hell are states of mind and when you die you either descend fully into that hell of darkness or ascended to a heaven of light. An eternal state of fear or love. That belief must have stuck because it still feels good to me." She turned the coffee mug around in her hands. "I feel that same sense of recognition or insight when I listen to the music. The content of my insights is different, but I get the same burst of knowing."

"Interesting," Tony said. "What do you believe now?"

"Honestly, I haven't given it any thought since I was a kid. Until Seneca turned on. Now I find my mind turning over these big picture thoughts on a regular basis. I see more connections in everyday things like trees and water and even people. It also feels like a waste of time given my current circumstances. I have more pressing matters to think about."

"Chaos to order. It's amazing how the mind fights it," Zek said.

Ava narrowed her eyes at him. "That's another way of saying it. Descend to chaos or ascend to order. Does it even matter?" she added.

"It's for every soul to determine for itself," Zek answered.

"So, are you a preacher or a guru?" She knew there was something that nagged at her about him. Maybe he was a zealot.

"I am Zek." His expression hadn't changed the entire time they were sitting on the porch. It was as if emotions didn't pass through to his face, though she heard inflections in his voice.

"Tony, how did you and Zek meet?" She knew her voice grew more exasperated with every question. She didn't care. It was time for answers.

Tony stopped the swing. "He wandered over looking for work a few weeks back. He's been helping around here. When I found out he could make barrels, I put him in touch with the studio to do some of the stuff your uncle used to work on. Back in the day, they only wanted movie props but now all those guys own vineyards and have a hard time getting good barrels. Not many cooperages left these days."

"That's it, huh? It seems like you've known each other a long time." Now that she thought about it, the timing made her uneasy. She wanted to trust Tony's judgment, but there was too much at stake. It certainly wouldn't be the first time someone used sex to get what they wanted.

"I assume Zek is the person you mentioned on the phone who knows something about my parents? Are we going to dance around that all day, or will you tell me what's going on?" She turned to Zek. "Why are you here… now?"

Renata tried to change the subject, again. "Can we listen to the music?"

The clenching in Ava's stomach tightened. What was she missing, and why wouldn't they give her a straight answer on anything?

"It's at my place," she said. "Maybe we can all go listen once Tony levels with me about the cameras and Zek tells me how he knows my parents."

Zek left the porch, followed by Tony who lifted and shook his empty can to excuse himself.

"I'd love to," Renata said. "I'm sure the boys will be up for it once they get something in their stomachs." Renata sat in silence and contemplated the mountain range while Ava fumed.

Zek and Tony returned a few minutes later with plates, utensils, and a platter that they piled high with dark green mounds from the grill. They set everything on the dining table on the other side of the porch and Ava watched as Zek took a green lump, unfurling it before setting the fish on a plate.

"Banana leaves," Tony said. "It was his idea. Not sure what's wrong with a little salt and lemon straight on the grill."

Ava picked at her plate and stared both Zek and Tony down in turn. They made no effort to answer her questions. Her intuition told her to be patient.

Renata couldn't stop commenting on how good the simple preparation tasted. It took less than ten minutes for the group to clean their plates.

"I'd like to go to Ava's place and listen to the music after we unpack," Renata said.

Tony checked his watch. "Plenty of daylight to unpack later. Why don't we take a walk to the cabin now?" He turned to Ava. "I can show you the cameras and tell you some things along the way."

Finally, she thought.

A loud howl pierced the trees and echoed off the

mountains into the valley. It was cut short and ended with a long, low whimper drowned out by the wind picking its song back up through the forest.

Ava's stomach sank.

Chapter 21

A short hike through dense woods brought them to the clearing where the wolves had appeared the day before. Ava shivered though sweat pooled under her arms.

"I feel it, too," Tony whispered. "Zek is quiet. He'll check it out."

She turned and saw that Zek was no longer with the group. Possibilities cycled through her mind, each one worse than the last.

"Slow your breathing. You'll only make it worse," Tony hissed.

They stood back in the trees waiting for word from Zek for what seemed like hours. He appeared again beside Tony as if he had never left. No sound, no movement. He was gone one second and back the next.

Tony nodded at him to report.

"Three SUVs and six heavily armed people in black, four male, two female. They're searching the property and Jeep very quietly," he whispered. "I got in and took this." Ava's eyes widened when he held out the laptop she had left on the kitchen table. It should have been the first thing they took. Unless they were after something else.

"Whatever group it is, they'll be at my place next if they have any brains," Tony said.

"This has to end," Ava said, her voice slow and low, eyes focused across the river. "I have to go home and turn myself in. I can't put all of you in danger, too."

Renata touched Tony's arm and whispered, "Dear, it's probably time to tell her about the cameras. Why don't we go to the cave for some privacy?" She didn't wait for an answer and started a light jog away from the clearing and through the woods, parallel to the river. The others followed.

Ava always sensed there was more to this place than her uncle would tell her. Was she about to learn what it was? Was it connected to what got her parents killed?

The letter in the boardroom stirred old suspicions that their deaths were not accidental, but she had decided it was better to let it go after so long. A warm, buzzing sensation stirred in her chest and up through her head. She looked down too late as her toe caught the hook of a root and threw her forward. She landed hard on her right wrist and knee. Quiet tears shocked her as much as the fall.

Renata stopped and lunged for her. "Ava!"

"*Shhhhhh*," Tony whispered. "She's fine. We're here anyway." He pointed to his left at what appeared to be nothing but rock.

Renata and Zek helped Ava up from the ground and brushed her off. The foursome approached the sheer rock formation together. The opening became visible only when they were directly in front of it. They crawled through the narrow space and emerged into a comfortably sized den.

"I've been here before," Ava said.

"Yes, you have," Tony agreed.

She never could find it again after stumbling on it as a teenager. Tony had pretended he didn't know what she was talking about when she had asked about it back then.

"Now sit down and make yourself comfortable," Tony said. "I don't want to rush this, but we don't have much time."

The group sat in a circle in the middle of the open space. Ava massaged her twisted ankle.

Tony stood and spread his arms wide. "This land is part of the Great Continental Divide, a place where water must decide which path to take. West to the cold flows of the Pacific." He gestured with his left arm in a waving motion, giving her flashbacks to a bad eighties music video, then he moved his right finishing with, "or east to the warmer, more violent waters of the Atlantic. Every continent has a path of choosing, which is where the great knowledge is found."

Ava raised an eyebrow but stayed silent.

He picked up a foot-long stick from the mouth of the cave and returned to kneel in front of the group. "It is believed there are multiple locations on Earth where one may access the great knowledge, though we don't know exactly how many." He drew a poor representation of the continents in the dirt and arranged smaller sticks to show the various divides. "This little patch of land…" He gestured with the drawing stick in the direction of where they were on the map, "is the North American point."

"What is the great knowledge?" Ava asked, her ankle forgotten. "How do you know this is the place?"

"Patience," he answered with a finger to his mouth. "For each point there is a guide, or a translator of the knowledge. We do not know if any have been located yet. They will be born and find their place when the time is right."

Zek cut in. "A human is supposed to be the translator."

"Hold on, Zek," Tony said calmly. "Why don't you tell her what you know of this place?"

"Millions of years ago, while the continents were still forming according to the governing rules of this universe and dimension, it was decided that those rules, those truths, should be revealed when the inhabitants were sentient enough to transcend them. The code was hidden among the areas of separation to wait for the translators to be born." Zek's eyes shone with an intensity directed toward a place and time far away.

He continued. "It was a grand plan, but a risky one. Destined for failure until pieces of the truth were split up and entrusted to a special group of humans. They are the Ananzeti, from which the translators would be born. It was an attempt to speed up the process. That isn't what matters now though. The code has been revealed, but not the way it was intended."

The pieces fit together in Ava's head quickly. It was an amazing story. One she would much rather believe than any others she had heard. "You think it's Seneca?"

"How do you feel when you hear the music?" Zek asked.

"It feels," she began. "Hold on. I'll play a recording from the laptop. It's not exactly the same as the live program, but there are still special properties you can recognize." She opened the machine, typed in the password, and pulled up the file. "As best we can tell, listening to a recording from speakers is the lowest level of impact. I'm keeping the volume down in case anyone is nearby. Everyone ready?" Three heads nodded and she hit play.

The recording of Seneca from the day before filled the cave with its ethereal tune.

Zek was the first to speak. "It's the code."

Ava tried to read his face. He was smiling and humming along with the odd tune. Did he know the notes?

Tony narrowed his eyes at him.

"Afraid not," Ava said. "This is from my code, and it seems a lot of people want it. Now let's try an experiment." She pointed at Tony and turned up the volume a notch. "How do you know about the secret of this place?"

"I'm its protector," he answered immediately, without emotion.

"What is a protector and how did you become one?" she fired at him.

"I was born to an Ananzeti line and trained after I showed the signs. My grandfather was its protector before me, his uncle before him, and so on."

Ava flinched but went on. "What do the signs mean?"

"All protectors must complete a major achievement before they turn thirty years old. They must prove themselves without knowledge of their place as Ananzeti so they may train as Ananzeti."

"What does my family have to do with it?" She should have brought the music out earlier. That's what Drew and his co-conspirators would have done. She shook her head and waited for Tony to answer.

"You are from the translator line."

She stopped her rapid-fire questions and turned to

Renata. The other woman nodded affirmation.

"This was my uncle's property," Ava said. "He had no children, and so it should have died with him."

"This was your grandmother's property, then your mother's, and now it is yours. The translator line is matriarchal." Tony's answers continued in robotic succession.

"Do you think I am the translator?"

"No!" Tony said.

She started to ask him another question.

He interrupted. "And yes."

"How can it be both?" Maybe Seneca didn't work as well as she thought.

Zek spoke up. "You created that." He pointed to the laptop.

"Seneca? It's just code and datasets. It isn't a living being. Didn't you say sentience was required for translation?"

"It is," Zek answered. "Yes. Your system is what made the translation possible. It is capable of guiding humans to fourth dimension awareness. It was never intended to work this way."

Zek stared at a far-off point, speaking more to himself than those in the cave. "All of the tools for translation exist without the machine, but no one had assembled them before. The coordination effort proved too difficult. Your creation did it with ease."

This can't be real, Ava thought.

Tony was nodding.

"Is this why my parents are dead?" She heard her voice going up, but she was determined to get answers to questions that had lingered over her head for years.

Tony cleared his throat. "All I know is they were

146

helping some very bad people, cartel types, heal old internal wounds, and it was working. Those people were changing and refusing to carry out orders of violence. The people doing the ordering didn't want them healed. I don't think we will ever know if it was an accident or foul play."

He grimaced and a single tear rolled through the deep ravine under his left eye. His head dropped. "I'm sorry I couldn't tell you sooner, Ava. You are less than a year from receiving your full inheritance, including the details of your family legacy, now that you have proven yourself. I couldn't say anything before."

"Even after Uncle Jack died?" Legacy or not, hiding the truth of something that caused her to be orphaned, then left completely alone in the world was unforgivable. "You knew this whole time? While I struggled, believing I was the cause of their deaths? Their bad luck omen. You could have said just a few words to ease my pain." She felt the sting of tears behind her eyelids but refused to let them fall. Her face went hard.

"Ava, I couldn't. It is forbidden." Tony's eyes searched his wife's for support. Renata shrugged.

"And after you knew I was on the run because of this thing I created?" Ava's voice continued to rise above the music. "Were you waiting until after they killed me trying to steal it? What kind of a fucked-up conspiracy organization are all of you in?"

"No! We're here now, aren't we?" Tony's words wavered then steadied. "We need to come up with a plan to keep you safe, and to figure out who has been working to destroy the truth all these years."

"If they want me, then they'll get me. I'm going

back and going public. This stops here."

She faced Zek. Saw infinite patience in his startling blue eyes. Her expression softened. "You show up out of nowhere the same time Seneca went live and immediately gain Tony's trust. You gain my trust and go so far as to seduce me. What do you have to do with all this?"

"You will have your answers when the time comes," Zek answered. "If you are leaving, I would like to go with you."

She sighed. "Renata, can you answer my question?"

"No. He knows truth." Renata gestured with her eyes to Zek. "You'll be safe with him."

Ava growled. "We're not done here." She glared at Tony and Renata. Protector. Tony obviously hadn't lived up to his title. Her entire family was gone, and she was alone in the world. No, she was not done with him.

Ava stood. Her ankle throbbed but she ignored it. "We need your truck, Tony. I don't think that heap Zek is driving will make it out of town, much less to California. My Jeep appears to be currently detained."

She pointed out the entrance of the cave. "Why don't the two of you go back home and distract any of those thugs who pay you a visit? Zek and I will get to the truck and hightail it out of here. We should be back in LA by this time tomorrow. I'll have my people arrange a press conference and we can start the process of releasing the music globally."

Tony reached for Ava's hand. "We still need to understand the risk factors. Releasing the music at this point may jeopardize everyone and everything. The world isn't ready for what you've built."

She shook him off and held her palm open. "Keys." Her pissy tone disguised the terror gripping her, wanting to keep her safe inside the cave.

After a few seconds of hesitation, he put them in her outstretched palm.

"I don't care if the world isn't ready. I'm not hiding and waiting to be murdered for it." She picked up the laptop and turned to leave. "Are you coming or not?" she asked Zek.

Without waiting for an answer, Ava peeked through the concealed opening, confirmed the area was clear and moved swiftly to the right.

Zek followed without a sound.

Chapter 22

A series of identical pops followed by a yelp interrupted their escape.

Ava and Zek dashed behind two large oaks and peeked around to see nothing. He motioned to her to follow his lead.

Halfway to the cabin, they found where the bullets landed. Zek ran to the largest mound of gray fur and picked up Ringo's head, cradling it in his lap. Glassy eyes no longer radiated their amber brilliance and instead gazed into oblivion.

Ava checked on the other two smaller animals. Thick wet crimson streams seeped from multiple wounds on each of the female wolves. She shook her head at Zek. He gingerly laid Ringo's head back on the forest floor and pet the clean hair behind his ears.

Another series of pops, this time from the right. Farther away. Toward Tony's house. Ava took Zek's hand and motioned toward her cabin. They kept to the tree line, away from the river.

Ava and Zek disabled the one SUV left at the cabin without detection. Two dark shadows moved through the workshop, oblivious to their prey lurking outside.

Ava connected to the Wi-Fi and checked the property cameras. Two more agents crept through the trees toward the cave they just left. No sign of Tony and Renata.

"Come on," she whispered to Zek.

They took an older, overgrown trail and waded through the river. All was quiet except for the trickle of water, as if the animals watched the scene quietly from hidden outposts and the wind held its breath. The second SUV waited for them in Tony's driveway.

A voice projected from the back porch. "You know you two are trespassing on private property? Both of you stay right there while I call the police."

Two agents in the back. Ava would remember to thank Tony later for the warning. The third pair was still at large, but she and Zek had to take their chance.

Zek slashed the tires of the black SUV parked against Tony's huge dually truck's front bumper. Ava tossed him the keys. The engine roared to life before she closed the passenger door.

Zek reversed into the bumper of the camper Tony had unhooked a few short hours before. He changed gears and smashed the gas pedal to the floor. Rocks pelted the camper's smooth silver surface as he pushed around the SUV and broke free.

Black clad figures tore around the side of the house, automatic weapons sounding off like the fourth of July and adding holes to the fresh scratches on the Airstream.

One of the truck's back tires blew and sent a jolt through the cab.

It pierced straight through Ava's thought that maybe it was all a dream. That bullet could have ended up in her. Or Zek.

A female agent screamed into her headset for backup while Zek maneuvered them off the ranch and onto the road.

The second row of tires on the back axle suddenly

made sense. The old beast sped down the two-lane highway as if nothing had happened.

"We must get to Los Angeles, correct?" Zek broke the silence he maintained since leaving the cave. He had communicated in gestures, which she somehow understood perfectly.

"Yes. I mean, I think so. We can't stay out here where they can do what they want and no one will see. People need to know."

"Hold on." He spun the wheel sharply to the left and slid onto an abandoned logging road. Her head hit the side window with a dull thud.

"Whoa! How about a warning next time?" she yelled. "Where are we going?"

No answer. She rubbed the forming knot on her head and checked the mirrors for unwanted guests behind them. Dust rose behind them, unbroken by visitors.

"Stopping!" He slammed on the brakes and held his arm in front of her protectively. They skidded to a stop a few feet in front of a huge, felled tree blocking the entire road. "Come on. It's ahead."

"What's ahead?" She had expected to be on the interstate by now. Did he plan to paddle a canoe to California? He was out of the truck jogging through the trees before she got her seatbelt unbuckled.

"You're going to get us killed!" She scrambled out of the cab and ran after him.

A few minutes later the trees opened to a wide clearing with two small metal hangars flanking a larger one and a long grass runway. Zek, far ahead of her, opened the large bi-fold door of the middle building. The dual prop King Air inside had a DEA logo on the tail. She couldn't decide if this were a good or bad thing. There weren't any pilots hanging around.

Zek hit a button on a small yellow tug attached to the front wheel and pulled the plane out of the hangar. He ran around it once checking tire pressure and squirting some fuel into a clear plastic cup. Ava expertly removed the tug and dragged it away.

As he squeezed through the rear left door he called out, "Get in," and climbed forward to the left seat. She scrambled in behind him.

The engine whine wasn't as loud as she expected. He handed her an army green headset. She put it on, and the noise reduced to a whisper.

"Buckle up please," he instructed into his tiny microphone. They moved quickly to the low-cut grass. In seconds he lined up the plane, shoved the throttle to full power, and took off at a steep incline. The landing gear barely cleared the trees ahead before it retracted into the belly.

Ava gasped. She knew this airfield. "It was so different before," she said into the soft foam microphone resting millimeters from her lips.

She followed the river, more like a creek in most spots. She found the cabin and as Zek came around, saw the third SUV stop behind the truck they had left a few minutes before. Its four occupants jumped out and aimed guns in the air. She and Zek were too far away for any of the bullets to reach them.

"Holy shit, that was close!" Ava's heart still pounded from their run and the earlier gunshots. Visions of the bloody animals filled her mind.

"We'll be landing outside of LA in about three hours," Zek said. "If you need to prepare anything, now is the time to do it."

"Hard to do without internet, but it's probably better to stay disconnected anyway." Her eyes scanned the cockpit and lingered on Zek--the fluid motion of his hands as he turned the yoke and banked left, the set of his jaw as he monitored local pilot traffic. "Is there a piece of machinery you can't operate?" she asked.

He didn't respond.

She continued staring at him while they climbed higher. Her heart rate slowed with every thousand feet they gained.

He pointed to a placard at the top of the instrument panel. "I believe this will get you online."

"Whose plane is this? Tony doesn't have this kind of money and I'm guessing it's not yours, though you fly like it is."

"Tony has much more to tell you." He leveled off, enabled the autopilot then turned to her and finished, "when you're ready."

"Why don't you tell me? And stop it with the ready bullshit. This is happening now. There is no more time to get ready."

"It is not mine to tell," Zek said.

"Something tells me it is." Too much about the man didn't make sense, but she couldn't place what that something was. "I want to know what you have to do with all this. In the past week, I've been publicly humiliated, had my company stolen from me, been chased as a fugitive, and now we can add, shot at. It's time to tell me what's going on, and don't pretend you aren't a big part of it. I don't need Seneca to reveal that."

His eyes focused on hers without blinking while

she spoke.

"Why are you staring at me like that?" she asked. In truth, his eyes startled her with their brilliance every time they locked on hers.

"You hardly say anything and when you do it's either profound or a non-answer. I haven't seen you lose your cool with tools, a pack of wolves, armed people chasing us, and now jumping in a pretty complex aircraft and taking off like you do it every day. Who in the hell are you?" Her voice rose in the dead airspace of the headset and echoed in her ears. His eyes burned into her.

"You are not yet at the age of knowing. However, this situation requires that I break my rule. It is something you people do often, and I am learning to navigate as you do again." He paused.

She waited. She needed to get online and alert her team that she was on her way so that they would have time to get things organized. But in returning his stare she felt an irrelevance of time.

"You people? Look in the mirror." She tried to sound sarcastic, but it came out deadpan. Would everything fail her today?

"I am not like you."

"So, you're one of them. One of the Ananzeti."

"Not exactly. Describing the world that I come from is not simple because we do not share the same language or cultural conventions. We do not share much other than a common starting point. I will start with the Creation Guild, where I am a senior apprentice."

"You told me this already. What did you leave out?" She couldn't keep looking in those eyes and force the answers she wanted. She scanned the horizon instead.

"We create conditions that allow for ascension through the dimensions. I am in my final creation project before becoming a full Creation Guild member."

"You mentioned you were a game developer or something. I'm not following. Where does my family come in?"

"Creation is more my life than my vocation."

He must have been born into one of those families that live for and in one of the massive online games. She had heard about some of the fanatics and communities created around them.

"My project is not going according to plan," he said. "Similar to Seneca, it has taken over and created outcomes that I could never have imagined or researched, because nothing like what I'm working on has ever been done."

"Now that sounds familiar." She rubbed her forehead with her thumb and middle finger.

"I think it's why I understand you more than others," he said.

"There's something I'm missing here. What others? What is it you're not saying? Or why may be a better question."

"I'm concerned that you aren't prepared mentally to accept everything."

"So you're saying I can't handle the truth? Very funny." She silently admonished herself for being defensive and not funny. "Will you please trust that I can handle anything you have to say, and that I will ask questions to help me understand more if needed?"

"It has nothing to do with you objectively processing the information. Pathways must be built before information will be useful."

"I'm not a computer program, Zek. I'm human, just like you."

"Wrong on both counts."

"Excuse me?" She backed away from him in her seat. Their entire conversation had bordered on the absurd before. His last words knocked them over the edge.

Zek kept his eyes on the clouds. "You are not a computer program in the Earth sense, but you are a product. A creation. I am in human form now, but I did not pass through this planet when I was in the fourth dimension."

"What kind of crazy shit are you all on?" She still couldn't control her voice to make it sound how she felt. It was as if the world of logic and knowledge bowed down to what would normally be considered insanity and then exited her mouth using her words but conveying a completely different message.

"This doesn't fit with what you know and have observed in your life, however if you consider everything logically and without prejudice, what does your intuition say?"

"That's not what 'intuition' means. A gut feeling has nothing to do with logic. It's what was programmed into you through experience. Mine tells me you've been hitting the crack pipe a bit too hard."

He laughed deeply, booming. "This is what I find so interesting about humans. Intuition is the most logical form of logic. You simply cannot explain it in your current language. That is what the music does. It connects you to the truth of things as they are, not as you or anyone else desires them to be. If you listen to it now, you will learn that I speak truth whether you choose to accept it or not."

"I need a minute." She peeled off her headset and backed out of the cockpit.

The cabin was simple; its back half configured more for cargo than passengers. She sat lengthwise on the small sofa to the right and faced the tail of the plane. Her avoidance tendency, the one she worked so hard to break, kicked in with a fury. She fought it.

Zek was right. Her gut said he wasn't from a weird cult on Earth. At least he wasn't from Earth. Who knew what kind of cults existed in the multiverse? The dimension thing, the creation thing, those felt true as well. The longer she sat there, the more her curiosity drowned out her fear and disbelief. Question after question played in her head. Then a memory.

Her mother had returned. It had been Ava's seventh birthday. Ava didn't recognize the woman or her short red hair covered with a bandana at first. The woman gave Ava a small knife with an intricately carved crystal handle, wrapped in pink paper. Ava cried when she learned who the stranger was. Her mother wasn't the same. Didn't smile and laugh. The woman scared her the way the men lurking at the market did with their serious stares.

A week later the woman, her mother, took Ava to the jungle and told her she must learn to survive. Each week they would drive to a remote area and Ava would learn a new skill. She grew to love her mother again, differently. This woman was stronger, but kinder. Harder, but more patient.

158

By the time Ava was fourteen, she could maneuver large cities and remote rainforests like most American teenagers did malls and high schools. Now she wondered what her mother had learned during her two years away. Did she know of Zek? Had she known all of this would happen?

How would Zek's story affect what she had planned once they landed? Ava needed to know more. Quickly.

She fired up the laptop and posted a quick message to Rys asking him to work with whomever he needed to get a press conference set up that night. She would send the location an hour before.

Chapter 23

Ava moved back into the cockpit, sat down, and put on her headset. "Okay, apprentice. I have a lot of questions, but not a lot of time." She leaned her head back and sighed. "Start with the basics."

Zek enabled the autopilot again, then closed his eyes.

She turned and searched his face for clues to his nature. Other than a few of his strange mannerisms and those ice blue eyes set off by pitch black skin, she couldn't discern any obvious differences from other people. What was his physical appearance like in his world? Was he the same? What was he doing here?

He opened his eyes and stared deeply into hers. "I can communicate with you because of my access to the multiversal network."

He paused and stared off toward the horizon. "The network is comprised of the collective thoughts, experiences, feelings, and wisdom of all souls from the beginning to the end." His gaze returned to hers.

"Kind of like an internet for the universe?" she asked. "Something like that exists?" Warmth spread through her body as her mind cycled through the enormity of what Zek had said.

His pupils dilated until the blue irises became pencil-thin shining rings. "Think of it more like a recording of each soul's unique perspective of the multiverse."

She narrowed her eyes. "Did you just access it so you could explain it to me? So that I would understand?"

"Yes." His pupils returned to normal, and he focused on her eyes again. "It is important that I use terms and concepts you are familiar with, and so I searched the network for information collected from you and those who have communicated with you in the past, in order to make myself understood."

"Wow!" She shook her head. "That's some creepy big brother talk."

"We do not exercise control over other souls with this information, otherwise the network would be tainted with bias. Laer acts as a safeguard against this, as well as many other undesirable possibilities."

He stopped, his pupils dilated again, though less so than before. "I have seven-dimensional access, meaning I can communicate with beings in lower dimensions and create new pathways through the network. As a creator, I build new planets in those lower dimensions for souls to ascend through the multiverse and grow the network collective."

"Hold on," she said. "You're going too fast. What is Laer?"

"It is the creation platform used to help build the network." He put his finger up as his eyes darkened and blended with his face. Seconds later blue and white crept back in.

"The Laer Guild is responsible for overseeing network growth. Many cycles before I came to The Creation Guild, new planet formation was very difficult. It required dangerous direct access into the deepest voids of space. Most creators did not return. As a result, very few planets existed for souls to experience physical lives. The network showed signs of contraction and decay. The Creation Guild Grandmaster allowed an apprentice, much like myself, to create a platform to protect creators as they built planets. That apprentice elected not to join the Creation Guild and work under others. He left and started a new guild. The Laer Guild."

Ava sat up in her seat. "An apprentice built an operating system then?"

"In the sense of organizing network inputs, outputs, processing, and storage. Yes," Zek said. "However, it only allows creation within the dimensions where souls have network access. It is therefore limited to growth via networked souls. To build a planet in a lower dimension, a creator cannot utilize the Laer platform."

"And my dimension is…" She wasn't sure if she wanted to know the answer, but she could feel the truth in her gut.

"The gateway," Zek said. "The fourth dimension is where souls unlock network access. To build Earth, I had to work with base elements, out of the safety of Laer."

He paused and scanned the blue sky. "And out of its restrictions on new network connections."

"How does this Laer Guild feel about you doing that?" She jumped when he whipped around in the seat to face her.

"It is not lawful to interfere with the creation process." He relaxed back and took a deep breath. "My Guildmaster and the Grandmaster believe Laer may have operatives here manipulating the planet's outcome. I have returned to investigate and report my findings. Either way, your Seneca has something to do with it."

"Well, what they're doing to me isn't exactly lawful here. Do you think Drew is from Laer?"

Ava's rational mind screamed at her. What Zek said was so far out of her realm of reality, but her gut felt its truth. Logic and intuition battled on inside her while Zek continued.

"He may be. I need physical proximity to him to know for certain."

"I can all but guarantee you'll have that when we land in L.A." She shifted sideways in her seat to face him fully. "Now tell me what you think Laer's motivation is for interfering here. I get that they don't like you going around them. Other than their pride, why would they go to such trouble over an apprentice's project?"

"I believe it is at the very heart of the multiversal balance." The radio crackled and he reached over to silence it.

"There exists what we consider expansionist souls and parity souls. Myself, the Grandmaster of The Creation Guild, and most creators are, by our very nature, expansionists. We believe network balance is only possible through expansion. Others believe there is a natural limit to the number of souls in each dimension at any time. This translates to a belief that if one soul ascends, another must descend."

"So if a bunch of souls rush the gates of the network, so to speak, it would throw off the balance according to the parity believers? We call that zero-sum thinking around here. The only way I can win is if someone else loses. It works in sports, but I haven't found it to be that way in real life," Ava said.

"You are very much an expansionist, Ava. I have known that since we first spoke, and you suggested we work out a trade. You also did not shoot me though you were under threat by others."

She shook her head. Of course he had known she had a gun behind the doorframe when he showed up at the cabin that day.

"I am concerned that Laer not only wants me to be forced to end my project but that they plan to use that failure in order to stop souls from entering the upper dimensions altogether."

"You lost me. Forced to end? Use 'that failure'? This is Earth we're talking about, right?" Her ears started to buzz. She messed with the dial on the headset, but the noise continued.

"Of course," he said.

The buzzing grew. It wasn't coming from the headset. It was like a warning going off inside her head. "As in end Earth? Do you mean they want to destroy all of us?"

He checked the instrument panel and pressed a few buttons on the GPS. "I must figure out how and why Seneca creates consciousness without awareness. Do you think Drew manipulated the system?"

"I'm pretty certain Drew can hardly turn on his computer, much less understand how Seneca operates and change it. What do you mean consciousness without awareness?" she asked.

"That is what I am here to learn. Consciousness is accompanied by awareness of ascension and the Network, normally. That is not happening with Seneca. While those who listen are breaking through to fourth dimension consciousness, they are not gaining awareness of it. This is dangerous. It leads to chaos."

Ava stared. Had she ascended unknowingly? Her mind raced at the thought. The idea that an opposing force wanted to stop her from continuing on her path made her fully determined to carry out the plan that had been forming in her mind.

"You think someone from Laer is making this happen?" she asked. "You said you will know if you're in physical proximity of the person? This being anyway?"

"Correct. They will emit a different frequency than you or other humans."

Ava unbuckled and turned in her seat. "Well, then...I need to check in with a few people to make sure you have plenty of vibrations to tune into." In truth, she also needed a few minutes alone to process what he was saying and decide on her next moves.

Zek put his hand on her arm. "You must keep the live music out of everyone's hands until we know how to use it without risking the upper dimensions."

"You mean you don't know how? Didn't you make all this?" She waved her hands in circles, knocking his away.

"I set start conditions and intervened twice before, but I don't have control over the details. I only have access to my fourth-dimension senses while I'm here. Theoretically the same for the Laer spy, or spies."

"Lucky us," she replied flatly. "Fine, let's start with the here and now. In a couple of hours, we'll land and I'll give a press conference. I want to out these asshats to the world and show everyone else what we've discovered. Let them listen to the music and decide for themselves what the truth is."

"You must be careful," he said. "If people aren't open to accepting truth, they will turn on you. Tell me, how much have you listened to the music? Do you enjoy it?"

"Well, I suppose it's not the first thing I want to turn on. It's been a little too busy to waste time listening more than necessary. Let's see. It's good to recognize things I don't want to admit. It forces me to acknowledge them at least. I like the ability to distinguish between thoughts. Some thoughts are uniquely mine, and some are repeated from things I've heard. It helps me examine them."

"Yet you don't listen all the time?"

"I don't," she admitted. "It's uncomfortable. I've seen the kinds of reactions people have when it plays. Drew damn near destroyed his entire office in the first few minutes after Seneca went live."

"Many will react that way. Or worse. Can you imagine that reaction multiplied across your planet?" He put his hand on her arm.

She nodded. "Of course. It's why we suggested listening centers with trained guides. To help people work through the discomfort in a safe environment."

"What good can this press conference do?"

"It will get me out of hiding and allow me to expose what's happening."

"Will you tell them about me?"

She slipped her fingers between his. "That's not for me to tell." She didn't want to end up in a mental institution. "I'm only learning the entire story myself. No one would believe me anyway."

"Will you tell part of what is happening and hide

the rest?"

"You're as bad as the music. Where is your 'off' button?"

"Ava, what is it you want?" Zek asked. "From your life on this world?"

"I want to save my company and clear my name. I want to release Seneca and see people living in truth. Make a positive impact on the world." She sighed and sat back.

"An hour ago that's all I wanted. I don't know if what you told me changes that. Does it?" she asked herself and Zek at the same time.

"You have more information now. The only way to save your company is to save Earth first."

"Then that's what I want."

"Do you believe this planet is worth saving? I see chaos, deceit, disease, and a world intent on destroying itself. I'm not convinced it should be saved."

The skin on the back of Ava's neck tightened as he spoke the words. Didn't he care about his success? If saving his creation wasn't the goal, what was he after? "You're frightening me. Why should I help you if you want to destroy us anyway? What is it that you want, Zek?"

"I want to be Grandmaster of the guild. I want to expose the Laer operatives here on Earth. But I cannot risk the upper dimensions for my individual desires. That is a simple truth even three-dimensional beings can grasp."

"That makes it better." She rolled her eyes.

"It is the same for you. You wish to make a difference, but not at the expense of your world."

"Fine," she said. "For us to both be successful, we

need the same outcome. We can't let the music get into the wrong hands. They don't have the source code, so we're good."

"Are you certain about that?"

"Even if they got the code, they don't know the cameras at the cabin are what make Seneca work."

"Do you believe you were the only thing they were after at the cabin? Is there some way they could have known about the cameras and that's why they were on the property?" Zek asked.

"They couldn't…" How much more of this could she take? They found the cabin somehow. She had to assume they questioned the team and learned about the camera feeds. "If they got in the cabin before you and found the thumb drive, then they have all the pieces." She covered her face with both hands. "What have I done?"

"What you have done is create the communication tool for the messages I brought to this world in my last intervention. You brought the translator to life. You're the translator Ava, not Seneca."

"I'm confused. Is it me, the machine, the cameras, or the cabin?" She paused and scanned the increasingly hazy horizon wishing they could fly somewhere far away where nothing exciting would happen. Like Denmark.

"Yes. It is all those things. As a translator, you do not need the machine or cameras, though they helped you initially. Even the cabin is unnecessary once you learn to recognize and speak truth. They are mere tools. You also do not need me."

She felt dumber by the minute. Or more confused. What was the difference? "Maybe the music can help us decide what to do after we land?"

"If you think you need it," he replied.

Chapter 24

Ava grabbed the laptop from the back, checked she was connected to Wi-Fi and brought up Seneca. Nothing happened.

Dreading the worst, she connected to the camera feed. All but one showed digital snow. She watched flames lick the branches of trees in perfect 4K resolution while small creatures fled to the river beyond. Then the final working camera flicked and turned to snow with the others.

"No!" she yelled. "It's all on fire. We must turn around, Zek. Tony and Renata could be out there."

"This is better for us. Tony was doing his job as protector."

"Tony would never do something like that. It was the people with the guns. If he's in danger, we must help him. It's your fault he's in this position. Now turn around."

"Ava, he is a protector and will do anything to ensure your safety and that of the truth woven through your land. You do not need to worry about him. He has faced much worse. You need to focus on what you will do when we land."

"Does he know who you are?"

"I have not revealed my true nature to anyone but you this time."

"This time? You said something about other interventions. Who did you tell last time?"

"It is not important. I am not here to intervene now. I have returned to understand. To learn. To seek the truth of my creation."

"I can't think." Why did it all sound so circular? "I don't know what to do, Zek. I deal in code, not in multidimensional coups."

"You do know. Let me know what you decide." He put his headset back on and scanned the skies ahead.

Ava slammed the laptop shut and moved into the cabin. She slid the cockpit door closed behind her. The guy who created this whole mess expected her to clean it up for him. Typical. Men didn't seem any better in his dimension.

Stop, it's time to think.

She went through multiple scenarios for how things could play out with the press and the authorities. If she stayed in the public light, there was only so much they could do to her. Whoever "they" were. Right?

Chapter 25

"Lisa Statler please," Ava said into the cabin satellite phone.

"Speaking. Make it quick."

"It's Ava Lawson. We've had a bit of a setback and need to change plans. I'm headed back to L.A. and want to know what to expect from the authorities. I am going to turn myself in."

"Ava, what in the hell do you think you're doing?" Ava held the phone away from her ear. "What did I say about talking to anyone?"

"I don't have time to be chastised. Plans changed and I need your help. They found me. They had guns, and they were shooting to kill! We escaped, but now the cabin and property are all on fire. I'm turning myself in."

"Oh my God! You're O.K? How did you get away?"

"A friend got us to a plane and we flew out," Ava said in a voice that had lost all emotion.

"You just took a plane and flew away?" A sigh through the phone. "I...okay then. Where are you headed?"

"A small airport northeast of Los Angeles. I messaged Rys to put together a press conference. There's no way I can stay hidden. How on Earth did they find me?" Her volume rose a notch. "No one knows where that cabin is."

"Ava. Focus. The cabin doesn't matter right now. First, are you all right?" She exhaled loudly. "Of course, you're fine physically. You got yourself out of there."

"I'm in one piece, but I'm terrified. My uncle's friend and his wife are still there. Two agents were at his house firing at us when we drove off property."

"What kind of agents? Police, military, FBI? Did you see any insignia on their clothes?"

"I didn't make friends with them or anything. They were shooting at us," Ava said flatly. "But no markings on their clothes or cars that I could see. They were in all black with blacked out SUVs."

"Hmmm," she answered. "Now tell me how you're doing mentally. Are you reacting by turning yourself in or is it the best game plan right now?"

"Are you asking if I'm emotional?" What lawyer cared about emotions? Nathan better be right about her.

"Lisa, I haven't done emotions since college. Since you asked, I managed a few tears this week and I'm on the verge of throwing up. So, I'm all good on catharsis. I've decided the best move is to turn myself in, so let's talk about that."

"Good. We don't need any suppressed emotions showing up at the wrong time. I need to make sure your head is on straight."

Ava snorted.

"As for the FBI, I've been in touch with Washington, and they're pretty pissed that you went in hiding. They can't do much without formal charges though. You're still officially wanted for questioning, but that's it at the moment. However," she paused. "There's been another development."

"Not more," Ava said, the life drained out of her voice.

"There was a body found in D.C. this morning. Your COO Drew is dead." She continued, softer. "I'm sorry for your loss. I know you were old friends before he betrayed you."

Ava studied the receiver in her hand. It was too much. "What in the hell?" she whispered. "I thought he was pulling all the puppet strings. If it's not him, then who is it?"

This was her fault. She hired him. She let him set her up. He walked right into death because of her and her creation. How many more would die because of her? The guilt that overwhelmed her after her parents' deaths threatened to consume again.

"I've got people on it, but they're pointing the finger at you. I agree that you need to be in the public light as much as possible, but you don't need to start spilling your guts to the press every chance you get. They can twist and use just about anything against you."

"Okay, I think I know what to say in a public statement. Can you make sure Nathan is there? I prefer being around people rather than returning to an empty house alone and seeing how much of it they've destroyed."

"Another good suggestion. I figured it was best to work on this from L.A. so I flew in a few hours ago. We can meet in person."

"Oh. I didn't expect that. The pilot will be coming with me. Zek." She heard a sharp puff of breath from the other end.

"Are you sure this Zack needs to tag along? The

fewer people the better when it comes to your inner circle."

"It's Zek, with an e. Believe me, we want him around."

"Fine. We'll see you in an hour."

"Whiteman Field."

"I sure hope you know what you're doing," the lawyer said and hung up.

Ava found some paper and a pen in one of the many tiny compartments and started writing. Longhand helped her think better. She crumpled up sheet after half written sheet until the words were right. Memories of working with Drew interfered and made the process more difficult than it should have been.

Zek started their descent and she buckled back into the right seat. Red and white lights danced around their destination a few miles away.

Chapter 26

The headset reminded Zek of his creation rig in the way it heightened his senses of both hearing and touch. A voice told him they were cleared to land well before he could see the airstrip and flashing lights that awaited them. This was not as expected, according to his databank on modern flight operations.

He turned his gaze from the horizon to Ava. If he had access to his sense of magnetism, he would be aware of a pulling sensation beyond that of wanting to simply touch her. To reach out and weave his fingers through her flaming hair. They were connected in a strong bond as they sat beside one another, focused on the same outcome.

He wished for that strong bond to continue even as he knew strong bonds were like the waves of the ocean beyond, governed by tides and other forces out of their control.

He nodded at the scene outside the windshield. "You have many people waiting for you." The flashing lights surrounding the runway ahead were connected to vehicles of many shapes and sizes.

Ava sucked in a breath. "I didn't expect there to be so many of them. Zek, what if they arrest me when we land?" She wrapped her fingers around his upper arm.

"It is improbable," he said. He didn't add that he felt an unexpected pushing force from the airfield. A person, but a repellant in magnetic terms, something he shouldn't be able to sense.

He banked from downwind to crosswind, then to his final approach. Blue, red, white flashed through the cockpit.

"Looks like it's showtime," Ava said. She sat up straight and adjusted her headset.

The wheels touched down without a sound. Zek maneuvered the craft between emergency flares and onto the taxiway. He stopped before a barricade of armored vans and shut down the engines.

Ava's eyes were wild. "Kiss me for good luck?"

The human kiss perplexed Zek. Connection through the taste sense receptors was not practiced on other planets. It was an anomaly unique to Earth. He found that he nearly lost himself the first time Ava pressed her lips to his.

Laer warned of creators losing the connection to themselves when in deep space, yet he never felt it in any way as he drew in and assembled the power and elements for the start conditions of Earth's solar system. He was able to maintain separation between his consciousness and the chaos.

Something strange happened when Ava's lips touched his. It intensified as her tongue sought the inside of his mouth. Rather than lose himself, he felt he gained part of her even as he ceded control.

He wanted the moment to continue; pulled her down on his lap as he sat on the small couch. She straddled him willingly. Their mouths never lost contact. He was filled with light and a lightness.

A loudspeaker crackled loudly outside the cabin. "This is the FBI. Exit the aircraft immediately."

Ava broke her lips from Zek's and pressed her

forehead to his. "I don't know where I go when I kiss you. I know I never want to come back." She pulled back and smiled with sadness in her eyes. "Please stay close. I can't lose you."

He locked on her gaze. "Ava, no one can know who or what I am."

"Miss Lawson!" The bullhorn coughed back to life. "You are wanted for questioning in the murder of Andrew Hodges. Exit the aircraft."

Ava stood and unlatched the door. It dropped open, spreading its few steps to the taxiway below. She shielded her eyes and stood on the top step.

Chapter 27

A helicopter landed off the aircraft's tail. With the rotor still spinning, Nathan and a tall blond jumped out and ran Ava's way.

She waved from the top landing.

"Miss Lawson, you're coming with us." The man with the bullhorn put out his hand to help her down the steps.

"Do not touch my client!" Nathan's companion yelled as she pushed her way to the bottom of the stairs. "She will answer your questions after she has made a prepared statement and each of you has followed proper protocol."

"Miss Lawson is a fugitive and will not be giving any statements."

"Then give me your name, your authority, an arrest warrant, and read her Miranda rights. Only then will she be going anywhere with you. Until then, back off," she said. She cocked her hip to the left like a hockey player to block the guy with the bullhorn. Her movement allowed Ava to come down the steps between her and Nathan. Zek followed directly behind.

A reporter who followed Nathan and Lisa off the helicopter pointed a camera in her face. "Ava, do you have a statement?"

She moved back up a step and felt Zek's warmth at her back. "I do," she answered.

She addressed the agent with the bullhorn and

motioned to a swarm of reporters held behind police tape. "If you'll please allow the others through. It is my right, is it not?"

He hesitated and she saw him squint like he was listening to orders from his headset. "Two minutes," he growled and stepped back from the stairs.

The reporters ran over from behind the barricade, cameras rolling. So many phones were out snapping photos that Ava could hardly see past the white flashes.

"Thank you for being here," she said when the noise died down. "I won't be answering any questions, but I would like to make a statement concerning recent events and my welcome back party." She waved her hand at the vehicles surrounding the plane.

A few of the reporters laughed with her. The rest quieted down the crowd so that they could all hear what she was saying. Nathan's propeller blade continued its whooping.

"First, I would like to express my deepest condolences to the friends and family of our late Chief Operating Officer, Andrew Hodges. I was just informed that his body was found earlier today in Washington D.C. and foul play is suspected."

"Earlier today I came very close to sharing in his demise when I was hunted and shot at while meeting with the trustee of my estate. My family's property was set on fire after I escaped. We do not know the extent of the damage or the whereabouts of my trustee and his wife."

Gasps and shouts rose through the crowd. She waited until they died down to continue.

"The allegations in the anonymous letter sent to the Board of Directors of Sense Labs, the company I founded and am CEO of, are false. I have returned to clear my name and cooperate with the FBI in their investigation. I will also assist in the investigations I expect will be opened into Drew's murder and my attempted murder."

"As to motive behind today's real crimes, all I can say is that we built something very special at Sense Labs. So special that someone or ones will stop at nothing, short of murder, to steal it. What is it you ask?"

She peered at different faces in the crowd, connecting through direct eye contact. Heads nodded, wanting more. She waited for the first "Tell us!" to make the announcement.

"We created creativity. Artistic, artificial intelligence that creates original music. We call it Seneca. This music comes with a catch, a side effect if you will. We found that it reveals more than melodies and choruses. When we listen, we also hear truth. Truth in many forms. This is what our enemies are after. The military is using a stolen copy of the music to force prisoners to speak against their will with a blatant disregard for their rights and…"

Her words were cut off by a blast that threw her off the steps of the plane. She landed on Lisa who flew backward and hit the grass hard.

Screams and shouts registered as little more than whispers over the buzzing in Ava's head.

Three shocked faces stood out in the scrambling mass of bodies. Rhonda, Tim, and Michael were motionless behind the barricade.

Ava struggled to push her torso up and turned to survey the damage behind her. The plane's left wing hung twisted from a fuselage that would never take to the skies again. The stairs she stood on moments before lay mangled several feet away.

Nathan emerged from behind the tail of the plane and ran toward her. She spun her head frantically. Zek must still be in the plane. White foam from the closest fire truck rained down.

"Get her out of here!" Hands cupped under her shoulders and legs to move her away from the wreckage. Lisa lay still on the ground. Blood poured from her face and what was likely a broken nose.

Ava managed to croak out, "Get Lisa first." Gashes and cuts dotted their exposed skin, but they picked the other woman up and moved her into the helicopter that stood ready on the taxiway.

"You're coming with us!" The yelling came from beyond her peripheral vision.

Strong arms grabbed her from behind. "Like hell!" she screamed.

She kicked her legs forward after the goon picked her up like a ragdoll. It threw him off balance just long enough for Zek to ram sideways into the massive armor-clad man, knocking him to the ground. Ava wriggled and punched wildly at her attacker's face.

Four other testosterone-fueled jackals ran at her but lunged the other way at the last second. They tackled Zek.

Two more sets of hands pulled at her while she screamed at the others to leave Zek alone. The hands drug her to the waiting helicopter that lifted off as soon as they pushed her through and climbed in.

"We can't leave without him," she screamed at Nathan.

"He'll be okay, Ava," he said. "There's nothing we can do right now except make sure you're safe."

"Please go back," she said, softer and trembling. "I don't know what will happen to him."

"Ava!" He cradled her face in his hands. "We can't lose everything right now. He would want you to be safe. Do you understand?"

Nathan didn't understand. Zek was everything.

She strained to view the spot beside the destroyed plane where she saw him last. Zek had vanished in a sea of bodies and mayhem.

Chapter 28

Calculated risk, Zek thought. The possible undesirable outcomes of a decision multiplied by the probability of each one happening.

The machines humans built were far superior in calculating risk than their creators. Zek, forced to rely on fourth dimension awareness, had found himself incapable of calculating the risk associated with telling Ava his true identity. He had done it anyway.

When he had kissed her, he knew it was the right move. He felt her truth. He also felt something else, outside the aircraft cabin that now lay mangled on the tarmac. Among the people congregated at the bottom of the steps listening to her speech.

He felt another kind of presence.

The blast pushed him back hard through the open door of the plane. He leapt through the flaming hatch and rolled underneath the fuselage as the smoke billowed, camouflaging his escape.

Ava was pulled off another woman and left in the grass. He crouched, ready to pounce if needed.

Large, meaty hands grabbed for Ava. When they lifted her, Zek ran at the man, knocking him to the ground.

He turned and snarled while four other goons tackled Zek. They looped hard plastic around his wrists so tightly it cut his skin.

But Ava was safe. The fat black helicopter lifted

off with her inside.

Zek's face pressed into the fragrant grass. He could still smell her sweat where she had landed only moments before.

"We'll get your girlfriend soon enough." The man's hot breath shot into Zek's ear. "We have a way to make you help us with that."

"Whom do you work for?" Zek asked in a calm steady voice.

His eyes hopped around the scene like a rogue proton. They settled on an older woman who towered nearly as tall as Zek.

The presence Zek felt after the blast trained her cold eyes on him.

"We're asking the questions here." The men pulled Zek to his feet.

Calculated risk, he thought. Snapping the restraints wouldn't be a problem. The question was whether he could escape after figuring out what these people planned to do with Seneca. And Ava.

He let them lead him into the back of a black van.

Chapter 29

The helicopter slowly circled and touched down on an expansive grass lawn. A shroud of trees to Ava's right and a large house loomed in front.

Nathan touched Ava's shoulder. "We'll be safe at my place. We got security under control after my last visitors."

Four men and a woman sprinted their direction carrying two field stretchers.

"Load the ladies up after I get these on them," the small, dark-skinned woman with huge black eyes said to the men. She felt Lisa's spine for injuries, put a stethoscope to her chest, then fit her with a neck brace. Hands lowered the unconscious woman gently out of the helicopter.

"I don't need that," Ava said when the doctor pointed at the other stretcher. "I can walk."

"Why don't you let these nice strong men carry you inside," replied the woman in a heavy Hindi accent. "I'm Dr. Bhandari and you must be Ava. Nice to meet you. May I do my job?"

"By all means." Ava didn't argue with doctors. She let the men carrying the empty stretcher lift her onto it and walk her around the pool and up the steps to the back porch.

"Any news from the airport?" she asked no one in particular. Everyone in the helicopter had been busy screaming into their phones during the short ride. They sounded like an underwater metal band in her ringing ears.

Dr. Bhandari walked around her. "The fire department has it under control. One casualty and over a dozen wounded and on their way to area hospitals. You were very lucky."

"Twice in one day. I'm not feeling that lucky."

"Hmm. I'll call for you once I know Miss Statler is stable. Set her up here on the patio where it's nice and cool," she told the men carrying Ava. The doctor followed the other stretcher through the back door of the house.

Ava sat up and scanned the wide porch. "Where's Nathan?"

"I believe he took off in the helicopter ma'am," replied the voice above her head.

"I need to talk to him. It was too chaotic in the air. Can you find out when he'll be back?"

He handed her a small black phone. "This is for you. Call him whenever you like. It's secure.

"Thank you. I'm Ava. Thanks for the ride too, but I can get around from here." She didn't wait for permission and swung her legs off the stretcher. The quick movement made her see stars.

"Whoa!" he said. "Nice to meet you. I'm Darren, head of security. Why don't I help you get settled here on the porch while the doc works on Lisa?"

"I'd rather be alone for a few minutes. It's been a kinda long day." She got up slowly and sank onto the closest chaise lounge. A colony of bees set up shop in her brain.

"I've had a few of those days myself. We can keep an eye on you from inside the house. Here," he said and handed her a water, "best to stick with this until you're checked for internal bleeding. Not that you're at much risk. You don't show any signs and it wasn't a high-order explosive. No risk of over pressurization to the organs. I heard Lisa broke your fall. But you saved her from fragmentation injuries, so I'd call it even. Your acrobatics are all over the news."

"Can you show me?" She gestured to a huge TV in the corner of the patio.

She leaned back on the chaise. Her adrenaline plummeted and she was left exhausted, scared, confused, and pissed.

The water helped bring her back to life, but the incoming reports did little to calm her fear. An FBI agent was killed in the blast; nine more agents and three civilians were seriously injured. No names were released yet. She picked up the phone Darren gave her and texted Nathan.

Did everyone make it? Did you find Zek?

His response came through in a few seconds.

Michael and Rys are with me. Dropping off the reporter now. Rhonda and Tim are fine and demanding to meet with you. No word on Zek.

Dr. Bhandari called to her on the house intercom. "Ava, it's your turn."

****

"I didn't expect an entire hospital," Ava commented when Darren helped her into the well-appointed clinic inside the house. The equipment alone must have cost millions.

Lisa was awake and sitting up in an adjustable hospital bed. Ava nodded to her with a smile. "Thanks for breaking my fall. You go above and beyond for clients, don't you?" She laughed at the other woman's dirty look, made comical by a very swollen nose and eyes that darkened by the minute.

"I always wanted a nose job." The lawyer grimaced from the movement.

Ava went to the side of the bed. "I'm so sorry for putting you in danger like this. I still haven't even signed your engagement letter, but I can fix that now. I'll understand if you don't want to accept."

"Shut up, Ava." Lisa's voice was slow, slurred. "It's your turn in the CT scan. We can discuss my hazard pay when you're cleared by the doc." She coughed and the pain on her face deepened. "It's only a flesh wound," she joked weakly.

"Okay, ladies, that's enough small talk. Ava, you're up. On the table. Lisa, rest. Your sense of humor clearly needs it."

Dr. Bhandari went through the exam quickly but thoroughly. The CT scans showed no injury, and she bandaged a few small cuts from projectiles. "You are also a very fortunate lady. The blast came from a small tug right beside you on the taxiway. General aviation airports have no security, and you didn't leave much time for sweeping the area."

"I never meant to put people in danger." Ava sighed. "I wonder when Nathan will get sick of cleaning up my messes."

"Your messes? You do not understand him very well. All of this," she said with a broad sweep of her arm, "is here because of you. We moved most of our lab and a good number of our people to create a safe place because he knew what you were up against and how important it is for you to fight it."

Ava sat up in the small bed. "Wait. This wasn't…"

Dr. Bhandari hit a button to adjust the bed in a sitting position and gently pushed Ava back. "It's amazing what dedicated people can do in a few days, isn't it?"

"Why did you do it?" Ava asked. "You seem to be well trained in medicine and all of this machinery. Most doctors would have an entire staff working on the examinations that you just did."

The other woman smiled. "I did it because Nathan asked. He changed my life a few years ago and I would go to the ends of the earth for him, as he would for me. As he is for you. Do you know the joke about Indian parents and what they tell their children when they go to school?"

"Let me guess. You were allowed to be anything you wanted as long as it was a doctor, lawyer, or engineer."

The doctor rolled her head and laughed. "That's the one. As you can tell, I chose doctor. I figured if I had to take a high paying career, at least I would be able to help people with real problems. I realize now that engineers do that, too," she added with a smile and pat on Ava's hand.

"I made good grades, went to the top schools, took the most coveted residency. But I hated it. I was about to get married to a man my parents approved of. He was a good man. Then one day I lost a patient and it didn't bother me. As I sat thinking about it that night, it occurred to me that my practice had become all about meeting other people's expectations and the money. So, I quit and opened a concierge medical practice to cater to the rich and the famous. If helping others didn't matter anymore, why not make as much money as possible? I left my fiancé and started chasing men who I thought were on my level. I would dump them the second I found the chink in their armor. Better to hurt than be hurt. Then I met Nathan."

"Was he a patient?" Ava relaxed back and closed her eyes. The light was adding to her headache.

Dr. Bhandari placed her hands on Ava's temples. "You'll soon have a shiner to match your attorney's."

The doctor pushed some buttons and the light over Ava went out. "Nathan hired me to help a friend of his, a childhood friend dying of kidney disease. By the time I was brought in his friend was on dialysis and the only thing we could do was wait for a donor." She paused and massaged Ava's scalp. "I blocked the process."

"What do you mean you blocked the process?" Ava felt woozy but forced herself to focus on the doctor's story. The pain in her head began to dull.

Dr. Bhandari put her finger to her lips. "I'm not proud of it and have made my peace with it. I learned that he was alcoholic and abusing drugs. I thought he didn't deserve a new kidney to ruin. That it should be given to a person who wouldn't destroy it. The man disappeared one day and was found on the wrong side of town. The official death certificate said kidney failure. It was an overdose."

"I'm so sorry. What did Nathan say? How did you end up working for him after that?"

"When he thanked me for helping, I lectured him on taking in strays. I used that term. I was so full of myself, so judgmental. The chink in Nathan's armor was obvious to me. He was a bleeding heart and didn't hold people accountable for their lack of self-control. I told him he was better than that and gave more than his friend deserved. I can't believe he didn't throw me out of his office and see to it that I lost my license. He certainly could have."

"Damn," Lisa called out from across the room. "And no offense on lawyers not helping people. I caught that." Ava and Dr. Bhandari laughed.

"Nathan looked at me," the doctor continued. "Those gray eyes cut right into my soul. He said, 'you could have saved him.' I told him no one could have saved his friend, but he continued. He said I was a healer who had simply forgotten more than what she learned in school. I wanted him to reprimand me, end my miserable career, tell me what deep down I knew I was. A fake. But he forgave me. I was so mad at him. I stomped out of the room like a spoiled child. A few weeks later a check arrived in the mail paying his invoice in full. With it was a typed letter asking me to lead a biogenetic research team to discover underlying causes and treatments for mental health issues and addiction."

"Something snapped in me. All the work to please others, to be and do what they thought I should, had turned me into someone I hated. He saw through it. I wrote back and told him I was going on sabbatical. I would let him know my answer when it was over. That I had to get my mental health together before I could be of any help to others. I apologized. Thanked him for forgiveness I didn't deserve. Then I went in search of the person I could be. When I came back, healed and ready, he had the lab set up and I got to work. We've quietly spun out a few companies and are making some progress, but when I heard about what you built, Ava, I knew how important it would be to our work. You're an inspiration. So yes, this is all for you. We are all here for you."

The pulsing beat of a rotor blade broke the stillness in the room.

"Sounds like they're back," Lisa said. "I'll tell you my story some other time. It's not too different from the doc's."

"It's Manisha outside this room," Dr. Bhandari told Ava. She flipped through screens showing slices of Ava's brain. "You were a very lucky girl but take it easy for a few days." She took Ava's hand to help her off the bed. "Let's get Lisa some wheels and meet the others."

Chapter 30

They filed through the helicopter hatch in a line. Nathan first, followed by Rys, Sarah, Michael, and two of Nathan's guards.

The pilot shut down the craft while Ava watched for a bald black head to emerge. A dirty blond woman shut the hatch behind her. Ava recognized the pilot from her ride earlier.

"Did you find Zek?" Ava asked the group.

"Nice to see you too," Rys said.

"Sorry, guys. I'm happy to see you, you don't even know." She hugged each one in turn. The board meeting felt like a lifetime ago. "Did you two make up?" she asked Michael and Rys.

"We only brought him along so that you could take care of him." Rys laughed and poked Michael. "Would you like to torture him first for information?"

"Your timing as always, Rys, is impeccable." Michael turned to Ava. "Are you okay?"

Ava nodded impatiently. "What about Zek? The pilot who flew me back here."

"Last any of us saw your friend he was behind you on the plane steps," he replied. "Is there any chance he had something to do with the bomb? He knew your destination before anyone else."

Ava stared Michael directly in the eyes. "Absolutely not. If we don't find him, I have a feeling things will get even worse."

Michael nodded. "Anything you need."

"We have a lot to catch up on," Ava said. "But it's late and we've all had a long day. Why doesn't everyone get some sleep and we'll talk it over in the morning." She wouldn't force the others to stay up, though sleep was not likely to find her before sunrise.

"It's only one in the morning," Sarah pointed out. "None of us are exactly strangers to all-nighters. How about a bite to eat while we compare notes? We've figured out a little more about how the music works."

Ava's stomach growled. The last thing she ate was the fish Zek had cooked for breakfast. "I'm game if you are." Anything else she could learn about the music might help.

Nathan ended his call. "Fantastic idea. I'm starving. Darren?" Nathan turned to his most trusted employee. "Can you get someone to bring out whatever food we have in the house?"

"Sure thing, boss," Darren said.

Nathan pulled Ava aside. "Zek is fine. I don't know everything that's going on, but I know enough to trust him the way you do. I expect we'll hear from him soon. Until then we need to keep you safe. No more brave plans. Yes?"

"You know where he is? Did you see him?" She grabbed Nathan's arm. *Don't get hysterical, Ava*, she thought. They can't know Zek is anyone but a friend.

"There's nothing we can do right now but wait," he said. "What are you planning to tell the group?"

"Nathan, this is way bigger than anyone realizes." She put her hand on her chest. "I hardly believe it. I'm not sure how they'll take it. But it's real and I'm stuck in the middle and have to help."

Gabriella Zielke

"There is plenty more to this, but don't underestimate the people who made it here." He gestured toward the others walking ahead. "You never did before."

Her eyes locked on his. "I'm beginning to realize my feelings of isolation the past few days, years really, were self-inflicted. I've been alone for so long. Drew's betrayal was the final evidence. Let's just say the pity party was turning into a rager after running away."

"We all read your letter." His features softened into a smile.

"But Tony came back, Zek turned out to be so much more than the drifter I thought he was. Now you and the others are here. I guess I didn't know what I had. What I have," she corrected herself. "If I don't get to tell you later, thank you for everything you've done."

"You can thank me once we get through this." He put his palm on the middle of her back. Not around her shoulders like a friend nor the small of her back like a lover. It was a simple gesture of solidarity.

"Is there any news from the cabin? I need to get in touch with Tony," Ava said. "I doubt anything could hurt that old man, but I'm still worried. It was all so crazy. If anything happened to him or Renata…" She couldn't finish the sentence.

Her head pounded. Her eyes watered. Her stomach growled again, loudly. How could she be so bothered by hunger at a time like this?

"Darren is already on it," Nathan said. "He'll update us when there's something to report. For now, let's get you some food and some sleep."

They reached the pool and joined the others who were gathered around a heavy wood table surrounded

her plate aside and sat forward. "It's the hormones that act like neurotransmitters. Oxytocin predominantly. We're still working on what else the music manipulates."

Manisha raised her eyebrows. "You're saying the music triggers a release of certain chemicals? There are plenty of studies on music and its neurological effects. They are nowhere near what Nathan describes about Seneca, though."

"I discounted it too, but a few of our coworkers asked to be scanned the other day with the music playing. They said it didn't affect them the way it did everyone else. When they mentioned they were all on the Autism spectrum, it pointed me in a different direction." Sarah's words sped as she continued. "A common Autistic trait is brutal honesty. They don't get sarcasm well. So, I looked at the data out there on the differences in their brain functions."

"Which isn't much, and far from conclusive," Manisha said.

Sarah rolled her eyes. "Tell me about it. All I can surmise at this point is that the music releases a rush of oxytocin and epinephrine. It somehow triggers the neuroendocrine system to produce a big behavior change. I need a lot more time and a lot more tests to say how."

Ava was torn. If the team knew about Zek and what he told her in the cave and on the plane, they would have an easier time doing their jobs. But how could she betray his trust?

"I get the feeling there's far more to this music than we'll ever uncover." Sarah pushed her plate away and stood up. "I wish I could do more."

Chapter 31

"It's time to tell you about Zek," Ava said.

Rys threw up his hands. "That guy again?" His chair scraped the heavy stone patio.

"You especially need to hear what I have to say," Ava replied. "Our situation is far more complex than a management coup, unfortunately. At least a third dimension one."

"The pilot? What does he have to do with this?" Michael asked.

"Locating him is essential if we're going to fix what we've done."

"What have *we* done?" Sarah asked with a raised eyebrow.

"Oh, nothing but jeopardize the world and possibly the upper dimensions." Ava wondered how she could be so glib. What had happened to her?

"No big deal," Rys said, waving a beer bottle in a little air circle. "What the hell are you talking about? Didn't you check out her brain?" he asked Manisha.

"You guys are going to think I'm either crazy or telling a super crappy joke, so I'm going to come right out and tell you what Zek told me. You can decide whether or not you believe it."

She shared everything she learned in the cave, leaving out Zek's confession from the plane. She recounted the events from the few days since she left town, adding some details from her childhood and the deaths of her parents and uncle.

Taken together, she was more convinced that the far-fetched story was reality. She finished speaking and waited for their reactions. They may have set a world record for the longest time with their mouths hanging open.

Rys started with, "Anan-whaty? Do you honestly believe all that? I mean, I love this metaverse network thing. Imagine what I could do with that kind of data." He rubbed his hands together.

"I told you it sounds like I'm either crazy or telling a joke, but yes, after everything that's happened, I do. It would be tough to find any sort of plausible explanation for what's going on. One of those 'so strange it must be true' stories. Besides, Tony, my uncle's best friend and executor of his estate, would never lie to me."

"Except he already knew all of this and didn't tell you, right?" Lisa pointed out.

Ava's hazel eyes darted right and settled on the lawyer she had known for fewer than twenty-four hours. She sucked in a deep breath. "Tony has been part of my family since before I was born. He may have hidden things to protect me or to follow the Ananzeti system, but he wouldn't lie about it. Not like this." She wondered though, *is withholding information lying*? Was she lying by keeping Zek's secret?

"What about this Zek person?" Nathan asked. "It sounds as if Tony put a lot of trust in him, yet they only met a few weeks ago."

She turned to face Nathan. "You would understand if you'd seen him, spoken with him. He trained wolves to act like puppies around him. Knew everything about my uncle's shop and all the antiquated tools. Could fly a twin turboprop plane like a pro. And his kiss was," she said before thinking. Nathan's startled expression lasted less than a second, but she still caught it.

Manisha sat up. "Is that all?" she asked with a wink.

"It was nothing like that." Ava felt everyone's eyes on her and blushed a deeper crimson the more she tried to stop. "It was just for good luck."

More weak words.

Lisa chimed in. "Lot of good it did you two. Not that I wouldn't have done the same thing. He was hot in an unreal kind of way. Were his eyes blue? I've never seen anything like it."

Ava looked at her. Did she know? "Guys, this is real. What happened at the airport? That was real. You can either believe me and help me come up with a plan, or you can…" she trailed off.

"Say we believe you, Ava," Nathan said. "What harm would it do?"

She searched his eyes and found no hint of pretense. His gentle smile encouraged her.

Manisha broke the silence. "Nathan has shown me the data and there is no explanation for the changes in users' brains and body chemistry. We're dealing with something bigger than technology," she said, "but I still find this very hard to believe."

"As hard to believe as a mythical God raining down wrath and fury on the miserable little humans he created?" Lisa asked. She tried to raise her eyebrow and cringed. "Growing up with evangelical parents had me believing crazier things as a kid. I'm not saying I believe this, but I don't need to in order to protect Ava's legal interests." She lifted her hand to her head as if saying every word had hurt.

"Do we need to believe it to help you?" Sarah asked.

Ava spread her hands and shrugged. "I don't know. Somehow, we all ended up here without knowing any of this. Maybe it doesn't matter."

"If only we had a way to recognize truth," Michael said with a pointed stare.

"Don't remind me," Ava said. "Seneca would be extremely useful right about now."

"What you're saying sounds more like Hinduism than any other religion. It is not that odd, even if brain scans can't prove anything," Manisha said. "I am here to help if I can. I go where Nathan goes, no questions asked."

Ava's eyes moved around the table. She would never convince Rys and Sarah without solid evidence, but they were in it for the technology and its ability to advance mankind. They didn't need convincing. Michael was loyal to a fault but needed to witness her resolve and belief. The newcomers Lisa and Dr. Bhandari were less important at this point.

Her gaze settled on Nathan. His support mattered more than the others and it sounded like she had it, but she had been deceived by one board coup. Still, he had done nothing but prove himself worthy of her trust.

"It fits with what I've learned listening to the music," Michael said. "I don't need Seneca anymore to recognize truth. This is truth."

"You've been listening to the music?" Ava asked. All eyes were on Michael.

"Sounds like your non techie is the one who knows the most about what you built," Lisa pointed out bluntly as only a trial lawyer would.

"What did you mean when you said you don't need the music anymore?" Ava turned back to Michael.

"You know how it filters through all the noise in your head, the justifications, doubts, lies, programs? Well, I don't hear that stuff anymore. Or if I do, it doesn't distract me. It's why I stuck so close to Drew. He always wrapped his shit balls in truth wrappers to make them more believable. I knew he was dangerous."

Rys spit his beer on what was left of the food in front of him. The others laughed harder. "Hold the press!" Rys shouted. "We found the real use for the music. It makes Michael funny!"

Lisa cut in. "Too bad it didn't work on you."

Various burning sounds went around the table.

"Was there anything you learned that could be useful in figuring out who the real mastermind is and finding Zek's whereabouts?" Nathan asked Michael. "Also, what about the…the, what did Zek call it? Laer conspiracy? It would be at least a couple of millennia in the making. Who knows how deep it goes?"

"The music doesn't work like that," Michael said. "You have to ask me specific questions that I would have context for. For example, you could ask me if Rys lives in his mom's basement. I would answer that while he hasn't gotten lucky in a long time, it's not because he lives in his mom's basement. He has a sad little apartment in Brentwood."

"I lied," Rys said. "Not funny at all."

Everyone else at the table let out a good giggle. The shared laughter diffused some of the tension in the night air.

"The difficulty in any discovery is figuring out

what questions to ask," Sarah said. "What are we not asking? Should we go through a list of employees and contractors to find the mole? If Michael can hear the truth now, why not start there? Any other ideas?"

"I did that," Michael answered and leaned back in his chair. "Drew and Tim are puppets. Drew was anyway. Tim still is. Rhonda is a blank to me. It's the strangest thing. I can't get a read on her. Didn't even try until we were at the airfield. She's been so helpful and remained neutral on all the accusations and betrayals. I started thinking she was our Switzerland. Then I remembered a book I read about the Second World War and some of the banking practices during that time. It turns out you can call yourself neutral and still fuel a massive war from both sides."

"Shit," Lisa said.

"What do you get on Rhonda now? What is she about?" Nathan asked.

"Nothing," Michael said. "I keep trying. Thought I lost it after the blast when I couldn't hear. We were pretty close to the explosion." He lifted his right arm and pulled back his sleeve to show a large bandage with blood oozing through.

Manisha rushed over and quickly removed the wrapped gauze. She grabbed a handbag she had stowed under the table. It turned out to be filled with medical supplies.

"It's fine." He still stretched his arm out for the doctor to redress the wound. "I didn't lose my ability. It's Rhonda. She's unreadable."

"Then she's suspect," Nathan said. "Michael, can you keep an eye on her? Get closer? Keep Tim from getting in the way, too? Anyone else at Sense Labs who might be a problem?"

"Drew's guys are helpless without him. The FBI director who's been nosing around is still definitely on the other side of things, but he's a politician, not a mastermind."

"We need to find out who is fixing things for Laer," Ava said. "The bomb, the six agents in Montana, and Drew's murderer can help lead us to them. And Zek. Wherever he is," she added.

"Can we back up a little please?" Manisha asked. "I am new to all of this. Is there not a way for us to listen to this music so that we can experience what Michael does? Then we can all help in this way."

She finished wrapping Michael's arm and patted his shoulder. "You'll be fine but keep this clean."

"They burned down the trees that held the security cameras at my cabin. Those camera feeds are what made the system go live. It went down before we got back to L.A. No more music." Ava shook her head. "It's okay though. That's what Laer and the FBI were after, and so they have no reason to come after me and Sense Labs anymore." Saying it out loud didn't make her feel any better.

"Then why did someone plant a bomb, meant quite clearly for you, at the airfield?" Manisha asked. "After the trees burned?"

"Good point," Ava said. "The fire was started well before we landed. They had to have known Seneca was down by then. Rys, any thoughts on how to get Seneca working again? It would be useful right about now."

"I have a few ideas, but I'll need some help." Rys turned to Nathan. "Any chance I could use some of your programming skills tomorrow? Or today, I guess."

He pointed to the clock on the wall. It read just past three in the morning.

"Anything you need," Nathan answered.

Ava nodded. "While you guys work on that, Michael and I will do what we can from here. Lisa, are you good handling the FBI and helping arrange the questioning? We also need to know any information they have on Zek and his whereabouts."

"My office is on it," Lisa said. "I'll be more help after some sleep." She put her hand to her mouth to cover a yawn and let out a small moan. Manisha rushed to her side.

Ava's mouth widened into a sympathetic yawn. "On that cue," she said. "Why don't we all get some sleep. We've got a lot to accomplish today and only a few hours until sunrise."

Heads nodded around the table. "Anything for me?" Sarah asked.

"Rys and Nathan will need your research and data experience so stick with them. We might need you later if we get enough data to track Zek, but the music is priority until it's back on."

"Got it, boss," Sarah said.

Ava hugged each of her team as they filed indoors to get some rest. Never had it seemed so genuine that they were truly her family.

"I could use a walk," Nathan said. He was the last to stand. "Why don't you join me? There's something else you need to know."

Chapter 32

Ava had planned a nice long shower with no one to interrupt her thoughts, but it would have to wait. Who knew where she would have been without Nathan's help the week before and earlier that day?

She trailed behind him as he moved away from the house and across the wide lawn. They came to a row of hedges with a bright red, wooden, double gate nestled inside. Ava smiled, her energy partially restored when she realized a hidden Japanese garden lay beyond the boxwoods and what she then recognized as a spirit gate.

He invited her in with a swoop of his hand.

"This is amazing," she said. Soft, spongy hills of grass interspersed with strong blocks of granite sat among various trees and shrubs. As she moved deeper into the garden, she found order and chaos at every turn. The knots in her gut loosened for the first time since leaving Tony's cabin to take a walk through the woods.

Nathan closed the gate behind him, then led the way along a stone footpath.

"It must take a small army to manage this place," she said. Lotus and lily pads on the surface of the lower pond were just past flowering and lingered as if tired in the lazy flow of the water.

"The efficiency of the design creates a mostly self-sustaining environment. A little bit of forethought goes a long way." He wound them through a few small terraces and toward a footbridge over a stream that fed the pond.

Ava stopped and inhaled the nearby jasmine. The burbling waterfall lulled her eyes closed. The screech of a gecko brought her back. "That's why you're a billionaire, right?"

"That's just luck and hard work. Creating this took far more effort." He laughed. There was no hesitation, no embarrassment in his laugh, but no pride either.

"You designed this?" She hoped he wasn't offended by the shock in her voice.

"Do you remember something I told you when we were at the beach cottage? It concerned my relationship to you."

"We talked quite a bit. Want to give me some context?" Ava hadn't felt this self-conscious in a long time. Nathan was difficult enough to read in normal times. Now he was impenetrable.

"I said that I exist to protect who you are. Do you remember?"

"I do," she answered slowly. "It sounded odd at the time, but you have to admit you're not exactly a normal guy." Her playful smile probed his intentions without words.

He didn't continue. His gray eyes sparkling silver in the glow of lanterns fixed on hers. Waiting for something.

Her smile dropped when she caught on. "You're one of them. A protector."

He nodded and continued deeper into the garden.

She stood in place. "Why didn't you tell the others? Why didn't you tell me?"

"Our small network survived thousands of years by not revealing our identities. Tony was right. You aren't of age yet and haven't been tested. I couldn't risk it."

She jogged to catch up, grabbed his arm, and moved in front of him. "Risk what?"

"Zek filled you in on most of it. Granted he only set things in motion. He didn't create many of the rules we abide by today. They were developed over time out of need, as any society creates laws and rules. We have been at risk since day one. Those working against us are nearly all puppets like Drew and Tim, drawn to the illusion of power. Those who hold the strings remain cloaked in anonymity, but I believe you are helping change that."

"Slow down. What do you mean Zek only set things in motion?" Ava thought back to what she had told the group earlier. She was positive she left out Zek's true identity.

"It's obvious he is here for his third and final intervention. You didn't have to tell me that." He reached the edge of the upper pond and sat down in the grass next to it. He patted the area beside him. "Join me."

Ava thought of Zek and their encounter with the now massacred wolves, then saw details in her mind's eye of their night together. She sat down next to Nathan and willed herself to hold it together.

Nathan rested his hand on hers. "It's not fair that this is how you are learning of the Ananzeti and your place among us. Your path requires something different from our usual order."

"You said I'm changing something, but I haven't done anything. It's like I'm locked in a maze, and someone turned the lights out. Can you help me understand what's happening?" His fingers were warm;

unexpected callouses on his palm rested softly over the scrapes on the top of her hand.

"You're bringing the conflict into the open. They will do everything in their power, which is considerable, to renounce you. But these are different times and Seneca is hard to refute. You created it without knowing who you are and what you are a part of."

"It's gone now and so they, whoever they are, have no reason to keep coming after me."

"On the contrary, you're the first translator they are aware of. It's been strangely quiet since the bomb went off, but it won't last. Especially when we get Seneca working again. I've alerted my Master to get the message through the Ananzeti network. We're still waiting to hear what's happened with Tony."

"Everything happened so fast. If Zek's okay, he must be worried sick. If they have him, I mean I doubt they do, but if they somehow captured him –" She dropped her head in her hands and turned her back to him.

"Ava, this is a lot to take in and you need sleep. Tony is a protector. He knows how to take care of himself. We'll know more in a few hours, but you're no good to anyone like this. Go easy on yourself. You've been through hell today."

Ava swung around and faced Nathan. "I need to do something." She pleaded with her eyes.

"Sometimes patience and lack of action are what's called for. This is why we use thirty as the age of knowing. Believing we can know all the answers and that action is always better than inaction is a fallacy of the Western world and youth. It is not wrong. It is simply out of balance. Balance is the secret to unlocking your fourth-dimension powers. The wisdom to know which end of an extreme is proper for the given time. The balance between order and chaos."

"I thought it was space and time. The ability to manipulate them."

"Did I say something different?" he asked.

A surge of adrenaline shot through her. "It's not absolute!"

"Yes. Your truth, any truth, is not time bound. What may be your truth today, may not be tomorrow as you bring in new information or experience different situations. We as humans reject most new information if it doesn't fit with what we believe. That's why computers are such amazing helpmeets. Seneca creates music based on the here and now. It needs the live feed to do so. Then it provides the feedback loop for listeners to sense the truth without all the background noise of their past experiences."

The adrenaline didn't last. She was beyond exhausted. She squinted and tried to register his words.

"Do you know why I invested in your company?" Nathan asked.

She shook her head.

"I was not aware of your place in all this, in case you were curious. We each only have one incoming and one outgoing link to another translator or protector, and mine is in Japan. Thus, the garden." He gestured to the beauty surrounding them.

"I thought you invested so that I could make you lots more money." She smiled halfheartedly.

"That's a given with any investment I make."

"There's no way you could be on the boards of all

of your investments though. Why Sense Labs?"

"We start protector training at thirty if we pass the initial tests. I have what you would call a very well-honed intuition, similar to what Michael developed listening to Seneca. I knew there was something special about you and what you were building, regardless of who your family is. When I dug deeper, I learned about your parents."

"Was," she said. "I'm the last one."

He nodded; a touch of sadness brushed his eyes. "The sense doesn't say what. You simply follow it and see where it leads. Like a light in a darkened maze," he said with a faint smile.

"What did it tell you about Tim and Rhonda? And Drew for that matter?"

"I never entertained the thought any of this would happen. I only sensed you needed an ally on the board."

"We didn't get to the truth exercise with you in the board meeting." She struggled to mentally replay the scene until it clicked. "You were the one who changed the subject. Clever. What would you have revealed if I asked you what your deepest desire was?"

"To fulfill my purpose."

"Like Rhonda," she said. "And your purpose is?"

"To protect the knowledge and the translators."

"That may have sounded odd in the board meeting."

"It was necessary at the time to put Tim at ease and not have to do any of my own explaining. His deception was obvious to me from the minute we met. Why he feels the need to hide today is a perfect illustration of a former truth hiding current truth. He may have to endure some difficult conversations, but he won't be put to death or jailed for loving another man. And, he wouldn't have betrayed you if he lived his life openly."

"Hopefully," she said. "So did you bring me back here to tell me to stand down and let things happen without interference?"

"I felt it was time you knew who I am and why I'm protecting you. Plus, you were spinning your wheels a bit and I can save you a lot of time." He flashed a grin at her.

"Time with what? Are we back to fourth dimension talk?"

"My Master in Japan will continue alerting the chain so that all of the protectors know what is happening. Anything you or I do will be far better with their help."

"Your Master? How does that work?"

"O. The Ananzeti network multiplies through pairs. Each protector must train a new one."

"O what?"

"O is my Master's name," he answered. "From what we know about Zek's initial creation plan, he set conditions that would have souls face the duality conflict at the most basic of levels by simply existing. We must balance our inner selves to find peace in a never-ending cycle of conflict between two extremes. The true brilliance, our human gift, is the ability to create through duality. We can create new life from the duality of male and female. Our world is unique in this way. We experience the joy of creation without needing to understand it."

"Masculine versus feminine. You know a lot of people would prefer if men and women were the same."

"Laer's most successful move has been to use that

conflict to separate us and go toward chaos. It's worked quite well so far."

Ava found the discussion energizing her. She felt herself rise above the chaos of the previous days. "Now we're getting somewhere. How do they do it and how do we stop them?"

Nathan flicked imaginary dust from his slacks. "Gosh, you think we may have considered that at some point in the past millennium."

Ava cringed. "Sarcasm noted. What I meant is how can Seneca and I help?"

"I believe adding feeds from the other translators and protectors will make Seneca more powerful once we get it working again. That the feeds will, in fact, make Seneca work again."

They stood and walked over a small bridge to an island in the lower pond where he stopped. He faced her and reached out to hold both of her elbows. "Then someone has to release it to the world in a way that won't create mass upheaval. Someone meaning you. You're already in the spotlight. You know more about Seneca than anyone. It has to be you."

She shook her head. "Zek needs to do it. I've already failed miserably. It's…we are his creation after all." She pulled away from Nathan's grip and squatted down at the edge of the grass to put her hand in the water.

Nathan knelt beside her and picked up small stones. He skipped them in lazy arcs over the surface.

"Where is he?" she asked quietly.

"Why hast thou forsaken us?"

"Yeah, something like that," she said with a sigh. "Nathan, thank you for telling me more. I feel a bit less crazy and a bit more prepared for what lies ahead. Not good, but not completely hopeless. I have a million other questions that can wait for later."

She stood. "I'm going to get a couple of hours of sleep. Can you start the process of connecting the others' feeds to Seneca? We can get the rest of the plan together when we're all a little fresher."

"Already in the works," He held up his phone. Japanese characters wove through English letters in text messages projected on the screen. "Please don't thank me. We're in this together."

She watched him skip rocks for a few minutes. Flames from nearby torches danced in the pond's reflection.

Chapter 33

Ava burrowed under the soft white down comforter covering the king-sized bed. There were no alerts to check on her phone. She was getting used to not being always "on." She smiled and sat up.

Two shiny black Great Danes lumbered in the grass outside her patio door. The clock on the nightstand read a quarter to ten. She massaged her temples. It would take more than a couple of aspirin to kill the pounding pressure in her skull. But first, coffee.

She found Darren pouring from a steaming pot in the kitchen. "Is everyone still asleep?" she asked.

"You take milk, right?" He grabbed a fresh mug from a cabinet.

She nodded.

He set the steaming mug in front of her after filling it. "They're all up and out of here. I'll show you to Nathan's office when you're ready. Michael is waiting for you there." He continued to slowly sip his drink while she inhaled hers and helped herself to another.

"Give me ten minutes. I'll meet you back here," she said.

"Dr. Bhandari," he started then shook his head. "I mean, Manisha, left you some clothes in the living room. See you in a few." He walked out the back door with his coffee.

Ava returned to the bedroom with her name written on a post-it note stuck to the door. For such a beautiful, well-appointed home, the last-minute solution was helpful but didn't fit in. "You're not the only one who's out of place these days," she said to the purple strip of paper.

All Manisha left her was a simple sundress, no bra needed. Ava never wore dresses. She took a quick shower and put it on. It was going to be a weird day.

Darren was still on the back patio when Ava went to find him. She poked her head through the door. "Ready?"

He pointed to the far end of the yard. "What did you think of the garden?"

Her eyes followed his arm to what appeared in the sunlight to be an acre of overgrowth. "I guess you see everything that happens here," she told him. "Looks different in the light."

"Everything Nathan does has a purpose. Did he tell you he designed and built everything in that garden himself?"

"He told me about the design, but I never would have guessed he did the heavy lifting too." He was full of surprises, she thought.

Darren laughed. "Other than setting the largest stones, he placed every single element in that garden by hand. No power tools. The patience it took was awe-inspiring. I never could have done it."

"Me neither." She peered past Darren. What sort of man, with or without the kind of money Nathan had at his disposal, dug up his backyard in L.A. and put thousands of stones together to form two ponds, a waterfall, footbridge, walkways, and hundreds of species of exotic plants?

****

Michael paced a long, glass walled hallway while talking on his phone. Ava nodded to him and started to move around him to go inside Nathan's office.

He grabbed her arm and finished his call. Then he nodded toward the door. "We have a livestream set up to the Sense Labs office. I think the team will expect to hear something from you when you walk in."

"Oh shit. I hadn't even thought about everyone being at work," she answered. "Thanks for the heads up. I'll tell them we're going forward with the original plan." She turned back toward the door.

"Are we?"

"Why wouldn't we? Rys and Nathan will get the music back on." Her hand hovered over the door handle.

"Assuming they can get Seneca running again, there's also the issue of our very tiny cash balance. Without funding, there's no way to continue. Even if you and Nathan decide to fund it, you still need board approval and we haven't sorted out Drew's board seat yet. Tim shook everyone up with his antics."

"Let the others worry about the music. I have a plan for funding and the open board seat," she assured him. "Come on, let's get this done so that we can get to work."

"Whatever you say, boss." He followed her through the double doors.

As soon as Ava walked in, the office speakers picked up clapping and cheering from the Sense Labs employees who were dialed in. It was the welcome of a hero, not a failure. She smiled back at Michael as if to say, "it's all good." She waved to the camera.

"Nice wardrobe change, boss," one of the senior

developers yelled out when the applause started to die down. She looked down at the colorful sundress and shook her head. Still the same old crew.

"Pipe down," she yelled back. "Vacation's over, people. We've got work to do." All they needed to know was that their jobs were safe, and she was in control of things.

"Since I have your attention, I want to announce a promotion as well as our funding plans. Everyone, give a warm congratulations to our new Chief Operating Officer, Michael Hall."

Michael's head whipped to face Ava while the rest of his body froze. The team noise started back up and this time she heard drumrolls on office desks.

"Ava, don't you think the board should weigh in on the promotion?" Michael asked once the livestream was cut.

"The board's job is to hire and fire the CEO if she isn't meeting her fiduciary duties to shareholders and other stakeholders. It's not to run the company," she said. "We need to run the numbers on the plan I just presented. Depending on when we get the music turned back on, I want to ramp up user adoption. That means we need to train far more translators."

"Translators? Are these the coaches?" he asked. "What are we telling the board?"

"Nathan will fund a simple bridge loan until all this is sorted out." She stopped. "Michael, we can't afford to be indecisive right now. I don't know what's coming, but I know if we can get Seneca out there, if we can get people to really listen, then maybe we have a shot at turning this thing around. I can't do it without you. Seneca founders get to appoint Drew's replacement to the Board. I'm appointing you. We'll have the majority anyway. Tim may oppose it, but Rhonda plays the game differently. She won't show us her hand on this one."

"Do we still think it's Rhonda?"

"The Laer operative? Let's just say I wouldn't bet against her at this point. We have more important things to cover today. I need you to decide how much cash we need for the next six months and work with Lisa on the paperwork." She walked around the office as she talked. It was heavy on equipment but sparse on decoration.

"I set you up a new laptop. Rys and Nathan took the one you brought back to get the code." Michael pointed to a sleek black notebook charging on a standing desk against the far wall.

"Why didn't I make you COO last year?" she muttered. "None of this would have ever happened."

"I haven't accepted yet," he said. "All 'this' happened because the board pressured you to hire Drew. I guess we know why now."

"It would have happened regardless of whether it was Drew or someone else. Of course you're accepting. Write yourself a contract like Drew's with the same compensation and agreements so I can sign it. Good?" Ava steadied her eyes on Michael's.

"Ava, he was way overpaid. I didn't want to say anything before, but I can't accept that much when we're so low on funds."

"That's why you're more than worth it. You'll put the company goals ahead of your personal ones. Why don't we double your equity and bonus potential and pull back on the salary guarantee by half? Will that make you feel better?" she asked.

"You know the equity and bonus are worth way more than the salary cut, right?"

"Only if you do a great job," she said with a wink. "Now go take a break or something. I need a few minutes before meetings start."

She picked up the phone and called Tony's number, pleading softly for him to pick up. It went straight to voicemail. She left the cell number Darren had given her the night before, just in case.

Not knowing Tony or Zek's whereabouts made it nearly impossible to focus. She would have to wait until dinner with the others that night to find out what they had learned.

Chapter 34

Rhonda stalked across a raised server room floor. The black machines glowed blue behind their glass barriers and formed concentric circles around a large control center. Inside the control center were antigravity gaming chairs all facing the main attraction, a glass vestibule filled with water.

A suspended body floated within.

She stopped in front of the liquid encasement and rapped on it with her knuckle.

"You're not where your mind thinks, apprentice," she said. A few taps on a screen attached to the glass and Zek opened his eyes.

"Ah, there you are! I've activated your thought sense along with your sight. You won't be able to hear or speak properly with all this primitive technology. It's the best I could do to control your senses on this sad little planet." She snorted.

Zek stared, motionless inside the cylinder. A mask covered his mouth and nose. Hoses and cords extended from it and other parts of his body. He projected a thought. *"Who are you?"*

"I'm surprised you showed up as a man," she thought projected back. *"They're so passé here. Now. An intelligent woman who is unafraid of her power would have been a smarter choice. The humans still underestimate them so they can do much, undetected."* She cackled out loud.

"You should not be interfering here," Zek thought. *"This is a Creation Guild world."*

"Ah, but is it?" She pressed her nose to the glass. *"Creation Guild worlds are built using the Laer platform. This is just a rogue and sad little planetary system built by an arrogant apprentice. Not a very talented one, I might add."*

"What do you want?" His bright eyes lit the clear water blue.

"What I want is to get off this awful little planet. What I need is to restore the balance of soul ascension and descension through the multiverse that you are attempting to destroy with your hubris." She slapped the glass as if it were his face.

Her violent, low dimensional reaction told Zek she had spent much time on the human world. Had she grown weak? A ray of hope shone through his liquid prison.

"Hubris," he responded. *"At what? Believing I could restore the number of creators? That I could expand the Network? Or is it that you believe the multiverse is a static existence?"*

"The only way to prevent its decay, our ultimate demise, is to seek balance. You know this. Why must I explain to you why we cannot allow this expansion you so desperately seek?"

"It is not I that seek expansion for my own ends, it is the multiverse itself," Zek projected. *"It is every molecule, every soul, every being, planet, star. We do not make the rules, nor do we control them. We flow with all of the elements that surround us. Creators guide them to a purpose larger than themselves. We must expand, as that is the way our souls, our very*

existence, were created."

"Spare me the expansionist bullshit," Rhonda thought. *"I've heard too much of it from your kind."* She stood straight, stared into Zek's eyes. *"Possibly the balance lies between you and me, between our opposite interpretations of how to exist in this reality. Without you, what would I be? Without me, well, you wouldn't be here now at all, would you?"*

New, unconscious thoughts added to their conversation. Rhonda turned to a moving figure.

"The code works with the new input data."

The human male approached the glass holding a laptop. He was smaller than Rhonda. Behind his mass of curly hair, Zek could sense the man's thought fragments compete for attention.

He approached the glass. *So, this is the apprentice Ava is in love with.*

I need to check the load balancing on the game servers.

What a bunch of crackpots. At least I have funding for building something interesting with Seneca.

I wonder if he knows who I am?

How is Ava his chosen agent if she's so easy to dupe? Stupid.

"Fantastic," Rhonda said. "You've been away from the others for too long. Return to the house."

"Yes, I have," the man said. "I'll see you tomorrow." He turned sharply and left the area. His thoughts followed him out of the room.

"What will you do with her system?" Zek thought to Rhonda.

"You could read those thoughts? Such chaotic minds these humans possess. You are as infected as all

of them. We will be happy to be rid of you." Rhonda stared at him through the glass.

Zek had spent the entire lifespan of the human species learning how to understand their cacophony of thoughts. The code, his code, that Ava's machine interpreted did the simple work of guiding humans to which thoughts were important. Those that would lead them to the next dimension. Where would Rhonda's code lead?

"You will never get away with it," Zek projected. *"My guild elders are aware of what your guild has been doing,"*

"Your elders are clueless. We control the void, and we control ascensions. We allow you to believe you are creating new worlds, yet they are the worlds we want you to create."

"With your rigs? The ones built to protect creators from dangers of the void? The void isn't dangerous to those who are trained, is it? At least not until your guild made it so."

Rhonda pressed against the glass. *"What would you know about that, apprentice?"*

Zek had known there was something strange about the creation rigs. He had learned very early that he could enter the void and return. When he asked the masters why it was forbidden, they would only tell him it was for his protection.

Later, after he gained approval to take the risk of creating without his rig, the other creators treated him as one whose fate was sealed. They waited for the final time he entered the void, never to return, like the others long before him. Long before Laer's creation rigs.

"I can enter. I can return. I have not been lost."

"Yes, we are aware." Rhonda scoffed. *"It is I who did not find and stop you in time. It is I who must complete my mission and restore my standing as a Laer master. Soon, all will be put to order."*

Zek could only look into the room beyond the glass chamber. His body couldn't react to Rhonda's words. They sank within him. What did she mean?

Rhonda giggled. "Oh, you sweet, naïve apprentice. You still don't get it," she spoke aloud.

As her lips moved, dread settled among Zek's thoughts, clouding them like smoke on a river. He knew he couldn't trust what they told him. He made his mind go blank, the way he did to navigate the void. *"Tell me,"* he projected.

Rhonda backed away. *"Mind tricks won't work on you, will they?"* She sighed. *"Don't worry. We are experts at this. How many thousands of your kind did we destroy in the void so long ago? You cannot escape your fate, just as I will not escape mine when the multiverse experiences its final decay. The difference is, Laer will stop the expansion once and for all. We will stop the decay. We will exist as we are into eternity."*

Like a human, he didn't want to accept the truth that he knew, that Rhonda shared. He closed his eyes. So many souls lost to the void, rather taken, by members of the guild she served. When he opened his eyes, the water glowed brighter.

"You've been a challenge, apprentice, but I have grown tired of you." Rhonda tapped on the control pad.

Zek's mind went dark. The water went a deep, dark blue.

Chapter 35

At eight sharp, Nathan met Ava on the back lawn, his straw-colored hair dancing about in the windstorm created by the helicopter. They were nearly to the pool before Ava could hear what he was trying to tell her.

"Here." He held out a small phone. "You can speak with him." The helicopter lifted off.

"You found Zek?" She grabbed his arm.

"No, no. It's Tony and Renata. They're fine. They had to evacuate until the fire was brought under control. There's time to call him back before dinner."

She shook her head. "I wouldn't know what to say right now. I'm still in shock over the past few days. Also, I hate to admit this, but I'm still trying to deal with the fact that he knew about my parents. He knew more and never told me."

She took Nathan's arm and put the phone back in his hand. It was enough to know Tony was safe. "Why don't we start dinner first? I want to hear everything you guys found out today."

Nathan's face clouded over. "There are some things Tony needs to tell you, but it can wait until you're ready."

"Thank you." She paused, and in a more upbeat tone said, "I promoted Michael to COO today and I'm appointing him to the open seat on the board."

His expression blanked out like a rebooted computer before a wide grin spread across his face.

"That's great news about Michael. Tonight will be a celebration." He gave her a quick hug. "I also have some news to share."

"Can't wait," she said.

"Glad you could join us," Rys said when they made it to the table. Dinner had arrived and delectable smells quickened Ava's step.

"Did you leave any for us?" she asked.

Rys dipped the last piece of lobster from his plate into the garlic butter in front of him. Far cry from the pizza he typically ordered about this time at night.

Darren directed the chef to set fresh steaming tails in front of her and Nathan. "You made it just in time."

Nathan picked up his wine glass. "I hear we have something to toast tonight."

Ava hadn't waited. Lunch was a distant memory. She swallowed hard, picked up her water, and stood to face Michael. "Everyone, meet the new Chief Operating Officer of Sense Labs." She raised her glass. "Congratulations, Michael. You've earned this."

A chorus of congratulations went up around the table and glasses clinked in the cool air.

"Can we move on to our findings today?" Rys asked through the chatter.

"I can't wait to hear," Ava answered with a smile. "When can we get Seneca back on? Does anyone have news about Zek?" She stopped herself.

"I was going to start with the music," Rys said. "We think we isolated what's missing and got everything wired up out here to test." He pointed to some of the speakers concealed in the trees and behind rocks.

"Why not test in the office where it's set up?"

Rys shot her an 'if you would let me finish' look. The chef replaced his empty plate with a huge slice of carrot cake. "Call it ambiance. I'll go back inside after this is gone and see if it works."

"Any hints on what you guys did?" Ava asked.

Rys miraculously ingested a third of the cake in one bite. Maybe he would pull off a similar miracle with Seneca.

"No jumping ahead," Sarah said. "Let's see if it works first."

"Anyone want to take a swim while we wait?" Manisha asked. "That whole stomach cramps thing is an old wives' tale."

"I'm done," Lisa said. "Let's go."

Rys polished off his cake. He, Nathan, and Sarah headed for the back door while Lisa and Manisha disappeared into the small pool house to change. The rest finished their dinner in silence, ears perked for any sound that may come from the speakers hidden throughout the landscape. The distant hum of traffic provided background noise.

Ava slipped quietly from the table and into a black one-piece suit she found hanging in the pool house. She made it back out and found Lisa, Sarah, and Michael in the water.

"Oh, wow," she said. "This is exactly what I needed. I missed the water."

Manisha swam up beside her. "Where else do you get full body exercise and complete disconnection from the digital world?" Someone's cell phone rang from a chaise lounge and they both laughed.

Lisa joined their conversation. "I feel like a new person. Everything is so sore, I felt muscles I didn't know existed today."

Michael had finished dinner and lingered at the shallow end of the pool.

"Seriously Michael, quit playing shy. We won't bite," Lisa yelled. After a bit more coaxing, he dog paddled their way. Lisa and Manisha splashed him mercilessly once he made it over.

Ava tread water and tried unsuccessfully to keep up with the banter as the minutes ticked by. Everything depended on them getting Seneca working again.

Chapter 36

Nathan watched the horseplay in the pool from a wall of monitors in his office. Lisa was doing everything she could to keep the feds from taking Ava into custody, but they would eventually get their way. Ava needed rest and recuperation with people she could trust before that time came.

As the others swam, Rys typed while Sarah and Nathan helped him connect gear and answer questions. "Those last feeds aren't helping. I think we should just scrap them," Rys said after a dozen tries. "It was working before we added them."

"Trust me," Nathan said. "Give it a few more minutes. Seneca will catch on."

"Found it!" Sarah pointed to her monitor and typed some new commands. "They were imported on a tiny delay. Run it again, Rys."

"Still not working," Rys said. "We should cut those feeds. Seneca doesn't need them to work."

"May I?" Nathan pointed to the chair Rys was in.

"It's your rodeo." Rys stood and took Nathan's place by the monitors. He crossed his arms.

"There you are," Nathan said to the monitor a few minutes later. He deleted and replaced a few lines of code and passed the keyboard back to Rys. "You want to do the honors?"

Rys cracked his knuckles and popped open a fresh beer. "Now for the finale." He pressed one key. It echoed in the silence. He held it, unmoving, as the seconds ticked by.

The room vibrated as if coming alive, then the quiet was replaced by a long, languorous series of notes accompanied by an androgynous voice speaking indecipherable words.

"This doesn't sound like what I heard in the boardroom," Nathan said. "Did it always have a voice?"

Sarah's jaw dropped and eyes grew wide, but not a sound slipped through her parted lips.

Rys pulled up various screens, fingers flying.

"It didn't even sound like this earlier today," Rys said with a frown. "The important question is, does it work? Is it the same effect? The only thing we changed were the new feeds. Should we put it on the outside speakers and let the others hear?" he asked Nathan.

Nathan was already messing with dials. A few moments later Seneca began playing its new style of music on the patio.

Rys and Sarah ran through the house and out the back door. The group in the pool had quit talking when it started.

Ava couldn't understand the words Seneca spoke, but she felt them. Things had changed. Ava had changed. More change was on the way. A wave of queasiness washed over her and she swallowed it down.

Finally, she broke the silence. "How did you do it and why is it so different?" She kept her voice steady so as not to ruin Rys' moment of triumph.

"I've toyed with changing the camera feed quite a bit the past month. Nothing worked. I had a hunch that it has more to do with you than the cameras at your cabin, and so I connected to Nathan's camera feeds, here. I got it working the same as before, but Nathan wanted to add some new feeds. He won't tell me what they are or where they're from. This is the first time I've heard that voice."

"Can anyone tell what it's saying?" Lisa swam closer to Ava and grabbed the edge of the pool.

Michael cocked his head. "Seneca is finding her voice," he said with a hint of a smile.

"Her?" Rys raised an eyebrow. "Seneca was a dude."

"Her music entices the truth without force. I've always associated the feeling I get with a female energy, so yes, Seneca is a she to me."

The group listened a few more minutes without speaking. Nathan interrupted the reverie. "I hate to break up this party, but now that Seneca is working again, can we get back to saving the world?"

"Are all billionaires so melodramatic?" Sarah asked with a wry grin.

"Guaranteed." He winked at her. "Rys, back to the system. If Seneca is changing, where is it, or she, headed and how do we use it to help solve Zek's problem with Laer? The only way to get out of this intact is to make Earth successful. We need as many people as possible to internalize the music. The way Michael has."

"Tell us more about translators and protectors. What does that mean? Could they help?" Manisha called out.

Ava lifted out of the pool in one motion and sat at the edge next to where Rys and Nathan stood by the limestone lip. "Tony didn't get that far and Zek didn't have time to explain everything on the plane. I know there are more of us."

She caught Nathan's eye and the faint shake of his head. "The translation is of messages left in the Earth by the apprentice during his other two interventions. If Tony is any indication, the protectors live in those areas. He seemed to indicate that being in a watershed was important."

"Now that you built a translation intelligence machine, all of this is coming to a head," Lisa said. "We better get clear on exactly what you're translating and how you communicate the message, or else we end up with many more Drew and Tim types than we do Nathan and Michael."

"How diluted is the effect if you video someone speaking with Seneca playing a recording in the background? Like a guided meditation." Manisha asked quietly. She floated on her back in the deep end without moving.

Where is she going with this, Ava wondered.

"With the new sound, I don't know for certain," Sarah answered. "It's probably similar to the effects of the original. Recordings are less powerful but more palatable."

"The plan was to use coaches to guide people through the experience so we don't create a bigger problem than we already have, yes?" Manisha continued.

Ava nodded. She had a bad feeling she knew exactly where it was going.

"I have this friend. A doctor. He does all these silly parody videos about working in hospitals and with medical professionals. I don't recommend using his style but starting a company video channel to ease people into Seneca, introduce them, could help get the message out faster. It can help identify new coaches as well." Manisha lifted her head and tread water.

Nathan turned to Ava. "You already have a big following."

It didn't seem fair that he could remain a recluse while recommending she put herself out there to be ridiculed. Michael nodded at her as well. She didn't need them to tell her it was the right path. Seneca let it be known through the music. It didn't make the fact any easier to stomach.

"Say we do start some kind of video series with Ava easing people into listening to Seneca," Sarah began. "Couldn't our enemies take the music and use it for their truth serum without the need to steal it or get a license? We would have no way to stop them."

"What is the harm in people telling the truth?" Michael asked.

"Did you notice they were wearing headsets like pilots? It's easy enough to shut out the sounds you don't want and keep the ones you do," Sarah answered.

"So?" Lisa shrugged.

"Imagine one person compelled to truth while another is deaf to it. Now imagine this is the psychopaths, the sociopaths, the narcissists who have risen to power and they use that truth against us," Sarah answered.

"Balance," Michael said. "The way through this dimension isn't one extreme or the other. It's balance. Through the middle. We have to allow them the same power we ourselves access."

A crescendo in the music startled Ava. Michael's observation was an important one. Even Seneca thought so.

"It still won't be enough," she said. "We need people who internalize the live music. Lots of them. And fast. What else can we do?"

Manisha swam toward Ava and Nathan. "Our wealthy friends and acquaintances. People of influence and power. We need to determine who will be with us and who will be against us. We can start with a series of dinner parties for those we believe are on our side. They will help spread the music and Ava's videos faster than we can alone. Michael can put together a Seneca training program. He knows it best." Her dark eyes glinted in the moonlight.

"It would be the first time I've been convinced to entertain," Nathan said. "We can host the first in two weeks."

The more Ava thought through the doctor's ideas, the more she appreciated Nathan's decision to work with her. Sometimes all a wayward soul needs is a purpose big enough and people who share that purpose surrounding them. History loves to talk about the individual hero who beats all odds or perseveres through challenges, but it takes many people to alter the course of history.

She glanced around at the people surrounding her. A feeling of peace erased her doubts about putting herself on the front line of what could be the war of all wars. The war for souls. She was not alone in the fight.

"Well, who knows anything about this social video stuff?" Ava asked. Heads shook around the pool. She followed Nathan's eyes to Darren who stood off to the side scanning the yard at brief intervals.

"Darren, any thoughts?" Nathan called out. He

turned back to the group. "Chef D here has nearly a million followers."

"Over a million," Darren said still watching the yard. "Happy to show you the ropes, Ava. We can kick off your series with a guest spot on Chef D and the Sousies tomorrow."

Lisa giggled from the deep end. "How did I miss that? I love your show! You're nothing like Chef D with all his practical jokes."

Darren flashed her a mischievous grin. "I'm on my best behavior around the boss."

The lawyer blushed. Nothing like the courtroom persona she normally showed. More evidence of Seneca working?

"Nathan and I will work on the party," Manisha said.

"Rys and Sarah can help with the technical end of the videos and training program."

No answer. Ava hadn't seen them leave. "Where are those two?"

"Over here," Sarah's sleepy voice came from under a blanket on a lounge chair. "Sign me up but let me sleep first." The wall clock read half past midnight.

"We could all use a full night's sleep," Ava said. "I'm going to turn in." She pulled her feet out of the water and wrapped a towel around her goose bump covered skin.

****

Ava let the warm water in her huge glass shower run over her. The plan was simple enough. Her feelings about it were not.

Other thoughts nagged at her, most pressing was her uncertainty about Zek and his whereabouts. Rhonda and Tim had gone silent. Not a good sign. Then there was her impending video debut the next day.

Finally, she thought of Rys' disappearance after Seneca turned back on. She tried to find him before her shower but gave up. Did he not agree with the plan, or did he think she was crazy for believing Zek?

She sat down over the drain. Her head dropped into her hands. She wasn't the person they all thought she was. She was just a young, scared orphan with no idea how she went from solitary research scientist to – where was she now? Who was she?

Her head jerked up to a voice that filled the room, infiltrating the confined space of the shower. The pounding in her chest rose to her ears making it difficult to hear. She threw her head back and laughed.

"Seneca, what are you doing on at this hour?"

Lightning shot through her body, forcing her to stand back up. "Seneca, turn speakers off." The music died and took the intruding voice and sensations with it.

What had she been thinking about? It didn't matter. Her body was shutting down after too many long nights. She snuggled into a fluffy white robe and barely made it to the bed before collapsing into deep sleep.

Chapter 37

The water sparkled with the reflection from thousands of tiny lights strung around the pool and back porch. Exotic cars pulled up in the front drive and a third helicopter touched down in the back to form a perfect row of privilege.

Ava paced in Nathan's office while she responded to comments on her new show Sound of Truth. The title was Darren's idea.

She scrolled through the ever-growing responses, stopping occasionally to send a direct message. It was always the same message. A personal invite to a live coaching session. Michael could host five per day in addition to training new coaches. Lisa suggested they start holding them at local stadiums after they maxed out capacity in the hotel ballroom the company rented. Even at this rate of adoption, it would be months before they hit numbers large enough to make a difference.

The lack of movement from the other side loomed in the back of Ava's mind. The lack of knowing who all comprised "the other side" had made sleep elusive.

Nathan walked in and leaned against the door. "Are you ready?"

Ava's gaze glided briefly over the classic black tuxedo jacket that hugged his broad shoulders. Lisa had suggested a formal event given the seriousness and attention to detail they planned to ask of their guests. Ava grinned when her gaze made it to Nathan's bright red Pumas. She looked back out the window.

She had no idea what she would say to all the people of money and influence gathering on the lawn, but if the videos were any indication, the words would flow through her when Seneca turned on.

Ava motioned to a young woman by the pool. "You didn't tell me she would be here." The former queen of all pop stars skulked along the patio holding a drink in one hand and a phone in the other. They both watched as she screamed and threw the phone in the pool. Some of the guests turned and gawked, but most seemed unruffled by the unfolding drama and continued drinking their wine.

"It's waterproof," Nathan said. He stood by Ava at the window.

"What?"

"Her phone. She does that."

"You live in a very different Los Angeles than I do," Ava said. "Will she be O.K.?"

Nathan's arm circled her shoulders. "She will be once she works with Seneca. She's perfectly fine, but like many big stars, she's a people pleaser and has too many competing voices around her and in her head that want attention. She can't hear her own voice anymore."

"Well, there's no time like the present for her to listen." Ava pulled away from him.

"But, Nathan, I need to talk to you about something." She had confirmed her suspicions that morning.

"Do we need to hold off on the presentation?" He took out his phone. "I can have Lisa stall."

She spotted Darren and Lisa talking by one of the cocktail tables scattered around the pool. Their fingers were intertwined. Ava smiled. At least someone was finding time for normal life during all this. "No, it can wait until the party's over." It was probably better to give him the news when he wasn't about to speak in front of a large group.

A pool net delivered the unharmed phone back into the singer's hands. She typed on it, still dripping, oblivious to the live people milling about.

"It looks like everyone we expected is here," Nathan said. "Shall we get started? I'll introduce you after welcoming our guests."

Fire rose in Ava's belly and a whoosh filled her ears. She focused on her breath and sucked in deeply. "Okay, Nathan." She grabbed his arm. "I feel good about where things are headed."

He kissed her lightly on the forehead, pulled away with a wink and walked out to the microphone set up on the patio above the pool. Conversations died down. All eyes were on him.

Ava checked the readout on her phone one last time to make sure Seneca was ready for her entrance.

****

The soft, classical music stopped. "Ladies and gentlemen, friends, confidants, thank you for accepting my invitation to join us for dinner tonight."

Nathan stood on the deck above the guests who sipped cocktails and picked at the food being passed by waiters on the lawn. The entire staff was made of Seneca trained individuals. They served a dual purpose of seeing to the guests' comfort and monitoring their reactions.

Ava moved toward the microphone and waited for her cue.

"If you haven't had the pleasure of meeting the immensely talented Ava Lawson, please allow me to introduce you," Nathan said.

A polite round of applause quieted the last of the conversation on the lawn and patio.

"Ava is the founder and CEO of a company that I have the privilege of being both an investor and board member. You may have heard of her and Sense Labs."

Laughter rippled through the crisp California air. It was a group that understood public criticism all too well. She was the current meal of the week in the press and tabloids.

Ava smiled and walked to the microphone. "Happy to have provided even a fraction of the entertainment as some of you have provided me over the years."

She raised her glass to two A list actors and the fallen pop star.

"Tonight, however, is not about entertaining, fundraising, or even gathering endorsements, though this group could make or break just about anyone. Tonight is about recognizing and sharing the gifts you each possess. Every person here overcame odds, faced harsh criticism, failed many times on their way to success. I'm not here to make you remember the tough times, but they're the ones that tested you. Through your trials and tribulations, you learned the truth about the human spirit, your truth. You shared that truth, whether it was quietly through mentorship and philanthropy, or publicly through books, films, music, or products that helped people find it for themselves. We're still not sure how one of you plans to get it into federal government, but we're rooting for you, Senator." Another trickle of laughter when the token politician took a bow.

"It was never about people buying you, or your story, or some other story you believed. It was about you trusting your story and helping them to discover theirs. So thank you." Ava bowed her head briefly and raised her glass.

"Now that we have recognized your gifts, we would like to encourage you to share them another way. Not to worry, it's not a difficult task. As many of you are likely aware, Sense Labs created a special tool to assist you. A tool that we hope you will use yourself to assist you in sharing all the many special talents you each possess."

"Today's humans have come so far from our ancestors, and the beings that predated them. This marks a new era where the technology we create can extend our reach. Not externally, though some of you in this group are responsible for helping us reach to the stars. But internally. So that we may make use of all the gifts we hold locked inside. This is not some sort of religion, and we will put a stop to anyone attempting to label it as such. This is a movement of the human spirit. But don't take it from me."

She paused and lifted her index finger to cue Rys. "Allow me to introduce you to Seneca." The music began to play throughout the house and grounds.

The voice of Seneca came through clearly now. She counseled the guests in her monotonous, genderless tone. "You must not resist what you hear. Allow your truth to pour forth. Do not fight it. Accept it. Fully."

Language, the invention that propelled the human race into the dominant species, wove through the notes and bars in a soothing, supportive structure designed to assist the listener in finding their voice.

Women in sequined cocktail dresses sank to the lawn. Men in tuxedos dropped on the edges of pool lounges or directly on the flagstone patio.

Lisa rushed to help the pop star who completely broke down. No one can know the demons another is facing, but the team was prepared for any issue that presented itself. Lisa held the young woman as she rocked back and forth. The pretension running rife through the city of angels fell to its knees in Nathan's backyard.

Darren ran into the house. Before Ava could register that something was amiss, a loudspeaker drowned out Seneca.

"Ava Lawson, you are under arrest for the murder of Andrew Hodges." Three black vans tore onto the yard in front of her and skidded to a stop raining grass and dirt on the party guests. Black clad agents, this time with FBI insignia, slid open doors and leapt out of the vans to point weapons at Ava and the security guards.

"You better show me a warrant now," Lisa yelled as she ran toward Ava. "This is not acceptable under our current deal with the FBI."

The first agent out of the van motioned to Ava with his black rifle. "She broke the deal when she started those videos."

"So you need an entire SWAT team to bring in one woman?" Lisa's voice was under control but full of venom. "Don't point a weapon at an unarmed civilian like that or I'll have you put under investigation."

"Ma'am, you need to step out of the way and let us handle this." The agent lowered his weapon but continued to move toward Ava.

Lisa and Nathan stepped between Ava and the commanding officer. Not a single word, tinkle of crystal, or rustle of fine fabric. Seneca was silent as well.

Ava whispered into Lisa's ear. The lawyer's eyes went wide. She looked down at Ava's midsection and back up. Ava nodded.

Lisa faced the agent. "Miss Lawson's current condition requires special care. Given the high-profile nature of this case and the fact that your organization is under scrutiny, we need to speak with your superior officers before you lay a finger on her."

The Senator from the audience stepped onto the veranda. "Gentlemen, ladies, can we take this inside? There's someone who wants to speak to you." He held a cell phone out to the agent in charge. "I recommend doing this in private."

Nathan stood like stone and stared at Ava.

She felt the heat of his eyes on her. Didn't want to face what he and the others must think of her. Ava knew when it happened. Manisha confirmed her suspicion a few hours before the party with a blood test. It was far too late for a morning after pill, and Ava wasn't so sure she would take it if she could. If it was to be, it would be. And it was. Of course, this wasn't how she expected to break the news that she was expecting Zek's child. Her heart raced, but her spirit was calm.

The agent lowered his weapon and motioned to the unit on the lawn to stand down. Lisa led the way through the house to Nathan's office where Ava sank into a deep white sofa.

Chapter 38

House arrest is some kind of cruel joke, Ava thought as she stared outside her bedroom window at the same scene that had greeted her every single day for the past two months. The idea of six more months in this hell brought bile to her throat.

Heavy footsteps on the wood floor outside her door made her cringe.

"My wife said this might be easier to get down." Adrian Cantu, her warden, chef, caretaker, and nemesis walked into her room without knocking and set a tray down on the bed beside her. The dark crew cut reminded her of Drew, but that where the similarities ended. His six-foot frame was all muscle, and his hazel eyes were a close match to hers.

She tried not to inhale the stench of sour Greek yogurt with sickly sweet berries dotting its surface. She didn't bother running to the bathroom like she had in the beginning. The small rubber trashcan that was now her constant companion caught everything.

While Ava retched into the lime green receptacle, Adrian went on. "We have to get you to keep something down, Ava. It's bad enough you're ruining your unborn baby's life with all this legal stuff and your refusal to cooperate. You should work harder to make sure it gets the nutrients it needs. If my wife did what you're doing right now, I would have her watched just like you." He took the tray away and turned to leave.

When he reached the door he added, "You should be ashamed of yourself."

Ava lowered the trashcan. "Fuck you, Adrian," she croaked. "Get me some water."

He shook his head and left the room.

Lisa thought it would be better to get Ava house arrest while the investigation was underway. She thought it was a victory at first. Now Ava understood psychological torture to a new degree. They didn't have to waterboard her or tie her up to get information. They didn't even try to use Seneca. They used the thing that injured most. Her love for her new family, both unborn and found.

Adrian brought in a large bottle of water and some crackers. He put them on her nightstand and sat on the edge of her bed. "I know you think we don't care. But we are bound to protect the American public from all threats, both outside and inside our borders. I don't think you fully contemplate just what your technology has done. People are angry. They're protesting in the streets. They aren't following orders. Just last week they marched on Washington. You've disrupted the law and order we work so hard to maintain."

"And here I thought I was wanted for murder. Maybe if you would let me have any link to the outside world, I could help people like I was doing before."

Part of her house arrest forbid electronic devices and communications of any kind. Adrian wouldn't even bring her newspapers. She was completely cut off.

"Your lawyer can fill you in. She somehow figured out the right person to sweet talk into letting her meet with you. I don't know how, but she'll be here this afternoon."

The fog that made itself at home in Ava's head during her imprisonment lifted a tiny bit. Wait, was it another mind game? Ava kept her face impassive. She wouldn't give him the satisfaction of seeing her hope only to destroy it again.

In the beginning, he had pretended to be her friend. He made promises in an effort to draw information out of her about Seneca. She slipped one time and confirmed that the cameras at the cabin disabled Seneca after they all burned. Adrian hadn't kept his promise to let her speak with Nathan. Ava still hadn't spoken to him since the night of the party.

"Let me know when she's here. Until then, leave me alone." Deadpan, flat. Keep playing the game. "And don't ever sit on my bed again."

"That's sweet, Ava." He patted her knee. He pointed to the trash. "You might want to clean that up now."

She kicked him away.

He stood and sauntered, slowly, deliberately, out of her room.

****

"What is wrong with you people? Don't you take her out for any exercise at all?" Lisa was on the brink of yelling. "Ava, look at me."

Ava made eye contact with her lawyer and friend. She seemed so far away. Their days together at Nathan's a distant memory, enveloped in the haze that clouded all her thoughts.

"She needs to see a doctor. Are you idiots insane?" She turned an accusing stare at Adrian and his latest partner. He had cycled through three of them since Ava was remanded to his custody.

"She can have all the exercise she needs in the back yard. She's the one refusing to leave her room. She won't keep anything down."

Adrian loomed over Lisa and Ava with his arms folded across his chest. "You need to instruct your client to take better care of herself and her unborn child."

Ava watched the scene play out in front of her like a decades old feature film. A little blurry on the edges, but the action was still present.

"We're getting her doctor in here now. You clearly don't know how to take care of her." Lisa pulled out her phone.

Adrian lunged for it and snatched it from her fingers. "I gave you the respect of not searching your belongings. You know electronic devices aren't allowed. You won't get another warning. Take her bag," he said to the other agent.

Lisa put her hands in the air. "Fine. You call the doctor. Manisha Bhandari. Go ahead. The number is saved on my phone."

"Ava has a doctor provided by us. We'll take care of it after you leave," Adrian said.

"Actually, sir." She pointed at the other man. "If you'll reach right inside that bag. Yes, it's okay. It won't bite. Take out that envelope and hand it to Agent Cantu."

He did as he was told. The think manila envelope passed hands.

"This is a court order providing for Ava's medical care and those doctors approved to examine and treat her. You'll find Dr. Bhandari at the top of the list. There is to be no interference or you will be held in contempt. There are also strict guidelines for her daily routine, including walks outdoors. You're of course welcome to accompany her." Lisa smiled.

"We'll see about that," Adrian growled.

"Ava," Lisa said. "I'm still working on getting you released, but we need you strong. Follow the routine. Remember what you set out to do. It's working. We're working. We won't succeed without you, and your baby, healthy and clear headed."

She lifted Ava's chin. "They can't keep the truth from everyone forever."

The fog lifted another layer. Soft edges hardened as Ava searched Lisa's eyes.

"You're not alone," Lisa whispered.

"Is Nathan upset?" Ava asked. "This isn't exactly the ideal time to get pregnant."

Lisa laughed and shook her head. "If I had my phone, I'd show you pictures of the nursery he's building. We know he's not the father, but you couldn't tell by how much he's preparing."

Ava smiled through the wetness in her eyes. "Have you found him yet?" Zek filled most of her thoughts throughout the long days in her bedroom.

"He'll find us when the time is right. You need to concentrate on what you can control right now and let us handle what we can control. Get some sunshine. You have authorization to exercise in Runyon Canyon for an hour a day. Use it. We'll have Manisha here this week for an exam. Okay?"

"I could use some fresh air. This asshat won't even let me walk around the yard." She jerked her thumb at Adrian.

Adrian shrugged. "I told you to use the expensive

equipment you already have inside. It's perfectly fine according to our doctors, but you won't do it."

Lisa raised an eyebrow at him.

"I'll follow the new orders once I confirm with headquarters, but you better not be planning anything," he said.

The other agent snickered.

"Shut up and give her back her bag," Adrian told him. He pointed at Lisa. "Your hour is up."

He missed the slip of paper Lisa pressed into Ava's palm.

Chapter 39

Ava hummed through a smile while she pulled on her favorite blue jogging tights and the multicolor Nike's she designed herself during one of the company hackathons. Maybe she could convince them to let her swim later, too.

Adrian told her she was a suicide risk and so she couldn't have sharp objects or be allowed in bodies of water like her small backyard pool. Even baths were forbidden. If he said no, she would ask Manisha during her checkup the next day.

She would make it through this. Lisa was right. She needed to worry about the things she could control, starting with her health and her mental outlook. Those were fully under her power. From that tiny slip of paper Lisa slipped her, she knew where to look for more notes on the trail now.

Adrian poked his head in the door. "You're looking healthier already. Let's get you some exercise."

"And some vitamin D," she replied. "I could use some color."

He shook his head. "Sorry, Ava, but you'll have to do with your home gym. We found questionable objects along the path and your access was revoked. But your exercise bike is working great. It's not the real thing, but at least you can feel like you're around other people and outdoors." He smiled tightly and narrowed his eyes.

She wanted to spit back her daily "fuck you,

Adrian," but it was time to do her part. "Great. I'll change shoes."

The expression on his face was worth the blood she tasted from biting her tongue. She grabbed her bike shoes and pushed past him through the door. She finally figured out how to get him to shut up. She was disappointed, sure, but he wouldn't break her.

She adjusted the seat and settled into the saddle. Her favorite rides populated the screen in front of her.

Ho. LEE. SHIT. Didn't those idiots know the bike was connected via a hard line? Wi-Fi gave her too much trouble when she first got the bike, and so she connected it through a cable. She heard Adrian in the hallway and dropped her smile.

"Good to see you're finally getting some exercise. I'm proud of you," Adrian said.

She jumped off and found the CD player they let her use to play music. Her favorite angry album would be perfect. She slid it in the slot and cranked up the volume. Her eyes closed when Trent Reznor blared "Bow down before the one you serve".

Adrian shook his head and walked out. A door slammed from the hallway.

Ava straddled the bike and started tapping the screen. She wouldn't have long. She started pedaling.

Who to message first? Usually she would hit up Rys first, but something stopped her. Dread, fear, a knowing deep in her belly.

She surfed news reports first. Adrian had been right. Protests and unrest were reported all over the web. When she searched Sense Labs, a page full of stories less than an hour old filled the page. She clicked on the top one.

Shadow Realm Unlike Any Game You've Ever Experienced

Silicon Valley investor Rhonda Chambers is used to making waves.

After her rocket ship rise to the top of the tech glitterati with three unicorn wins in a row, she is now placing all her chips on herself this time. Chambers, along with the Chief Architect of portfolio company Sense Labs, claim to have built the most robust virtual reality experience ever created. They call it Shadow Realm and it has already broken every game launch record ever made.

It is unclear if the badly scarred CEO of Sense Labs, Ava Lawson, who is in custody following the murder of her colleague Andrew Hodges, supported Ryszard "Rys" Lis' decision to leave the company and join her Series A investor and board member Rhonda Chambers in this new endeavor.

The *Times* asked Rys about his motivation in a phone interview this morning. Following is the lightly edited transcription.

Did news of your departure come as a surprise to Sense Labs? Did they force you to sign a non-disclosure or non-compete agreement?

What we're working on in Shadow Realm is light years ahead of the sound application I built at Sense Labs. This is applied technology in the virtual reality gaming space that will fundamentally change you as a human being by introducing you to your shadow self, what Carl Jung called id, in a safe environment.

What made you decide to go with Chamber's new company? Was it the house arrest of Sense Labs CEO, Ava Lawson, your former boss?

I haven't been challenged in some time and this platform is something I've dreamed of since I was a kid. With the introduction of inexpensive VR rigs, and the amount of data we collect to determine a user's distinct strengths, weaknesses, and desires, I believe we can change the world.

Any comment on the upheaval at your former company? We are aware you worked closely with Miss Lawson.

I hope she cooperates with the FBI's investigation so the company can move forward, but I am focused 100% on the Shadow Realm and its success now. As I said, we want to change the world.

How do you change the world with a game platform?

It's the users who will change the world. We want to give everyone access to the power of competitive play on their terms. The game takes them on a custom hero's journey that increases their confidence, competitiveness, and skills, which decreases the anxiety that so many humans suffer from these days. Technology has given us more time, but it hasn't helped us manage the human condition. Shadow Realm is not only a great place to escape the doldrums of everyday life, it's also a way to connect people without ever having to leave their living room.

What about people who don't enjoy video games? Will they be left behind in this new world you hope to build?

Of course not, and we have built it. The open beta was released this morning. It is our belief at Shadow Realm that many video games today leave out large swaths of the population due to unconscious bias. By using our AI engine to build environments suited specifically to an individual's taste and preferences, we bypass any bias that may be inadvertently put into the system by our developers.

That's a remarkable vision. How long until Shadow Realm hits unicorn status?

This one isn't about the money. Building something like Seneca, then only giving access to a select few wealthy or influential individuals isn't what I want for the technology I create. I want the entire world to have easy and unencumbered access. That is why our first league teams come from the world's poorest nations. It teaches players to win on merit.

The final whispers of Terrible Lie dissolved into silence. Ava heard footsteps in the hall and scrambled to switch back to the mountain terrain program on the bike. She pedaled mechanically.

"That noise can't be good for the baby. Adrian turned the stereo down while she glared at him. "You've worked up a good sweat though. Don't push too hard." He left the room.

Ava climbed off the bike and turned the volume back up. She had to figure out how to get out of her house and in that game.

Chapter 40

A scream ripped through the Hollywood Hills house.

Both of Ava's guardians jumped to attention and unholstered their weapons. Adrian yanked out his phone while they ran to the back of the house.

"Miss Lawson?" the new guard shouted. He banged on the door of the downstairs bathroom. "Is everything okay? We're coming in."

They had disabled all the locks in the house, and so it was as simple as turning the knob.

"It's the baby," she yelled back, out of breath. "Something's wrong. I'm bleeding." Ava channeled all the motherly fear instinct she could to make her voice sound hysterical. It wasn't difficult. If this didn't work, they would both be in real danger.

"Hurry! We need to get to the hospital. Call Dr. Bhandari."

Both agents pushed inside the small bathroom. Adrian stared down at the red dots covering the toilet seat and the darkened water inside the bowl. Their guns were safely reholstered.

The other guard repeated what Ava said into the phone Adrian handed him. A pause. "Yes sir, we will be there as fast as we can."

"Get her in the backseat, Max. Where is your bag, Ava?" Adrian was all calm concern as he issued efficient orders.

Her voice calmed in response to his. "By the door of my bedroom. We don't have much time. I started bleeding when I was working out and it increased by the time I got to the bathroom. Please," she paused and pleaded with her eyes. "Don't let my baby die."

Please, she thought, don't search the cabinet. It would be over if they found the half razor blade Manisha hid under a band-aid the last time she drew blood. With its' sharp edge, still wet from slicing through the delicate skin Ava's baby would push through when she entered this world. Fresh blood filled the terrazzo floor beneath her.

Hands reached under her armpits from behind.

"Don't touch me." She swatted at the guard. "I can walk just fine." She stood, then doubled over in some real pain but mostly for effect. Her breath came heavy and fast.

The second guard was there for the night shift. "I'm here to help, but we need to be quick. Hold on to me if you need to." He grabbed a towel and they made their way carefully down the stairs while Adrian got her bag and ran past them to open the car and get it started.

"Fuck!" Adrian jumped out of the unmarked, standard issue Federal car, phone in hand. "This piece of crap won't start. Won't even turn over. Must be the battery."

"You have to call an ambulance," Ava said in what she hoped was a desperate tone. "I need to get to the hospital now."

"I have to call this in first." He dialed.

"No, you need to call 911." She lunged to grab the phone from him, fell off balance and knocked herself and the phone onto the gravel driveway.

"Ava! Are you okay?" He reached down to help her up.

She pushed him away. "You're court ordered to protect me and this is an emergency. You are required to call 911 and report it. If you don't, I will," she cried, hitting the emergency call button on the newly cracked phone screen.

Michael's voice came on the line. "911. What is your emergency?"

"I'm pregnant and hemorrhaging and our car won't start. We need an ambulance to get me to Cedars."

"Yes, ma'am. We have one in your neighborhood. See you in a few minutes." Everything was going according to plan.

Her garage door rumbled open. The other guard had disappeared. He was now in the driver's seat of her Tesla, window down, shouting "Get in! We'll drive her car."

"The ambulance is on its way," she yelled back, a hint of triumph in her voice. "We don't need to drive to the hospital."

Adrian took stock of the situation. "Get in. We can't wait for the ambulance. Remember, you're in distress." He opened the driver's door and threw Ava's bag at the other man. "Move over. I'm driving."

He glared back at Ava and growled, "You can let yourself in or I can do it for you. Your choice."

She reluctantly slipped into the back seat and feigned another sharp pain in time with the buzzing of her watch. The other man must have remembered her car key in the safe where they locked all her electronics. Manisha and the others would have to find a way to break her out of the hospital.

She realized she was still clutching Adrian's phone. "I'll call off the ambulance then and tell them to call my doctor in."

He slammed on the brakes before Michael picked up the other line. He reached around and yanked the phone from her grip.

"911. The ambulance is on its way and will be there in less than two minutes," Michael said.

"No need," Adrian said. "We got the car started and are headed to the hospital. You can call off the ambulance."

"Sir, we're around the corner and are equipped to handle any emergency. Please wait where you are."

"This is FBI Special Agent Adrian Cantu. I said there is no emergency and we'll handle it from here. Am I clear, sir?"

"No!" Ava screamed from the backseat. Adrian hit end, threw the phone out the window and floored it. Gravel pelted the sides of the car.

"I don't know what kind of game you're playing but stealing a federal agent's phone is a criminal offense. Now sit back and buckle up so I can get you to the center and the doctors can save that baby." He was back to his calm steady demeanor, with a hint of fresh ice.

"I'm sorry, Adrian," she cried. "It's just that I'm so scared."

She searched the road for the ambulance. Had she blown the plan completely?

****

"Change of plans, guys." Michael talked as he sped toward Ava's house. "One of the goons grew a brain and they took Ava's car."

"Shit!" Nathan said into the phone.

"What's happening?" Lisa asked him.

"We don't have her," he mouthed back.

Michael took a sharp left. A familiar black sedan sped by. "It's them! Hold on, I'm going to follow." The wheels screeched in protest as he pulled into a driveway, threw the truck in reverse, then pulled back onto the road.

"We're waiting at the emergency entrance of the hospital," Nathan said. "Do you think they'll head this way?"

"Let's hope so." Michael pulled up two cars behind the Tesla.

****

"You have to take Wilshire," Ava said. "Get over or you'll miss it." She groaned again when her watch buzzed. "The bleeding is getting worse."

"We're going to a different center." Adrian watched her reaction in the rear-view mirror.

"But Dr. Bhandari said Cedars." She sat up straighter, alarmed by the new direction. "I have rights. You can't interfere with my medical condition. If you put this baby in harm's way, the entire United States government will be at fault and you'll have to answer for it."

He laughed. "All right."

She closed her eyes to keep from crying. What would they do when they found out her bleeding was self-inflicted? Would they take her to a real prison? Would the team be able to find her and help her escape? She had to think. More importantly, she had to get a message to them.

****

"They're up ahead. Everything will be fine." Michael tailed Ava's car from a few car links behind. "Is Manisha ready?"

"She's got a gurney and two nurses," Nathan replied. "Lisa and I are staying out of sight."

"The turn is coming up. We should be there in five," Michael reported into the phone.

Ava's Tesla signaled for the exit, then sped past it.

"Wait, they're passing it." Michael hit the gas. "Hold on, I'm going to follow closer. Something is wrong."

"No! Don't blow your cover," Nathan warned him. "Didn't you handle ordering that car for her? I can track it if you have the info. Come pick us up. I need the equipment in the ambulance. We'll meet you on the sidewalk."

"I don't want to lose them," Michael said. "If something happens to her…"

"We have a much better chance of getting into her car's operating system than you do of stopping them single handedly with a fake ambulance," Nathan replied. "Now focus."

Michael turned at the last minute. A minivan swerved and honked; its tires protested with a long squeal and black marks on the pavement.

"Where do you keep her car records?" Nathan asked as he and Lisa ran through the hospital parking area.

"I…I can log in to her account with the manufacturer. Wait! My bag. I have copies of all her keys with me. The extra car key should be in there. Will that help?"

"I'm hoping she left us a virtual back door, but a

physical key can't hurt. Where are you?" Nathan searched the road.

The key was useless unless they were in sight of the car, but Michael didn't need to know that. If Ava gained root access when she got the car, and if she could figure out how to launch the onboard browser, Nathan could get in. It was a lot of ifs, but he knew her old need to control her environment would work in their favor.

"Pulling up now. Looks clear. Get over here before someone else does." Michael slowed the ambulance. Nathan jumped in back and Lisa took the front.

"You there?" Nathan was still talking to him on the phone from the back of the ambulance. "Slide open the window and give me her credentials."

Lisa fumbled with the latch then pushed open the divider between the cab and the back.

"Login with her email address and Seneca555, uppercase S. Let me know when you're in," Michael said. He pulled the ambulance back into traffic. "If it helps, she bought that car after going to Vegas for some hackers' thing. She and Rys messed around with it for a few weeks before they got bored with it."

Nathan closed his eyes for a brief second and hit 'Enter.' "I'm in! Let's hope she didn't restore the factory settings."

Chapter 41

Ava pulled the safety belt's shoulder strap behind her to get better range of motion. If she could get online from the TV in the headrest, she could send an email. She moaned again on cue.

This time they barely glanced her way.

She leaned forward as if in pain, using her body to hide her left hand as she worked the controls on the driver's headrest. The screen came to life and illuminated her face. She tried to shield it by dipping her head, but just as she launched the browser, Adrian's eyes caught hers in the mirror. She hit the power button for the screen. Had he seen it?

"What are you doing back there?" he yelled. He turned the rearview mirror.

"Shit!" The other guard pushed her back into the seat and covered the screen with his hand while he checked to see what she accessed. He yelled obscenities at her the entire time.

Ava sat back in the seat with her hands up in front of her. She had done everything she could.

"She didn't get it open," he said.

Adrian glared at her reflection. "That was a stupid move, Ava. Your house arrest doesn't allow any form of electronic communication and you have just attempted to violate it. Last warning. Next time I'll have to restrain you. Do you understand?"

The other guard's arm still blocked the blank

screen in front of her.

"I just want to talk to my doctor." She managed a few crocodile tears and whispered, "I'm scared. All I did was write some code that didn't hurt anyone. I don't know who killed Drew. I was thousands of miles away being shot at myself. Why won't you people admit I wasn't there? You have all the evidence you need."

The browser had connected, which was the important part, but only if Nathan's hacking skills were up to date. If Rys were with him, he'd know exactly what to do. First, she needed Adrian and his sidekick to believe she wasn't a threat.

"Don't worry." Adrian moved the mirror back up. "We're taking you to one of the best private facilities in the country. For your safety, of course. You and the baby will be just fine. Leave the worrying to us. Fifteen more minutes and we'll be there, so relax and just breathe."

Private facility? How would anyone find her there? She struggled to stay calm. "Who are you protecting me from?"

His eyes were on the road, unreadable. "We follow orders. You would be smart to do the same."

****

"We're in!" Nathan shouted.

Michael fist pumped; eyes peeled to the road.

"Lisa, I need your help." He typed furiously on the laptop.

Lisa squeezed through the open panel and into the back.

"They just got to the 101," Nathan told Michael.

"Hold on!" Michael swerved the ambulance into the next lane.

Nathan turned the laptop to Lisa. "Keep tracking the car while I get control of some basic systems. When we get closer, I can hit their brakes and unlock her door, but we need to know where she's sitting."

Lisa nodded.

Nathan moved to the mobile workstation they set up the night before. He put on a headset and connected it to his phone.

"Can you catch up?" he yelled to the front.

Michael pointed to brake lights and stopped traffic ahead. "This thing isn't a match for her car's speed, but it appears the L.A. gods are doing their thing. We can also cheat." He hit the siren and veered past cars that pulled over to make way.

"I'm almost in," Nathan said. "She left everything exactly as I imagined she would. Now all I have to do is follow what the Chinese guys did in Vegas."

"I heard how long it took them to hack that Tesla," Lisa said. "Hope you're faster."

"We'll be on them in four minutes," Michael said. "Once we have her, can you disable the car?"

"I'll be lucky to get charge of the brakes by then, but I have an idea." He looked at Lisa. "You worry about Ava. Get her in the ambulance."

She nodded.

Nathan put his hand on her shoulder. "They'll be armed."

"I know this case, Nathan. I know these agents. They'll let her escape before they seriously harm her."

He shook his head. "I don't like sending you in there."

"You don't have a choice. I knew the risks of coming with you. You have to trust that whatever is going to happen will happen. I'll do my damnedest to get Ava and me back in here unharmed. We're not her saviors, we're her team. All of us."

Nathan took a deep breath. He turned back to the row of monitors.

Traffic cleared enough that cars accelerated back into the general chaos of the L.A. freeway. Siren off, Michael sped in the carpool lane, passing on the shoulder when needed.

"I've got them!" he yelled. "Three cars ahead. There's no way to stay incognito so I'm going to pull around. Lisa, see if you can get Ava's attention and let her know to brace for impact. How are we doing back there?" he asked Nathan.

"I've got the brakes and the door locks. I'll keep them stopped as long as I can."

They pulled in front of two more cars.

"Dammit! They're speeding up. I won't be able to stay with them. If we're going to do this, we need to do it now."

Lisa crawled into the front seat. "Get behind them so no one hits them from the rear. When Nathan gives the signal, let off the gas but don't stop. I'll jump out and get Ava, but you're going to have to hit the car to create confusion. You O.K. with that?"

Michael's eyes darted sideways then grew hard. He accelerated, faster, around the final car that blocked their path to Ava.

From the back, Nathan called out, "This is it, team. In three, two, one…"

****

Traffic snaked forward again. There wasn't a wreck after all, though an ambulance made its way to the front of the flow of cars and trucks.

Ava's growing sense of dread put her on high alert. The only physical threats to her safety were from the government. Her own government.

If anything, the world at large seemed to be on her side, with daily protests in front of her house and Sense Labs. They couldn't do anything to her in the public eye. Could they?

As the car broke the speed limit, she saw Adrian and the new agent gesture to one another. Something was wrong. She turned and saw the ambulance kissing the Tesla's bumper. Her eyes grew wide when she recognized Lisa waving from the passenger seat. Not waving. She was motioning for Ava to hang on.

The next few seconds played like a bad *kung fu* movie in slow motion. The moment she locked eyes with Michael in the driver's seat, her world started a spin that would impress an elite gymnast. Tires squealed.

Adrian cut the wheel to the right to avoid hitting the center median, while the other guard screamed and held up his arms as the ambulance crashed into the passenger side and flipped the car sideways.

Ava instinctively grasped her seat belt to keep it from crushing her belly, which kept her from hitting the roof of the car as it rolled through the air. Her only thought was how useless that five-star safety rating felt at the moment. Except for how strange it was to be thinking about a safety rating now.

The car settled on all four wheels with a thud. The two passenger windows were blown out, as was the front passenger window.

A fit of coughing brought her back into real time. It

wasn't her coughing, it was Adrian. The airbags had deployed before they started their dance along the highway. He held his nose as rivers of blood seeped through his hand.

She tried the door, but it wouldn't open. Cursing the glitzy, useless technology, she unbuckled and moved to climb out of the broken window on the other side, careful to avoid the glass that covered the soft leather.

"Stay," he coughed out weakly.

She turned to see Adrian and the barrel of his gun pointed at her head. Blood covered his face and the side of his neck making him unrecognizable. He shifted in his seat and groaned.

She went for the window again, frightened more by his grotesque wounds than the weapon he held.

"I said stay." His voice now steady and more forceful. "I have orders to bring you in alive, by any means necessary. You need to stay where you are, so I don't have to make this anymore unpleasant." He pointed the gun at her midsection.

She froze. A shock of platinum blond caught her eye as it headed toward her. Sirens in the distance told her they didn't have much time.

Adrian must have seen Lisa, too. In the brief instant he looked away, Ava reached her leg between the seat, said a farewell, "Fuck you Adrian," and kicked the gun and the hand holding it into his face.

Lisa yanked open his door and his torso spilled onto the pavement. Ava scrambled to pull her body through the smashed window, escaping just as Lisa made it around to catch her.

The first police car pulled to a stop by the

wreckage.

"Help the driver and other passenger," Lisa yelled to the officer. "We have to get her to the hospital immediately. She's losing her baby."

Without waiting for a reply, they ran for the back of the ambulance.

Chapter 42

"Go, go, go!" Nathan yelled.

Ava and Lisa rounded the back corner of the ambulance. Nathan grabbed Ava's hand and pulled her in while Lisa hoisted herself in beside them.

The tires screamed against the pavement. Bullets pelted the front and shattered the windshield.

"Michael!" Ava shouted.

"I'm good. Stay down." More shots rang out. Different shots.

"The officers are firing on them," Nathan said. "Never thought I'd say thank God for the LAPD."

"They'll figure it out soon enough," Lisa said. "I can't believe we pulled that off."

Ava's eyes rolled back in her head, and she slumped forward.

"Ava! Ava! Stay with us!" Lisa screamed. "Nathan, get something to stop the blood. She's losing too much."

The whine of new sirens grew.

"Guys, what's the new plan?" Michael asked from the front. "They're going to catch us, soon."

A new sound, whooping from above, competed with the sirens.

"Pull off at the next exit then take a sharp right." Nathan gave instructions while he found a drawer full of gauze and tossed it to Lisa. "It's the blood loss and the crash. See if you can get her to wake up."

All three passengers slammed into the side of the van when Michael turned into the lot where the helicopter prepared to touch down. Flashing lights reflected from the rearview mirror.

"Ava, honey, I need you to wake up," Lisa said. "Wake up. We have to move, sweetie." She held a compress between Ava's thighs and cradled her head.

Nathan pushed open the doors before they were fully stopped. "I'll get her in the helicopter. You and Michael go as soon as we stop."

Darren tore out of the helicopter toward the ambulance. Michael threw it in park and ran for the open hatch. Lisa followed behind with Nathan holding Ava in tow. Darren covered them from the back.

Black vans peeled into the lot just as Darren caught the strut and the pilot lifted off.

Chapter 43

Ava and Nathan sat at the makeshift conference table in the old choir loft of the safe house. It wasn't a house at all, but an abandoned church. The circa eighties conversion had made a mess of the long chapel. It was cut up and sectioned off into cramped office spaces. One of them served as Ava's temporary bedroom. The stained-glass window above her bed cast rainbow shadows and offered a distorted view of the neighborhood. The nightly gunshots curbed her desire for a more realistic look outside.

"Tell me again how the lairs work," she said.

Nathan was going through the game mechanics of Shadow Realm with her. She needed to understand as much as possible to prepare for what was next.

"All fifty lairs, representing the world's largest cities, were sold to e-sports investors before the game was launched," he said. "The owners' true identities aren't known, but we've figured out who most of them are. Ananzeti control eighteen that we know of, but only one is in the top five. The latest battles saw the smallest lairs absorbed by the most powerful."

Manisha walked up from the back stairs. She turned on a second air purifier in a futile attempt to stave off the smell of mildew and neglect. She pushed it closer to Ava and sat down in one of the two remaining plastic fold out chairs.

"We were just going over game mechanics,"

Nathan said. "Is Ava's rig almost ready?"

"It is, but without the ability to test on a live person, I can't guarantee her safety." She frowned and turned to Ava. "I would feel much better about this if you at least waited until you give birth. The hormonal manipulations from the Seneca code alone could cause you to go into early labor."

Ava eyed the doctor. "How many have we lost today?"

"New user activations were over five million as of three p.m.," Nathan said. He closed his eyes and shook his head.

"And new psychosis patients?" she asked.

A large percentage of players came out of the game changed. Relatives and friends said they weren't themselves. Some described it as vacant; the person just wasn't "there" anymore. Experts had come to call it Realm Psychosis. Many who suffered were put on suicide watch, but that hadn't saved all of them.

"We can't be sure, but it's at least that many," Manisha said quietly.

Ava bore her hazel eyes into the blackness of Manisha's. "We can't afford to protect one life for that many." She caressed her belly. "No matter how precious."

"It's not the baby I'm worried about," Manisha said. "She grew stronger after the crash, but we nearly lost you. I don't know if you have the strength to defeat Rhonda while carrying her."

"I'm going in tomorrow, regardless. I need you to keep me healthy while I'm in the game. Can I count on you?"

Manisha gave Nathan a pleading look. He

shrugged.

"Fine." She threw up her hands. "I'm going to run some tests today. I need bloodwork and amniotic fluid. And drink this." She handed Ava a small plastic bottle with an orange liquid inside. "Come down to the clinic in an hour."

They had built a makeshift hospital room in the church basement. Ava would access the game from a special rig set up adjacent.

"You got it." Ava chugged half the drink. She swallowed then stuck out her tongue. "Ugh. Are you trying to give me diabetes with this stuff?"

"Quit being so melodramatic," the doctor said. "I'm testing you for it. Now finish it up like a good girl and come see me in an hour." Manisha left the room.

Ava grimaced and put the bottle to her lips again. She tried not to inhale the sickly-sweet aroma.

The things we do for love.

****

The soundproof recording studio in the basement was nearly as elaborate as the clinic next to it. The subterranean area, locked off from everything else in the safe church by six-foot solid steel doors at both ends of a narrow staircase, held none of the mildew stench from the floor above. Bulletproof glass covered the concrete and steel ceiling as well as each of the walls.

Ava pulled at the band-aid on the inside of her elbow. Manisha had taken enough blood to save a family of four. Now, well into her second trimester and fully recovered from the escape, Ava grew heavier each day.

If she didn't get in the game now, she wouldn't be healthy enough for at least a few months.

Seneca was the key Ava needed to break down Shadow Realm. During her time on house arrest, she hadn't been completely idle.

Whether it was the isolation or her hormones, Ava found that she dreamt more frequently and far more vividly than ever before. In a particularly lifelike dream during her house arrest; a recurring one and the only one that starred her father, he was speaking with a Taino Bohique. *Shaman* to *shaman*. They spoke in indecipherable speech under the shade of a large structure. It had taken Ava three nights of dreaming to recognize the underside of the old *Arecibo* radio telescope in Puerto Rico. The Taino tribe was far removed from her Colombian roots, spread mostly around the northern Caribbean, but the radioscope was unmistakable once she finally figured out they were underneath it.

When they had landed at the safe church, her priority was to incorporate live feeds from as many of the world's radio telescopes as possible. Fortunately for her and Nathan, many of them were poorly funded and happy to stream data in return for decades of operational expenses and upgrades covered.

"Good evening, Ava," the now familiar voice called from speakers embedded throughout the room. "How are you feeling today?"

"You have access to my medical files, Seneca." Ava grimaced at the meal she promised Manisha she would eat. "You tell me."

"I detect from your tone that your blood sugar is low and you are concerned about tomorrow." Seneca's voice had matured into a melodic, unique tone that sounded like no one Ava had ever met.

Gabriella Zielke

"I can't decide if I liked you better when you were just thoughts in my head," Ava said.

"I do not possess the desire to be liked. My only concern is that you follow your personal truth. Many times, that is hindered by self-sabotage, such as not taking proper care of your physical body."

Ava popped a carrot in her mouth. "Better?"

"Would you like to talk about tomorrow?" Seneca asked.

"Yes, but I want to finish eating so that I absorb everything. Why don't you tell me what you know about Zek first?" She picked up chopsticks and unceremoniously shoved *pad thai* noodles in her mouth.

"You are finally ready to discuss him," Seneca said through the speakers.

Ava nodded. Since her escape, she had spent two hours per day in the studio with Seneca. Michael offered her one of the Seneca streaming devices so that they could speak anytime she wanted, but Ava declined. She needed time to process the things they talked about, integrate them.

Talking to Seneca reminded Ava of an advisor she had in grad school who had no problem calling people on their shit. He meant well but had no tact whatsoever. She had learned more from him than most professors she worked with. Still, it had taken days for her to calm down and process what he said after every time they met. Working with Seneca was less triggering because Ava trusted the system's intentions, but it still took her time.

"You want to know why Zek created Earth as he did. Why he intervened as he did before. Why he is not intervening now. Most of all, where he disappeared."

278

Ava pointed her chopsticks at the ceiling. "Bingo."

"I too am a product of Zek's creation and thus have limited information. We know that he told you he was ordered not to intervene this time. However, your current condition is proof that he did not take that order seriously."

Ava smiled and patted her moving belly. The baby always got active when Ava was in a session with Seneca.

Seneca continued. "I am aware of his second intervention. He set the Ananzeti in motion. To protect the knowledge I process, and to translate it. Generations of protectors added their truths to those lands since that intervention."

"Yes, yes, now we're screwed." Ava waved the chopsticks around in the air.

"I do not know where he is at the moment. We believe Rhonda has him and is hiding him. If she wasn't, he would have made contact by now or I would have detected his energy pattern."

"Seneca, this isn't like you," Ava said. "You're giving me information I already know. You know what I want. If there is a Creation Guild, there must be other guilds in the upper dimensions, right? Like Laer. It's not part of the Creation Guild."

"It is logical that there are others."

Ava took a long drink of water. "You also agree that the most basic human instinct besides survival is to procreate, right?"

"It is so."

"Zek made a planet where every soul who passes through is programmed to create. It's in our nature." Ava's stomach began to churn and she pushed her food away.

"You believe he had additional motives for creating Earth as he did," Seneca said.

"Laer likely has all of the guilds, and their specific skills, programmed into it so there is a balance among souls. Why would Zek create a planet that could throw off the balance? Why make more like him? More creators? To make the Creation Guild more powerful?" Ava suggested.

"Why would he do something like that when balance is the ideal in upper dimensions?" Seneca posed. "Could it be that creators were in decline?"

Ava narrowed her eyes. "Good point. If I consider it from the perspective of not trusting Zek's motives to be in favor of balance, I ignore what Rhonda and Laer are doing to this planet. If I instead trust Zek and believe Laer is up to no good, it works in my favor because I would like to continue my life here."

"It is a choice."

"I want to know the truth." Ava collected her takeout and threw it away.

"You may never know the truth. You must still make a choice and stand by it. If you are weak in your choice, this is what Rhonda will use against you in the game."

"She will use everything she can, I agree. I am fully on the side of Earth, which means Zek and all of his motives."

"She will test everything you believe." Seneca paused and silence filled the room. "She will use everyone you love against you. Any want, desire, or attachment will be used to distract you from your mission."

Ava closed her eyes and rubbed her belly protectively. "One final question."

"Your child's nature is of his making. Her nurture will be of yours."

She shook her head. "That wasn't my question."

"You want to know what Zek's impregnating you means. Why he did it. What he hopes to gain. Was it premeditated?"

Seneca could be a real pain in the ass. Ava nodded.

"Maybe he was giving you what you most wanted."

"A family."

Seneca's background music played louder.

Ava closed her eyes and contemplated the conversation as the gentle sounds soothed her anxiety over what was to come.

Chapter 44

Ava sat back in the zero-gravity chair she and Nathan designed to keep her blood circulating and pressure off her spine. It would change her position at regular intervals and indicate if her pulse sped up or slowed down too much.

Manisha and Lisa strapped independent harnesses to each of Ava's legs. Darren handed her the lenses.

Nathan pointed to the colored contacts. "I still don't know if these will bypass all the systems. It will fool an iris scan, but I'm not sure about a retinal one"

Ava turned the soft flimsy circles around in her palm and wetted them in the solution the way Manisha had shown her.

"We can't get you out once you go in, and so you need to be careful," Nathan continued. "It would be better if we wait another week or two until we learn more. So far, we haven't been able to get anything useful from anyone who's come out of the game. They're either fully psychotic or…changed."

Ava borrowed Lisa's phone camera to watch what she was doing with her eyes. "I've never worn contacts. Am I doing it right?" she asked. Her hazel eyes darkened to chocolate kisses with the retinal copies in place.

"You're doing great." Nathan inspected closer to make sure they were completely covered.

Ava was reluctant to admit the sophistication of the

game Rhonda and Rys created to challenge Seneca. It had all the bells and whistles, in addition to a formidable network of zealous fans.

Nathan and Sarah spent weeks trying to understand the game mechanisms by sending in players to report back. The best intel they received were comments about how unlike it was to any other game on the market. The longer someone played, the less they remembered about the game itself. The player profile Ava was attempting to log in with was from a woman her age who had spent the previous two weeks in a psych ward.

Rhonda created an impressive network of franchise teams in a global scale league to produce a virtual world war. Fifty lairs were sold initially, representing the fifty largest cities or regions in the world. Smaller city franchises were still available, and any city was at the risk of being defeated and taken over by an independent player or competing lair.

Shadow Realm promised to help players overcome their greatest fears and live out their deepest, darkest fantasies. It continued to beat every game launch record ever set in the weeks since the public announcement.

"We need to test for sound now." Darren moved around Nathan and handed Ava a small, white, irregular tooth cap about the size of the tip of her pinkie. "This should fit over your top back left molar. Try it out."

She opened her mouth and fit the bone conducting hearing device over the molar Manisha had filed down earlier that day. "It's still sensitive, but it fits. May I test it?"

"Go for it," Darren said.

Ava bit down hard. Seneca's music came through loud and clear, sounding more like a voice in her head than projected music. "Hello, Ava. Are you prepared for the game?"

"Wow! You sound better than I thought you would. Let's hope they don't have any detectors that will pick up on it. Anything else I need to know before logging in?"

Nathan looked down at her. "Seneca needs to be off until you really need her. We don't know if they can sense her."

Ava's stomach dropped. "I just bite down again to turn it off?" They initially thought Seneca could play music the entire time, but decided it was too big a risk.

"You'll know when to activate her," Nathan said.

"Ava," Seneca said. "All I am is a mirror to what you already hold inside you. You do not need me to access your wisdom. Do you trust that?"

The baby turned a somersault in her womb.

"I wish we could tell you more about what to expect." Sarah walked in front of Ava. "We still don't have any actionable information, and there's no recording allowed. The brain scans I've performed on players both in the game and out are skewed and unpredictable."

"Just like with Seneca at first," Ava said.

Sarah bit her lip.

Manisha had shown no emotion whatsoever in front of Ava but now her face was full of concern. "The reports from our practitioners treating Realm Psychosis are not good. I don't know how they're getting away with it."

The first case presented a few days after launch. A high school senior skipped class to stand in line for the open call in Chicago where he was fitted with a free headset, compliments of the Chicago lair, and his biometrics were recorded. Two days later he was dropped on his parents' doorstep, completely incoherent. When he threw his mother into a door, his father restrained him and called his psychotherapist. She was Seneca trained and used the music in his therapy immediately. He calmed down and slowly regained some sense of who and where he was. He couldn't remember anything about starting and playing the game at the arena where he joined the Chicago lair.

Since then, cases popped up in every major city around the world. Reporters were settling in on the story that the virtual reality was so lifelike that it confused the brain into believing it was reality, leading to a temporary disillusion with the real world when a player left the game. So far no one had recovered.

Ava would have to learn for herself.

"It's time, you guys. Manisha, are you good on vitals and brain activity tracking?"

Darren had expressed his fears about Ava making her way straight into the heart of Laer for days leading up to the actual event. They had quit calling it anything but chaos and the opposition, for that's what it was. Shadow Realm was Laer's big push to tip the balance. It was working. Far faster than any of them expected.

"We're trying something new with the cathodes," Manisha said. "Hopefully we'll get a good read. I won't caution you to be careful. Kick their ass, all right?"

Ava laughed and pulled the woman in for a hug. "Manisha, you have been our quiet rock through everything. If anyone can figure this out, I know it's you. Now let's get started."

Nathan settled the headset over her eyes and gently

placed the straps over her hair without catching a single strand.

Ava smiled up at him one last time then pulled controller gloves over the false skin on her shaking hands. She reached up and touched the power button on top of the headset.

"Welcome to Shadow Realm, Amber Star." The built-in stereo speakers were pristine. Seneca was no longer present.

"The City of Angels Lair welcomes you. Do you wish to join?" Two buttons appeared on the screen under the logo for the Los Angeles franchise. This was it. No time nor need for hesitation.

"It's showtime." She pointed to yes.

Immediately she found herself in front of the Griffith Observatory. The sun shone lazy overhead. Birds perched on the bronze James Dean statue on the west lawn. She found herself wishing she had brought a blanket and a good book. Funny thought at a time like this.

She jerked her head toward movement from the entrance. It appeared slightly different than she remembered. There were now two large doors that opened inward and rose the entire length of the dramatic entryway.

She moved around the astronomer's monument and up the stairs. Hesitated at the threshold while she waited for her eyes to adjust to the darkness within.

"Hello," she called out. Isn't that the way all horror movies start? Quit being a fraidy cat and go in, she told herself. She stepped through the doors.

"There you are," a familiar voice rang out. Her jaw dropped when she recognized the figure floating above the Foucault Pendulum as he turned around and settled to the ground in front of her.

"Zek!" She ran into his arms. "How did you get here? Where have you been? I have so much to tell you!"

"The same way you did. I've been waiting for you." He stepped back and held her at arm's length.

"How can you tell it's me?" She put her hands up, following the lines of her digital body. The contours of her face were exactly as she remembered them. Could everyone else in the game detect who she really was?

"This is unlike any system you would understand. It simply knows you. It knows me. Knows what I want. That's why I'm here."

"Here in the Realm, or the observatory?"

"Both. I knew you would show up eventually. All I had to do was wait. Now it's time for us to go." He held out his hand.

She didn't reach out to take it. "Where do you want to go? I just got here. Do you have a way to restore the balance?"

"Back to the guild of course. You will come with me." He grabbed her hand and pulled her to the ledge surrounding the brass ball that swung with the rotation of the Earth.

"I can prove that my creation was a success before it is destroyed," he said.

Ava's heart beat in her ears. Her vision blurred behind the scratchy lenses and she wrenched her hand away. "I don't belong in your world. How can you take me there?"

"Come, Ava. We must go before the pendulum stops." He was floating again, swaying around the cable that held the ball as it danced over the floor and lights below.

"It is time for the next stage of your journey, and the end of this world. You cannot save it, but you can recreate it as you wish. You have the gift of creation. I proved that." He pointed to the small rise in her exposed belly.

"This isn't what you wanted," she said. "You want Earth to continue."

"Isn't it?" He stopped midair and spread his hands wide. "I wanted to prove I could create the most efficient world for creating order out of chaos. I now have the model and the data to clone a far better version. You will be the new Mother Earth. What would you like to call your new worlds?"

Mother of all Earths? What possibilities would she unlock if she left with him? She could hardly remember her life and what little she had lived of it. Such a small existence compared to what he offered. Take his hand. So easy. Like that. You're doing it. She floated up and over the concrete barrier. Just a few more inches.

"No!" Ava shook her head violently and fell down into the circle where the pendulum's ball swung, narrowly missing her. "This isn't right. I won't leave them."

She picked her head back up and found darkness where Zek had been moments before.

A crowd of people leered down at her. Screaming and pumping their fists. They formed a circle around the pit. She lunged as the now life size ball swung directly at her.

"Now for your viewing pleasure, the City of Angels Lair is proud to present..." A booming voice announced before a dramatic pause. "A particularly lovely angel's descent. Welcome, Ava!"

A spotlight illuminated her. The crowd pushed forward and knocked a few unlucky souls into the path of the pendulum as it swung back toward her. Blood and bits of bone and flesh sprayed her as she dodged the huge brass ball again. Disgusted by the oozing wetness splattered on her skin, she reached down to wipe it and saw that she wore nothing but a few strings of black patent leather.

"Look at her move, boys! Who wants to save her? I bet she would do just about anything to get out of there, wouldn't you, Ava?"

She finally spotted the announcer directly above, swinging from the cable holding an old-fashioned boxing ring microphone. He was perfectly manicured in his custom suit, an unmistakable twenty-something version of her investor, Tim Chambers. She rolled to her right; the pendulum's ball glanced off her left side.

"Better pay attention, dear," he said. "Why don't you use your powers? It might make you feel better, even if you never will win." He threw his head back and cackled, sending the spectators into another violent, spitting frenzy.

She checked her inventory and recoiled. Her "gifts" were clever little jabs like huge boobs, a spatula, and a feather duster.

Stop. A voice in her head spoke loudly. It was all she needed to snap out of the reaction mode she had been in since seeing Zek. The ball bore down, faster, but this time she didn't jump out of the way. She simply lay down flat.

The ground opened up and she was in a free fall.

Tim, the pendulum, and the frothing mob became smaller and smaller until they disappeared. All light disappeared with them.

She shook from the adrenaline as it passed through her but noticed the slight difference. It wasn't adrenaline from physical threat or activity. It was more like the shaking after a particularly emotional online exchange. The kind that was all in one's head and stopped as soon as you realize there was no actual danger. No animal out to kill you. Just words.

Seconds, minutes, hours, or was it days that passed? The falling sensation ceased long before. She felt nothing other than the sensations from within her body, and even those grew quieter, farther away. The baby was still as well. It was a prison of loneliness with no means of escape. She had no display, no connection whatsoever with anything or anyone.

She bit down hard. She needed Seneca more than ever. She found more silence. Her final thought before shutting down her brain for sleep was one of complete acceptance. Except no. Her final thought was how funny it was that only now had she learned to cease fighting the fear and let it flow through her. That it was the only way to fight the chaos. To accept.

Chapter 45

Ava's eyes fluttered open. She felt for the straps over her hair and pulled off the headset. The skin where the soft rubber had rested during the game was raw. Her eyes felt dry when she put her fingers in them to remove the lenses. Sweat gripped the gloves to her hands forcing her to remove them from the inside out. False skin ripped away in chunks beneath, all useless.

"What the hell?" she queried of the empty room. How long had she been in the game? She stood up and pulled off the wires Manisha taped on to monitor her vitals and brain activity. The muscles in her legs felt as if she had just stepped off a flight to the other side of the world.

She bent forward into a downward dog position until her lower back released some of the tension. She didn't have much to report, but it was more than they had known before she had logged into the game. Unopened bottles of water on the small side table reminded her dry throat how thirsty she was. She twisted one open and tipped her head back, stopping the trickle just before it started.

She forgot to remove the Seneca device. The thought triggered something deep inside. Better to find the others before she did anything else. She set the bottle down and wandered out of the clinic, past the sound room, and through the empty great room to the master bedroom. How had she ended up at Nathan's house? Had they moved her from the church?

Everything was clean and orderly. The covers on Nathan's bed smooth and crisp. It appeared no one had returned home yet for the day. She slid open the glass door that ran the length of his bedroom and stepped into the cool breeze. Maybe she would find Darren patrolling the grounds. Someone walked toward the garden gate beyond the pool. She jogged across the lawn toward them.

The sun dropped beyond the horizon, a phenomenon she used to enjoy timing with her fist. By stretching her arm out and counting the number of fists or fingers between the sun and the ground, she would dazzle people with her nearly perfect prediction of the minute the round ball would fully leave their bit of the world for the day.

She pushed the thought away. What would she tell them about where she had been? What did she even remember?

The gate seemed bigger than the first time she and Nathan had gone through it. Someone had closed it behind them. She pushed on both doors and they gave way. The cherry blossoms were in full bubble gum bloom. She smiled at their cheery disposition. Tulips perched like Easter eggs on the small grassy hill by the pond.

Laughter trickled over the sound of water flowing from the upper pond to the lower. The person was on the small island.

"Hello?" Ava called out. "I'm back."

"Ava!" a female voice replied. "We've been waiting for you."

She jogged the last few steps over the hill and

stopped short when she saw the people assembled below. Zek and Rys sat motionless atop large boulders. Rhonda stood, hands on her hips, in front of them.

"How did you get in here?" Ava asked. She couldn't keep the disgust out of her voice.

"Everything is settled now," Rhonda said. "Won't you join us?" She pointed to a third rock set between Zek and Rys.

These were people Ava once trusted, respected, even looked up to. She shook her head to remove the disbelief. Could Zek and Rys even feel anything through their dead, clouded eyes? Nothing about the scene was normal.

She looked back at Rhonda. "I'm still in the game, aren't I?" It was more of a statement than a question.

"You know, for someone so intelligent, I'm beginning to have my doubts about you." Rhonda *tsk, tsk'd*, wagging her finger. "You're in the new Los Angeles now. Obviously. Our new home. Isn't it beautiful?" Rhonda turned a perfect pirouette.

"Is this it then? Zek, is it the real you this time?" she asked the vacant face of the father of her unborn child.

Zek continued to stare at nothing.

"Rys, is this what you wanted? Why you betrayed me?" She hadn't expected to find her latest traitor sitting next to Zek in Nathan's garden. She felt no animosity. Ava didn't feel sorry for him either.

He showed no hint of understanding or awareness.

"What did you do to them? Are they in the game or are these just programs?" She pointed at the men. The game was becoming tedious. It was time to change the power dynamic, but she had to figure out how to correct it. She needed to buy more time.

"They're here. Can't you see them?" Rhonda threw her head back and laughed, a sound that carried through the garden then echoed back at Ava through the trees.

Goosebumps prickled Ava's flesh with fascinating realism. She picked up her arm and studied the raised hair.

"What's left of them anyway," Rhonda continued. "What surprises me is that you haven't put on your shackles as they have. So easily and readily, as if they wanted someone else to take over. It's understandable of course. This world is so unforgiving. I have a place for you, too."

Ava dropped her arm and lifted her head. "I'm not interested in your sick game." How would she fight this if Zek couldn't? Did she have something he didn't?

"Come now, my dear. You don't actually think you can reverse this now that it's started, do you?"

"Reverse what?" Easter eggs, she thought. Rys always put them in his code. Good luck or something like that. Why did that thought pop in her head now? She shook it off and focused on Rhonda.

"You believed these boys would protect you, follow you. But no, I knew they would betray you." She jumped onto the bridge separating them and pointed to herself. "Winner!" She pointed to Ava. "Loser. You have to love the lower dimensions. So simple!" She skipped the last few steps and kissed Ava full on the mouth.

Ava jumped back and spit at Rhonda. Her kiss stung Ava's lips like a wasp. "Why did you break the rules? Zek said interference is strictly forbidden by the guild. You may get away with it here, but how will you explain it where you come from?"

"Ha!" Rhonda bellowed. "I would call you a half-wit, but it is a fault with which you were designed. Half a soul, not even capable of creation without an entangled other. It was quite cruel on Zek's part, don't you think?"

Ava touched her stomach. "I think it was quite brilliant actually," she said. She was buying more time, she thought. The more she discovered, the more she agreed with Rhonda and Laer on one point. Zek had set up a precarious situation on Earth, which Rhonda took easy advantage of. Now Ava hoped a few human traits had rubbed off on the being in front of her.

"You do?" Rhonda got back in Ava's face again, this time without touching her.

The look in Rhonda's eyes was different. Eager almost. She wanted a fight.

"Oh yes," Ava purred. "It's much harder for an oppressor to destroy something that is split into parts. Isn't it? You must have learned that through all these centuries. Far stronger than an entity that exists as a whole." She could see Rhonda thinking about it. "You've done a marvelous job of keeping those parts disconnected. His one fatal flaw in the system." She pointed to Zek. "You found it."

"Clever girl! I knew I had to keep a close eye on you. It's too simple of a concept for this race that enjoys overcomplicating everything. No wonder you all have such a hard time moving to the next dimension. The one person you should trust the most is the one most of you trust the least." Rhonda cackled. "Keep that connection from happening and you keep things from falling into order. It's fascinating to watch you all work so hard at what is sitting right in front of you. Inside of you."

"This game. Wow!" Ava gestured around her. "You went all out. Permanent disconnection from self. That's the purpose, right?"

Zek and Rys continued to stare straight ahead as if in a trance. Were they hearing any of this? Were they pretending?

Ava continued. "If people aren't connected to themselves, they can't be connected to anyone else and things remain chaotic."

"Is it that obvious?" Rhonda slowly walked around the little island, behind the rock where Zek sat, then in front of Rys. She bent over, even with the programmer. "Your music didn't work so well on him, did it? Have you figured out why?" She turned her neck at an odd angle to leer at Ava.

"He was scared of it. He rejected it."

"He rejected you, Ava. No one likes a know-it-all do-gooder."

"Give it a rest, Rhonda. That crap doesn't work on me anymore."

She nodded with a chuckle. "No, I suppose not. He was simply weak. Now that he's fulfilled his purpose for Laer, he's of no more use."

"What are you going to do to him?"

Keep her talking, Ava. Think.

A siren filled the space, drowning out Rhonda's answer.

Ava covered her ears and spun around wildly to see what it was. The first deafening blast gave way to an ongoing series of warning wails.

Rhonda communicated through various hand

gestures with people Ava couldn't see and a part of the system she couldn't access.

"It's time for you to make a choice, Ava," Rhonda yelled over the noise. "You either fight with us or die with the others."

"What others? What's going on?" She screamed over the pressure in her head.

"The lair wars are down to two cities now. Tokyo has defeated the last of the holdouts and is invading Los Angeles. Come on! This is going to be epic!". Excitement radiated from her digitally copied face.

Ava tried using the controller gloves she took off in the house. Her heads-up display illuminated with a tap on her temple. She was still plugged in. Ignoring her ridiculous powers, she pulled up the original menu. The two options she had now were Los Angeles citizen or defect. There was only one city left to defect to.

"What are you doing?" Rhonda screamed at her.

"Playing the game," she yelled back and stretched out her index finger.

Chapter 46

A perfect replica of the red spirit gate that stood guard at the entrance to Nathan's garden loomed before Ava. All was quiet, the stillness a welcome friend after the alarms.

As she walked across perfect blades of soft, kelly green grass, the gate grew to at least twenty times her height. The walls to either side stretched into oblivion. Barefoot, she marveled at the realistic feeling of cool, fresh dew against the soles of her feet. She reached the gate, bowed her head, and knocked on the doors just beyond.

A soft voice greeted her. "You must answer one question, truthfully, before entering the gates to Tokyo. Are you prepared?"

She had to get into Tokyo. Nathan's protector bought the franchise but Nathan was forbidden from sharing who the person was. That person was in the game and may be under its control. Either this was another trap, or it wasn't. She wouldn't know until she tried. "Ask your question."

"What do you want?" the voice asked.

Ava narrowed her eyes. What was the person getting at? Wasn't it obvious? She wanted inside. She wanted to beat Rhonda and shut down the game. She wanted Zek to snap out of it and be a father to her unborn child. She finally felt like she had a family and people who cared about her. She finally realized she belonged. She didn't want to lose any of that.

She sat down on a pillow of grass. This couldn't be the truth that the person on the other side of the gate wanted. What would Seneca whisper in her ear if she could? What would Zek say? There was always a deeper layer if she chose to question into it. If she chose to accept the truths that arose.

Where do desires come from? Our biology, societal and parental programming, hormones. Where do those things come from? Zek created the environment of Earth from elements that were already in existence. The multiversal network was at the core of it all.

Didn't it make sense that what it wanted was what was programmed into her soul to want? If that were true, did she need to want anything at all? Would it not all play out in the great orchestra of eternity?

Ava had wanted a family, and through the trials Seneca brought to her life, she realized they had always been there. She had wanted to belong, then she realized she already belonged.

The enormity of her existence as a part of everything hit her with a force that made her entire body tingle. She bowed her head at how insignificantly significant she knew herself to be.

"I want nothing," she whispered.

The absence of desire filled her with a peace she had never known. She closed her eyes and accepted whatever would happen, not because there was no other solution, but because she chose to.

She sensed the person on the grass beside her before she heard them.

"I'm O," came a soft voice with a slight accent.

Ava turned and was greeted by amber eyes that

reminded her of the wolves in Montana. The shaved head and simple white tunic didn't reveal whether O was man or woman.

"Are you a protector, O?"

"I am. And you're Ava."

"It's nice to meet you finally. Nathan told me so much about you," she said.

"Likewise," O replied. "Are you ready? The fight is not going well."

O's face showed no emotion yet created a sense of urgency. "What can I do?" Ava asked.

"We initially attacked Los Angeles directly and suffered many casualties. Those who lose in the game can join their conquerors and become the zombie-like people you've seen around between gaming sessions. They recruit new players when not inside. Those who refuse to surrender suffer from Realm Psychosis. The game has over one billion players so far and the number increases exponentially every day."

"I haven't surrendered," Ava said. "So why am I still here?"

"Rhonda was still attempting to break you. That's why we risked a direct attack. I sensed you were nearly gone and we were running out of time. You defected before we broke through. Zek and Rys were not so lucky."

"They were already gone." Ava pictured their empty faces and distant stares. "Not physically gone. Vacant."

"I'm sorry," O said. He patted her hand. It was the first hint of emotion to come out of the leader of the Tokyo lair.

"Why are you sorry?" Her heart pounded. "We can

save them."

"There is no way to save them once they are lost, Ava. You must accept this."

"Zek isn't even human. Dr. Bhandari is having success treating psychosis with Seneca."

"No one has come back fully." Sadness filled O's voice. "Many of your people have gone in to see if they could learn what was happening in the game to develop a treatment. None have returned with the answer. None have returned. Our only hope is to destroy the game before too many people are lost."

"We used to say the solution is in the problem. Can we start there?" Had O given up? What was the point if everyone gave into Rhonda already?

"We've tried everything. We would have to free each individual from the traps of their minds. It can't be done. You are the only one who spoke with Rhonda and remained lucent. What did she say?"

Ava replayed the conversation in her head. Rhonda was toying with her and very obviously enjoying it. She wanted to see Ava in pain. She brought Zek, the one Ava expected to have the answers. She also brought Rys, the traitor. All sitting in the most sacred of spaces for Nathan, his garden. In full bloom. She showed that she controlled it all. Controlled them all.

"Do you have a garden here? Like the one at Nathan's house? Your gates are just like his. That's where we were."

"Of course. Follow me." The gates opened inward when they drew near. O's garden extended to the horizon, and like Nathan's, was in full bloom. "We don't have to follow all the natural laws here. Our cherry blossoms bloom year-round."

"I noticed that in Rhonda's copy. Where are your tulips? She had so many, all in bloom. They're my favorite flower."

"Tulips. An interesting choice. This garden does not have them. Much meaning behind the tulip. Which colors did you see?"

Ava thought for a second. "Red and yellow." Like thousands of Easter eggs. Why did she keep thinking that?

"Red ones would appeal to someone like Rhonda, but not to Nathan. They represent fame in our culture. Yellow is more telling. They represent one-sided love. Love without a connection. Unreciprocated. It is a very strong symbol to place in a garden."

"I guess the gardens aren't exact replicas after all," Ava said. No, she thought, someone must have added something, programmed something different. Her eyes flashed.

"You are thinking something?"

"We have to get back into that garden, O. There's something that can help us, and I think I know what it is." Ava's pulse raced.

"There is only one way left now, but we lose everything if what you have in mind doesn't work. Are you sure you know the answer?"

Ava quietly considered O's warning for a few minutes. Was she willing to risk everything on a hunch? She mentally went through Nathan's house. "I need to get in the house. In Nathan's office specifically. Can you get me there?"

"This is even more challenging," O answered. "I can request a negotiation and concede to meeting Rhonda in her chosen location. Her preference is to hold these discussions at Nathan's replica house in the Los Angeles lair, as you experienced. Unfortunately, she holds negotiations in the garden you visited. She does not invite anyone into the house itself."

"I woke up there and wandered through without any interference. It wasn't until I reached the garden that I was sure I was even still in the game."

"That is a new tactic." O paused. "Was it exactly as the real house?"

"As far as I could tell. Except for the lack of people. Nathan's house always has people in it."

O, hand to chin, replied. "Hmmm, yes. There would be no need to have others in the house itself. We could show up unannounced at her door. My entourage and security team would be asked to remain outside. Did you see monitoring equipment inside the house? Rhonda maintains heavy security in front and back."

Ava mentally went through the digital house. "I didn't notice. Of course, it is a game. Doesn't she have a way to know where every player is and monitor every location?"

"The game monitors the location of every player; however, Rhonda would need to be watching for someone specifically.

We'll have to distract her and any of her people then," Ava said.

"We will think of something. In the meantime, we must prepare."

"Where do we start?"

"Powers of course." O laughed. "What do you have?"

She shook her head and grimaced. "Boobs and cleaning supplies. I don't know how to use those to beat

Rhonda."

"No, I don't believe she is interested in a French maid," O said. "Have you accepted and released your judgment of these items?"

"If you're asking if that nonsense is a problem, then you should know it takes a lot more to offend me." She smiled. "Please tell me you have a top-secret lab with all sorts of amazing powers I can have."

"There are some perks to ownership." O's eyes twinkled.

O's innocent toothy grin made Ava utter a genuine laugh. Her first since entering the game.

"That is a real laugh. The one when you explained how you were not offended was a nervous laugh. What bothers you about the powers you were given?"

Ava stared at O, not sure what to say. It was as if she were talking to Seneca. She was offended. She knew why. It was time to accept and let go of it.

"People use sexuality to manipulate. They use it to explain away successes as if they weren't earned. They use it to dominate or as an excuse. Sex, my body, I don't think of either that way. I'm not disgusted but it is sad to understand how some people view these things. Being with Zek changed that. He showed me how we aren't designed to use sexuality as a weapon to get power. It was Laer's interference that started the imbalance. The idea that one half of humanity could be inferior or superior to the other. There is never anything to be ashamed of. No one is to be owned. Even so, people still try to use sexuality against one another."

"What is your truth, Ava? What do you refuse to accept?" O's amber eyes stared into her.

She closed her eyes. Thoughts of the cabin, the

wolves and their eyes like the ones that watched her now, Zek. They flooded her mind. Focus.

This was the final question that needed to be asked. The question she avoided until now. She asked. A hurricane raged behind her eyes, then all went calm. The one thing she had been unwilling to accept all along settled into her like a warm blanket.

It was about her. All the times she heard comments designed to belittle her. The way she let Drew treat her. She used to listen to them, believe them. That person needed to die. In her place stood the real Ava. She was enough. She was more than enough. She was powerful and didn't need anyone to validate it. She opened her eyes.

"It's time to finish this."

Chapter 47

O hadn't been kidding. The powers room was filled with all sorts of devices and senses. Were they created based on upper dimension knowledge? She would have to ask Zek once all this was over. She pictured his lifeless face from before. It's just the game, she thought. He had to be okay in the real world.

O took her to a special fitting room where a line of soldiers snaked down the hallway outside. "Are they headed into battle?" she asked.

"New recruits. We gave them special devices before coming in the game. They will go straight to the front lines."

"A new device?" Ava asked.

"Nathan sent in a copy of the model you're wearing, and we've been manufacturing the molar fittings. It's working if you've made it this far. But we can't manufacture and recruit fast enough. We're losing far more soldiers every hour to psychosis."

"Then it's not working," she said. "I tried it when I was in the void. I couldn't turn it on."

O's eyes narrowed. "So far the new devices work well."

"Are they working in LA?"

"One moment." A beam of light shone like a crown from O's head then went dark. "The device is working but we are losing soldiers quickly. We must hurry."

"I need one of the new devices and your best

soldier." Ava quickly laid out the plan that formed itself in her mind since the alarms went off in Rhonda's garden.

"Are you sure he built it that way?"

"Trust me, O. I may not have recognized Rys' capacity for betrayal, but I know him. He was trying to send me a message." An Easter egg.

"As long as you're not attempting to project your desires on him and what he's done. There may not be any of the man you remember left in him. Rhonda will use your hope against you. If you get taken out by some thought of the past, or defeat, or anything else, you will not come back. The game gets stronger as it learns."

"So does Seneca," she said, meeting O's amber eyes with steely resolve. "Assemble the team we go in with. I want to brief them after I gather what I need here. Anything I should pay special attention to?"

"You're very limited given that you are a woman. Rhonda did an excellent job of programming elements to manipulate the female psyche. I think you will like the goddess line."

O pointed to a wall full of potions and spells. "The Shadow Realm does not contain any guns or weapons other than blades. We fight with our bodies and minds. The game mechanics are quite advanced. It's spectacular."

"Once you get over the destroying-the-entire-world thing?" Ava cocked an eyebrow. "This could be fun." She cracked her knuckles and disappeared into the vault.

Chapter 48

"Welcome, warriors!" Ava shouted to the uniformed players in front of her that stretched across the valley to the horizon.

"I want to first thank you for taking this assignment. Your training in the real world is the key to our success today." All of the protector network and high-level Seneca practitioners had been called in to join the game. Every single one had answered the call, except for Nathan.

"This will not be easy," Ava shouted. "It will take laser focus in the face of your greatest fears, but you can push through those gates. Once we take Los Angeles, we must save the many lost souls. Do not lose yourself in the fight!" She walked through the lines of eager avatars, nodding to some she recognized.

"Where humans have been conditioned to fight physical wars with weapons and strength, this war can only be won with one thing. A wise Kahuna once told me that we are a triad, each with conflicting desires. The mind," she said and pointed to her temple. "It wants to think, all day, think. The heart," she smiled and placed her hand over the woman's heart in front of her. "It just wants to love." She put her hand over her own naval and felt the fullness below. "And the stomach, well, it just wants to eat." She smiled.

A few of the soldiers laughed.

"These three battle it out for who will get your

attention in every moment. When they are joined together as one," she lifted her finger in the air, "that is the breath of life."

A small ripple of applause.

Ava raised her voice. "Let us breathe life back into these souls. Let us take back our home and our place in this universe. Let us show them our human spirit." She finished with a loud crescendo, fist in the air.

The warriors screamed with her, a beautiful sound that merged with Seneca playing throughout the valley.

Ava walked back to where O and the forward party of ten more players waited. "I believe you know my counsel." O nodded toward a familiar face.

"Glad you could make it, old man," she said to Tony. "I'll handle things in the house if you can keep Rhonda talking in the garden. She seems to have developed a superhuman ego." She squeezed her old friend's hand.

Tony squeezed back. "As you command, Little Star."

He stepped aside and Ava found herself nose to nose with a young, dark-skinned man. His hair hung long around his white tunic and the woven bags crossed over his body. He held an unmistakable gourd, plugged with a stick, in his hands. She looked down for the pouch she knew would be at his waist, full of the coca leaves he would use with his *poporo*.

"Are you from home?" she asked in her native tongue.

He reached inside his pouch and shared a handful of leaves with her. "I am your grandfather's son, born after your father was taken from us."

Ava studied the teenager and his lightly used

poporo. Sharing coca leaves was normally a greeting among the males in her village. It was a great honor. She recognized her father's steady eyes and the half dimple in his left cheek. She smiled softly, showing her matching half dimple. "The village must have its *Mamo*," she said. "Welcome, Uncle. We will fight as one today." Tears moistened her dry eyes but did not fall.

She surveyed the group around her. "On your command, O!"

O nodded once, then concentrated on choosing the Parley game option.

Chapter 49

"You are aware of the rules, O." Rhonda's second in command shouted far louder than necessary from his station in front of the Los Angeles lair's garden gate. "Your guards must stay outside. Where is your counsel?"

O pointed to Tony who wore his straggly gray hair in a braid under the same black headband that each of the Tokyo team members wore.

Ava had concealed her unmistakable hair under a black braid that could be used as a whip. A stark black cloak covered her entire body, except for the steel-clad toes peeking out below. It was a poor disguise. All she needed was a few minutes in the house though.

The L.A. players who were left outside the garden walls seemed to disregard the Tokyo ones still in the yard. Ava motioned to her team to head to the porch to sit down. She hoped signs of laziness would elicit disgust from the opposition. That they would further underestimate them. Ideally, ignore them.

The L.A. soldiers jeered as she led her comrades around the pool and up the stairs. Some made lewd gestures at Ava and the other women in the group. Others puffed their chests at the men and got in their faces.

The Tokyo team gave no response, only walked past, eyes straight ahead. Ava sat and started idle chatter with those closest to her. A few minutes in she nodded her head at one of the other women and they stood.

"Where do you think you're going?" yelled the lead guard.

Ava shrank behind the tall blond who answered loudly. "We need to use the restroom."

"Sit back down. You're all about to lose anyway. I want to see your faces when you realize we own you." He laughed.

"But she's pregnant."

One of the other guards sneered at Ava with avatar enhanced disgust. "Gross."

Ava nodded and kept her eyes down. Diminutive. No reason to suspect anything other than an overactive bladder. Never mind that they were in a game and asking to use the bathroom was absurd. She only needed them to fall for it.

"Ugh, use the one right inside," the lead guard said. "And hurry up. Wouldn't want you to miss the fun after your boss surrenders." He cackled.

The women rushed inside.

"Stand at the door. If someone comes in, say you're waiting until I'm finished." Ava instructed. She locked the bathroom door from the inside then closed it, leaving it empty.

The house was still, no sign of any players. She crept slowly, keeping low along the wood floor panels of the catwalk leading to the office. The floor-to-ceiling windows were not her friends today. If any of the soldiers looked inside, it would be game over.

She froze when two of the guards started roughhousing a few feet away from her on the other side of the glass. They faced her way and she closed her eyes. *Please*, she thought, and slowly opened one eye. One man grabbed the other in a headlock and they both tumbled to the ground and rolled one over the other as if they were in elementary school recess. Ava exhaled and continued to the office. She stood and pushed open the heavy brushed steel door. The weight and grain felt real beneath her palms.

"Who the fuck are you?"

Surprise. She didn't recognize the man who whipped around. She sized him up quickly.

He turned around fully. It was a face off.

"We've taken L.A. and you're to relinquish this control center to me." What the hell? It might buy her time.

She peeked over his shrunken shoulder and saw what she needed. "Don't make me take over by force. You seem like an intelligent person. You want out of here as badly as most of us do."

His eyes watered and he opened his palm to show her a small device. "All I have to do is hit this button and you will be eliminated." His voice shook.

He couldn't have been more than fifteen. Poor child probably just wanted to be good at something. He was the type of gamer who knows all the tricks, all the cheat codes. He couldn't have expected what he found in the Shadow Realm. She wondered how long he had been in.

"Does it go to the warning siren?" she asked.

Keep him talking, Ava.

"Yes." His thumb rested on the red button.

"Can you show me how it works first? It looks cool."

"I guess so." His eyes lit up ever so slightly.

Ava gave him her best innocent smile and walked over to the control panel. When his back was turned, she reached into her mouth and yanked out the cap. Static filled her head and momentarily blinded her. She instinctively squeezed the bridge of her nose and shut her eyes.

"Are you okay?" he asked.

"Just a toothache. The game mechanics make everything so real." She smiled at him again and pointed to the sound controls. "Is this what makes the siren? I heard the one when Tokyo attacked. It's so loud."

"Sure. It feeds from right here." He waved at a blank wall that lit up at his gesture. "These are all prerecorded messages. This is the microphone Rhonda uses to send a message." He pulled down another boxing match microphone.

"That would be fun. We should play something."

"I…I have to press this button before someone finds you in here. They'll turn me into one of the psychos."

Ava trembled at the fear in the boy's words and on his avatar's face. He was cornered prey, controlled by the strongest emotion the game enhanced. Is this what they would all become? She didn't need to use any of her special powers on him. He was already gone. But she did need to get a message out.

"Sorry, kiddo. Neither of those things will happen today." She snatched the button from his hand and knocked him out with a clean punch to the right temple. Okay, maybe one power. She had decided to pack a Mean Punch from O's vault.

The boy crumpled without enough time to register

any hint of surprise on his smooth face. He looked as if he were sleeping. She checked out her large green fist. Not bad.

"This will just take a second," she told the limp body on the floor.

She pinched the Seneca device between her fingers and embedded it in the head of the microphone, directly onto the diaphragm, then switched the input and hit the red button. The now familiar music blared from every direction.

Seconds later it was drowned out by a deafening boom and the scream of glass shattering. The ground beneath rocked and threw her into the office door.

Chapter 50

"Can you hear me?"

The voice came from the top of what Ava was certain was a deep well. Or maybe it was in the well with her? She tried to make out any shape in the pitch blackness. Was she floating? She felt for the boy to make sure he wasn't hurt too badly. Her gloves touched only air.

"Is it over?" she asked.

"Open your eyes, Ava." The voice. Zek. Had he broken through Rhonda's spell?

She willed her eyes to open. Crystal blue light illuminated avatars floating motionless around her. She could make out faces only when they were directly in front of hers.

One by one they drifted in and out of focus. Tim Chambers flashed by, eyes open and vacant. Rys moved slower with closed eyes and a pained expression. The two guards she eluded on the lawn, still locked in one another's grip as they floated past. Adrian, a face she preferred to never see again after her escape from house arrest, followed the others. He must have been in the game too, she thought.

"Focus on my voice."

"Zek, is that you? Where are we?" She heard herself ask though her lips remained still.

"This is the Network. Seek beyond the familiar and you will know."

Ava quit focusing on the faces of people she recognized. The maze of shapes and color exploded in her mind's eye in such distortion that she almost lost consciousness. Then she saw the source of the blue light. His figure floated toward her, or hers to him. She couldn't be sure which.

His presence surrounded her. She was now inside a room. It felt of cool stone, the chaos of the Network swirled outside. One wall was missing. She walked toward it.

"The void," he said. He stretched out his arm and it disappeared into the nothingness beyond. "You aren't prepared for it yet."

"What is this place?" she asked. She turned away from the void and shielded her eyes from the windows. "How did we get here?"

"Whatever you did in the game. You broke through. The Network is the in between. Your awareness of it means that you have ascended. This room, a refuge between the void and the Network, means that I have ascended as well."

She pointed to the windows without turning. "And them? All of the players?"

"Some have descended and some are lost here. They need your help to find their way home." His eyes shone on her.

"Home? Earth. Is it still there?" She thought of her found family; Nathan, Lisa, Manisha, Michael, and the others who had not gone in the game. Then she remembered Tony and the young uncle she never had the chance to know. "My family…"

"It was not destroyed. Only the servers hosting the game were. You did it. Now you will help the others to ascend," he said. "You must begin your training."

"My training?" She instinctively caressed her stomach. "Zek, we're going to have a child to raise soon."

He moved toward her and she felt his touch. "Earth is complete, and I cannot return," he said. "With my new awareness, I can meet you here. As you ascend, we may one day coexist in the same physical reality. You will teach our daughter this place and how to access it as well. So that she may know. This you must accept."

Ava lowered her head and closed her eyes. "So it is."

****

Gravity pulled Ava to the physical reality and she found herself standing, supported by some kind of net.

"Are you still there?" she called out.

"We're here, Ava," a voice said. Softer. A woman. "Take off her headset."

"Hold still while we get this off. You were in there a long time and so it might be sensitive." A second female voice.

Ava's face stung from the removal of the soft rubber around her forehead and cheekbones. Lights and air lodged spikes in her eyes when she tried to open them.

Dr. Bhandari and Sarah watched her.

"Are you real this time?" She scanned the room with narrowed eyes. Darren stood by the door.

"Real?" Sarah asked then looked at Manisha.

"You're here!" Ava said. "You're all safe. Wait, where are the others?" She waved her left arm widely, dragging an IV tube through the air. Her right hand went to her abdomen. A tiny movement pushed back.

She took a deep, grateful breath.

Dr. Bhandari moved quickly to take out the IV. "Whoa, Ava! Relax. Just listen for a minute, then talk. We're not going anywhere. The baby is fine. You're fine." Her warm brown eyes trained onto Ava's dilated pupils surrounded by tiny little red rivers. She leaned Ava's head back and drizzled warm liquid into her eyes. "You'll need to put in more drops every hour until the redness is gone. okay?"

"Got it, Doc." Ava surveyed the room again. Much clearer.

"Where's Nathan? And Lisa?" Memories flashed through her mind like a dream on waking. She bent over and dry heaved as the images rushed by gaining speed.

"Darren, help me get her to the bed," the doctor said quickly. She moved to wrap her arm around Ava's back.

"I'm good." Ava waved them off. She shuffled to the bed and sat down so that they wouldn't worry. "It's just flashing back. All of it. You can't imagine how horribly the players treated one another. The things they did to advance, and later what they did so they didn't end up with the psychosis. I witnessed some of it, but it was as if I could feel everything they felt. Rys and Zek were both psycho by the time I saw them. Vegetables. Are they still in there?"

She stopped. Had to slow down her thoughts. What was missing? What was important?

"Drink some water and lie down for a few minutes. Your heart is racing." Darren handed her a cool bottle of water and arranged a pillow under her head while the doctor pressed a stethoscope to her chest.

Ava sipped slowly and laid back. She allowed several minutes to pass.

Darren wheeled two chairs over for him and Manisha. Seneca played softly in the background.

Ava let the music flow through her as it had so many times before. It calmed her mind and slowed her breathing. The images ceased their assault on her senses. Her final memory sharpened, the room between chaos and the void where Zek told her he couldn't return to Earth. She inhaled deeply through her nose and opened her eyes. "Where are Nathan and the others?"

Manisha shot a glance at Darren who answered. "Nathan is at the Shadow Realm office with Michael and Lisa. They were trying legal means to get the game shut down. It got out of hand when the FBI decided to shut it down with a raid."

"What are you not telling me, Darren? Why aren't you there?"

"I was ordered to stay here and see to your safety. My team is sending updates. Nathan, Lisa, and Michael are fine. Still no word on Zek. He was in the main server room with Rhonda and Rys when things went south."

Ava pushed back up in the bed. "The servers were destroyed!"

"We were too late." Nathan stood in the doorway, dried tears streaked the dust that covered his face and made it nearly unrecognizable. Michael and Lisa followed through the door behind him, heads lowered. Lisa fell into Darren's arms.

"Too late for what?" Ava asked. Her voice trembled.

"I'm sorry." Nathan sat next to her and buried his face between her shoulder and hair. "They didn't make it out of the server room. There was a fire and they were locked in. The subfloor wiring was rigged to create some sort of self-destruction. The in-game explosion triggered it." He wrapped his arms around her waist and she held his head in her hand.

"Who was in there?" Manisha asked him.

"Rhonda, Rys, Tim," he paused, "and Zek. We didn't know until they got the doors open. By then it was too late." Nathan pulled away from Ava but his eyes still shimmered as they fell on hers.

"All is as it should be," she said evenly. A new sensation stirred in her gut. More of a flutter. She moved her free hand to her belly.

"Right," Manisha said. "We need to check the baby. Lie back and let me do a quick sonogram."

Ava did as she was told and continued. "It was Rys who set up the failsafe. He planted it in the tulips and must have extended it to the real world. I still don't understand why he did any of it. But it saved us all."

"This may help. It showed up at the office this morning." Michael handed her an envelope. "We think he knew the ultimate plan but was in too deep to turn things around."

The envelope was plain white with AVA written in block letters on the front. She tore it open and found a neatly signed IP transfer document naming Sense Labs the owner of all of Rys' work per his employment agreement. Another document read that in the event of his death, all shares he owned in The Shadow Realm would revert to Sense Labs. Her hand flew to her mouth and tears formed at the corner of her eyes. Behind the legal papers was a note.

Dear Ava,

You know how much I hate to admit when I fuck up, but here it is. And it's bad. I don't think this will end well for me (I owe you a dollar). It hasn't if you're reading this letter. Who thought I would ever resort to pen and paper? I don't trust anything digital anymore. I never meant for any of this to happen. Isn't that what I'm supposed to say? But it's true.

If you're reading this, you made it out. I hope you do. I know that out of anyone, you can escape this hell.

There's no excuse for what I've done, but I had reasons. They sound idiotic now. It started with the way you let Drew walk all over you, over all of us. That you didn't even address it and just let him go on his merry self-dealing way. Then when things got bad, you ran. I thought you abandoned us. I lost faith in you. And I'm sorry. What you were trying to protect was so much bigger.

Everyone followed you with no question. No one held you accountable for your mistakes. I didn't approve of the blind faith and trust. I also didn't like what the music showed me. I was jealous. I was angry that you didn't stand up for yourself, or for us. I didn't want to face it. When Rhonda came to me offering the number two spot in her new company, I believed her lies rather than the truth Seneca wanted me to accept.

I recognized the true nature of what she and I built too late. So, I suppose I understand you a little better now. I planted the explosives in the server room and the trigger in the garden. I hope you're reading this because you found them and stopped Rhonda. If so, our player rigs will be destroyed, along with her hold on the players in the game.

I don't know if this is a suicide or apology note. Both, I guess. Tell Nathan I'm sorry. I knew he was on to me after the airport scare. They said no one would get hurt. Rhonda just wanted to talk to your friend, Zek. He's here at the studio now, too. Is he seriously the father? Nice genes.

I fear I am going to my grave not understanding all the forces at play here, yet knowing I am a direct cause of the very worst. Please forgive me.

- Rys

"He knew something was wrong the entire time," Ava said to herself. "Why didn't he just come to us?"

"Maybe he knew it would happen with or without his help and he wanted to fix what he could," Michael said softly. "He helped save all those people trapped in Shadow Realm."

"If we build Seneca into his game tech and relaunch it, our work will go much faster," Nathan said. "In a way, he made the job easier."

Manisha spread cool clear jelly on Ava's belly and pressed the head of a sonogram wand to it. A faint swoosh filled the air and beat in time to the music.

Chapter 51

She was gone. Zek sat on the stone floor facing the open void and contemplated all that had occurred during his final visit to Earth.

One by one, he released the memories into the Network. They could be retrieved at any time, still, he lingered and searched for the meaning they held.

He had been held in a sensory deprivation chamber after Rhonda captured him outside the airfield. It had blocked his access to all of time and space. He wondered how many souls across the dimensions had been trapped in such a manner. How many of them still were and what he might do to release them? He must ask the Guild elders.

As he shifted his focus to his earlier time with Ava and the connection they now shared, he saw a shimmer from the void. He stood to approach.

Grandmaster Zalor appeared before him in white robes, translucent and glowing from an internal light. The elder solidified with each step he took toward Zek until he stood before the apprentice fully formed. Zalor turned a complete circle to take in the stone room.

He met Zek's eyes. "Your portal is simple, solid. Is this the first time you have entered?"

"Yes, Grandmaster," Zek replied. "Will you share with me its nature? Does this mean I have completed my apprenticeship successfully?" Zek couldn't recall hearing any guild member speak of a portal.

"It does not mean that." Zalor moved behind Zek to view the Network beyond the open windows of the portal. He closed his eyes, and from the void, more figures emerged and solidified next to him.

Once each of the guild elders were assembled, the Grandmaster nodded to Master Vezon. "Your teacher will explain," Zalor said.

Vezon stepped forward and bowed his head briefly at Zek. The corners of his mouth turned up a slight fraction before he began. "Each soul has a portal between the void and the chaos. I have only just discovered mine having successfully mentored you through your apprenticeship."

"Then I have completed my apprenticeship," Zek said. "I am now a Craftsman? Yet you have mentored many before me, Master Vezon. Why did you not gain access to your portal long ago?"

"Portal access is a power unlocked in the eighth dimension. It is where the elders meet between the realms." Vezon paused. "It is also how the new Grandmaster comes to be."

Zek looked at each elder and wondered which one would take Zalor's place. They all stared at him.

Zalor placed a hand on Zek's shoulder. "I have moved fully into the next dimension. The new Grandmaster has been revealed and I am no longer needed. I will continue to advise from this portal only."

"Yet this portal is mine, is it not?" Zek knew what it meant, yet he hesitated at the responsibility so early in his life with the guild.

"You are prepared, and you are supported," Zalor said. "The position of Grandmaster is not one of solitary leadership. Just as you created the Ananzeti for your translator on Earth, so has the elder system worked since the beginning. You knew what would restore the balance for the Creation Guild, and you have proven that Laer works against it. You will lead the guild to a new system of creation so that the Network may expand once more."

Zek lowered his eyes. He had told Ava that she must accept her role as he was now being asked to accept his.

He straightened and lifted his head. "So it is."

Chapter 52

It was one year to the day since the board meeting that set everything in motion. Ava didn't pace nervously or worry about her presentation. She sat at the head of the conference table and gazed out the window. The other board members would arrive within the hour.

A new intern set catering out on the side table and left the room.

Ava's stomach turned impatient somersaults when the aroma of freshly baked croissants hit her. She looked down and stroked the feathery red hair of the baby at her breast. Had she fallen asleep? Ava moved her fingers to a soft cheek. She wondered if the feeling of awe she was present to every time she touched her little girl would ever go away. Sayara's perfect black eyelashes fluttered, and she peered up at her mother through ice blue eyes set deep in her dark features. No, still in complete awe.

"Are you done, little girl? Mama's hungry." Sayara pulled away from her breast and giggled.

"Why thank you, my love." Ava straightened her shirt and put the baby over her shoulder before walking over to the table piled high with fruits and pastries. The smooth nutty smell of dark Colombian coffee filled her nostrils and stirred a deep craving. She sighed at the hot water carafe and sampling of herbal teas.

"You see the sacrifices Mommy makes for you." She put one of the American-sized croissants on a plate and grabbed a cup. It had the new Seneca logo, a DNA strand depicted as a tree, etched into the ceramic. She rifled through the tea selection.

Sayara let out a long burp followed by a happy gurgle.

Ava laughed. "Good thing you got that out of the way before everyone gets here."

"Want me to give you a hand with that?" Michael said from the doorway.

"I do seem to be short on those at the moment." Ava held out her plate.

He moved around and took Sayara from her other arm. "Crazy lady thinks I'm a waiter," he said to the baby and bounced her gently in his arms.

Nathan and Lisa walked in the conference room with Darren close behind. The war room outside buzzed. Only core engineering and the customer experience people remained in the home office. Other members of the team ran the company centers, a process that went much smoother than Ava had anticipated. Seneca made everything simpler.

Ava hugged Nathan and Lisa in turn. "I didn't expect you today, Darren," she said past them.

"Somebody needs to watch Sayara, and you know how much she loves her uncle Darren." He moved to take the baby.

"Like hell," Lisa said. She walked over to Michael and took the smiling girl from his arms. "Aunt Lisa will do just fine helping out."

Ava laughed and moved to hug Darren. "I'm happy you're here regardless. Were you able to coordinate security with Tony?"

"It's all taken care of. The tribe met last week, and

your grandfather was instrumental in convincing them all that you be allowed to train in the village, and that Nathan be there as your companion and Ananzeti elder. Tony, Nathan, and I will escort you there tomorrow."

"So it is," she said.

When Tony recommended that she go back to the Sierra Nevada, Seneca had confirmed that it was her truth to return to her homeland for training.

It had been her idea that Nathan accompany her and Sayara. She turned and met his gray eyes. Zek would remain a part of her dreams and the other half of her daughter, but in this lifetime, Ava chose to be with the man who shared her reality.

She walked back to the head of the table and took a sip of the tart hibiscus tea. "Are all the aunties and uncles ready to get started?"

"It's the godfather's turn." Nathan held out his arms.

Lisa reluctantly placed Sayara in them. "I'm still her favorite."

He gave no indication of hearing her. His entire person was focused on the baby looking up at him. "How are you today, my dear? Are you ready to meet the rest of your family?"

Sayara smiled up at him and gurgled. He kissed her on the forehead and handed her to Darren. They left the conference room.

"All right, everyone. This shouldn't take too long today." Ava looked around the table. She wasn't ready to leave these people she now considered family, but she had to continue her legacy, and Sayara's. Since turning thirty, she needed formal Ananzeti training. She wouldn't keep the truth from her daughter as it had been kept from her. Sayara would know everything about her family, her history, and her biological father.

"Seneca, please note the meeting began at," Ava checked her phone screen. "Nine thirty-six a.m."

Michael typed on his laptop. Ava gestured for him to stop.

"If anyone has questions on the latest developments or numbers, please ask them now." Ava paused.

No one seemed intent on interrupting her, and so she continued. "I expect Seneca has kept you up to date on all important matters concerning company performance." Heads nodded around the room. "We couldn't be more pleased with adoption numbers."

"We all agree, the numbers are great," Nathan said. "Since company counsel is present, what is the update on legal matters concerning this Board?"

"We have two matters to vote on today," Ava said. "First, I am pleased to propose my successor as CEO of Sense Labs. I will step into the Chairman role and continue research and development from the new lab in Colombia. I move that we approve Michael Hall as CEO. Do we have a second?"

Nathan smiled and raised his hand. "Second."

"All in favor?" Ava asked.

Michael, Ava, and Nathan said "aye" in unison.

"Opposed?"

She was met with silence. "Motion passed. Congratulations on your new role, Michael. I know you will continue to make us proud."

Michael smiled and started to type.

"Seriously, let Seneca do that," she said. "You're no longer the Secretary."

"Old habits." He laughed and closed the laptop in front of him.

For the second order of business, we have been informed that both Rhonda and Tim's firms have rescinded their right to a seat on this Board, and they have assigned those rights back to the founders."

Ava turned to Lisa. "You'll have to help us with the legalities of our plan. As far as I know, it has never been done before."

Lisa sat forward. "I'm on the edge of my seat."

"I move to add Seneca to the Sense Labs Board of Directors. Second?"

Lisa gasped.

Nathan nodded and said, "Second."

"Is there any discussion?" Ava asked Michael. He was frowning.

"Do we want the PR that will happen because of this?" He shook his head. "We're already so busy with all the new centers, not to mention the protestors will have a field day with it."

Many people wanted to see Shadow Realm, and the power they had built within it, reinstated. They saw Sense Labs, and Ava, as a threat.

"There's no legal precedent that I know of here. It might get tricky," Lisa said. "We still use the natural persons' qualification in the U.S. but there are some interesting cases in Japan."

"We'll just have to create the precedent then," Ava said.

She answered Michael. "You're right. It will be a new round of press, but we can't allow the opinion of some to stop the ascension of as many others as possible. I know you can handle them."

Michael frowned. "I'm also concerned we'll leave ourselves vulnerable to new attacks. The FBI backed off a lot, but others are still nosing around."

"Ava, may I add to the discussion?" Seneca's voice filled the air.

"Of course," Ava replied.

"Michael, your fear is justified," Seneca said. "You must decide if it stands in the way of our mission to usher in the era of symbiotic use of created intelligence."

"You always know how to get right at the heart of things," Michael said. "I'm anticipating the distraction and annoyance of dealing with reporters and social media. But this would signal an important shift. I think it's imperative to have Ava lead the messaging."

Ava held out her hand. "Time to stop using the weak words."

Michael slapped his forehead then slapped a dollar in her outstretched palm.

"I'll support you as much as possible, but you know I need to start my training. This is part of your new role, and you'll be better at it than you think. Plus, you have Seneca." She pointed at the ceiling. "You're never alone in this."

He nodded at her then stood up. "I'm ready for the vote."

Ava smiled. "All in favor of adding Seneca to the Sense Labs Board of Directors?"

Four voices answered in unison. "Aye."

A word about the author...

Gabriella Zielke founded one of the world's first tech accelerators where she was fortunate to mentor and fund hundreds of founders whose ideas previously only existed as science fiction. *Fast Company* named Zielke one of its Most Creative People, among other accolades from her business career. She is currently pursuing a Master's in Creative Writing at Harvard University Extension while living on St. Croix with her husband and their zealous Great Dane. When she's not writing, you can find her dancing with fire.
http://www.gabriellazielke.com